THE SANDS OF KALAHARI

THE SANDS

OF

KALAHARI

A Novel by

WILLIAM MULVIHILL

G. P. Putnam's Sons   New York

For Nancy and Mary Ann

Fly over South-West Africa and you will see desert: a third of a million square miles of sand. From the Angolan border south to the Orange River no water runs regularly into the sea; the beach stretches a hundred miles inland and there is almost no rain: the Namib Desert.

In the interior great escarpments rise and there are nameless bleak mountains and great empty savannas, desolate and dry. Then another desert, the Kalahari, the Great Thirstland, larger than Texas. Southward is five hundred square miles of parched bushveld.

In all this vastness there are towns, ranches, mines and settlements but they are far apart, like atolls dotting a vast ocean.

THE SANDS OF KALAHARI

CHAPTER I

DURING the night Detjens died and the rest of them were almost glad. The crash had broken his back and fractured his skull and he had died without once gaining consciousness. Now there were six of them, five men and a woman, standing around the blanket-wrapped body in the early morning heat.

When the plane crashed the day before, Detjens was the only one hurt. He was unknown to the rest of them as they were to each other, but his slow dying had drawn them together around him. Now they felt that they had known each other for a long, long time. They had nursed him, prayed for him, sat with him through the long black night. Because of him they had stayed near the wrecked plane, not moving; because of him they had not tried to reach the low black mountain off on the horizon. He was dead now and they were free and they stood around the body, waiting. They were nervous, strained, aware of each other's impatience. Some of them stared at the body and then at the distant hills. Sturdevant, the pilot, cleared his throat.

"I think we should bury him here," he said without looking up. "Right by the plane. No sense in going off anywhere else."

They agreed. If Detjens was buried where he lay it meant that Sturdevant was planning to move, to reach the hills, the black mountain far away. And he was their leader. They studied him for an instant: a tall rangy man in his late thirties with a sharp, tough face. He was a redhead, an ex-fighter pilot, a South African. A few days ago they hadn't known him; now their lives depended upon his judgment. He looked up and past them, studying the awesome desert, slowly rubbing the red stubble that covered his lean jaw. He adjusted his peaked cap and slapped at a fly that settled on his bare leg. He wore a brown sport shirt, khaki shorts and rubber-soled shoes. They waited for him to speak but he turned and walked away studying the pieces of debris that lay around the smashed plane. He picked up a curved piece of aluminum and came back to them, knelt in the sand and began to dig. The semicircle broke up. The woman turned away, walked wearily to the tilted fuselage and went through the low door. The men found cans and pieces of metal and joined Sturdevant.

The pilot studied the other four men as the grave grew deeper. His responsibility . . .

Grimmelmann was the eldest, old enough to be the father of all of them, a white-haired German who walked with a slight limp and carried a heavy, rubber-tipped cane. He was in his seventies but still strong. When they got on the plane back in Mossamedes he had been wearing a heavy, belt-in-the-back European suit and a stiff white collar. Instead of a suitcase he had carried a cheap bulging brief case, which Sturdevant always associated with Germans and refugees and displaced persons. The old man was heading for Windhoek, seeking a brother who owned a vast sheep ranch. He spoke English in a slow, precise manner like an old schoolmaster. Digging in the sand now he was in his shirt sleeves and from the depths of the brief case he had found an old peaked hat of military cut which almost covered his wispy white hair.

Jefferson Smith was the youngest, probably in his late twenties. He was an American, a Negro, a professor and a scholar doing some kind of research on Africa. Tall and graceful with an easy smile. When Sturdevant had first seen him he was carrying two heavy suitcases and his light seersucker suit was damp with sweat. He was alert and talkative, his voice deep and pleasant. Sturdevant wasn't used to him yet; the other Negroes who had been in his plane were mine boys, laborers. It was difficult to realize that Smith was an American with a lot of money and a lot of education.

Next to the Negro, scooping dirt out of the hole with a tin can, was Mike Bain, another American, in his late thirties. A good guy, Sturdevant mused, but one he'd have to watch. He was flabby and soft and there was a nonchalance in his movements and remarks. Grimmelmann was old but he was strong and high-spirited; Bain was neither. He was shorter than Smith, under six feet, and good-looking in a haggard way: a face that had seen a lot of good times and a lot of bad times. Sturdevant knew he was an American engineer who'd been knocking around in West Africa for some years.

The last man was O'Brien, big, handsome, capable. He stabbed into the earth with a sharp piece of metal, loosening it for the others and then scooping it out himself with a flat piece of plywood. He was hatless and the heavy stubble of his beard merged with his raven-black hair. He, too, was American, close to Sturdevant's age, and he had come to Africa to hunt. Along with a big leather suitcase he had carried two expensive hunting rifles and a pair of binoculars. He was taller than the pilot and heavier through the chest and shoulders. When they had met back in Angola the big man had been wearing a bush jacket and a wide-brimmed hat. When they shook hands Sturdevant had sensed a latent strength, a power surpassing his own. He was glad O'Brien was with them.

The grave grew deeper. They did not speak, for there was nothing to say; a man had died and he had to be buried. They dug and grunted and were silent. At last they broke through the gravel-filled hardpan and the earth became softer.

Sturdevant brushed away a trickle of sweat from his upper lip. Very soon now, unless they found water, they too would be shriveled and dead. There was water in the plane, almost two tins of it, but when that was gone . . .

There wasn't going to be any search plane.

He told them a few hours after the crash. It had been a private flight, unrecorded. He had agreed to take them to Swakopmund and they had left Angola without ceremony, a lone plane winging south over the dry, barren land. There would be no search plane, for no one knew that they were lost. They had to save themselves and they had already wasted one precious day.

People died in deserts. It was a strange way to die in the twentieth century but it happened. The world was still filled with great blank spaces where men died for uncomplicated reasons: thirst, hunger, heat, cold. Not long ago he'd read in a newspaper about a party of geologists who had come upon an awesome sight in the Libyan desert. A World War II American bomber sitting on its belly in the drifting sand. It had sat there undisturbed for over fifteen years; the logbooks and clothing and guns were untouched; some water jugs were still full. There was no sign of the crew but investigators believed that they had left the plane seeking water and died in the endless desert, four hundred miles from the sea.

All at once they stopped digging.

"It's deep enough," Sturdevant said.

They stood up and arched their backs to take out the stiffness. Sturdevant and O'Brien picked up the corpse and placed it into the shallow grave. They all knelt down again and began to push the soil back into the hole.

Grace Monckton sat inside of the plane in a deep bucket seat, eyes closed, half-asleep. She had been up most of the night with the dying man and she was dizzy now with shock and fatigue.

Her face was aristocratic; even in half-sleep there was alertness in it, an indefinable assurance. She was a young and beautiful woman with heavy golden hair. She groaned and murmured; as terror came into her dream, she shivered; she was young and she did not want to die. She reached out and pulled a faded raincoat about her, for the night chill was still with her. When she got on the plane she'd been wearing madras shorts and a light blouse. During the night one of the men had given her a great bulky sweater. Now, wrapped in the raincoat, she fell into a fitful sleep.

The men left the mound of earth and walked to the battered stump of the plane, to the shade, to hide from the rising sun.

Sturdevant was last. Like the others he ducked through the low doorway and lowered himself into one of the tilted seats. He closed his eyes. He was a fool. He had killed little Detjens and wrecked his plane and made a final mess of his life. And he had the lives of five others in his hands, lives for which he was responsible. If only the plane would shiver and roar and roll forward, take off and fly away, get them out . . .

"I think," said Grace Monckton, "that we should try to do something now. I think some of us or all of us should try to look for help."

Sturdevant nodded, his eyes still closed. It was cooler here than outside and he was grateful.

"We will," he said. "When the sun goes down we'll all head for that mountain."

"Will we find water?" she asked.

Sturdevant's hands rose and fell in a limp gesture of ignorance. "Who can say?"

"We don't have any choice," O'Brien said. "We can't stick with the plane any longer."

The others listened and agreed and remained silent, sitting in the same seats they had occupied during the flight. Grimmelmann began to snore quietly.

"Let's all try to get as much rest as we can," the pilot said. "We'll be walking all night."

Mike Bain smoked his last cigarette. He recoiled from the thought of moving. The walk to the black mountain would be tough, maybe too tough for him. It might be better if he stayed. When the plane crashed he'd been thrown around like the rest of them and he'd cut his thumb. Now it was beginning to throb and bother him; he'd have to look after it when he felt better; there had to be something left in Sturdevant's medical kit. He should do it now but the seat was too comfortable and he was too tired.

The cigarette burned his fingers. He had saved it for hours and thought about it and finally smoked it, sucking the pleasure from it, knowing there were no others. The reality of it frightened him. For years and years he had smoked two packs a day.

He flicked the tiny butt out of the shattered window and watched it die in the sand. He closed his eyes, slept.

There was still some food in the plane, and the water that Sturdevant always carried. Africa is a dry land and the plane was his home and he kept it well supplied. One of the tins had burst open when they crashed and they had drunk another; now there were two left, almost ten gallons.

Sturdevant's bellylanding had been something of a miracle. They had glided over the table-flat desert for an eternity, noiseless, the ground closer each instant. The wheels touched at last and were ripped off—then the screech of tearing metal as the tail went, the left wing. They swerved and spun around, almost turned over. Then silence. They had survived.

Jefferson Smith had made a HELP sign. He picked up pieces of the smashed plane and started on the first letter. The other men joined him until they ran out of manageable debris and then, exhausted and dizzy, they sought the shade and darkness inside the battered fuselage, gratified that they had worked for the common salvation.

And they did other things. O'Brien set fire to one of the wheels, which had been snapped off and was three hundred yards from the fuselage. He poured oil on the rubber and touched a match to it and they watched the black column of smoke rise higher and higher into the still air; they added debris to the pyre, but in the end it died down and no one came to save them. Just before dawn they burned the other tire, hoping the glow might attract someone.

O'Brien took one of his rifles and fired three shots in quick succession but there was no one to hear and he stopped. It was a waste of time. They were utterly alone in a great sand sea.

When they left, the sun sat on the flat line of the horizon. Several plans had been proposed and rejected. O'Brien had wanted two groups; one of the younger and stronger to go first as a scouting party. The others would follow at a slower pace, carrying most of the water and the other things they would need. Some of them had thought this a good plan but Sturdevant vetoed it. He didn't want the group to break up.

It wasn't easy to leave. They stood around the smashed plane adjusting the nondescript packs and bundles they would take, making petty decisions, discarding one thing for another. They would warn each other of the danger of carrying too much and a moment later would point to the value of some other object and hope that it would not be left behind. O'Brien knew clever ways to make tight serviceable packs with a blanket and a few pieces of twine and he helped them all. Grimmelmann walked among them urging them to be sure to take all the shoes they had; in the desert shoes were almost as important as water. O'Brien's rifles and ammunition were distributed among the men and Sturdevant decided to carry the two water tins himself. He had always carried plenty of water in the plane and now it was keeping six people alive. In three or four days it would be gone.

The old man was the first to leave. He stood for some time watching the others, impatiently leaning on his heavy alpenstock. Then he turned and walked off into the desert, looking toward the far mountains. There was a faint chance that there might be something on the far side of them—a mining settlement, a railroad line. There might be a spring; they might run into some Bushmen or Berg Damaras or even some good German sheep ranchers. It was all a matter of luck.

And the others followed him, one by one. Grace Monckton came striding forward, confident, optimistic. Then O'Brien, strong and purposeful, a huge pack on his back, a rifle in each hand. Then Jefferson Smith hurrying to catch up.

Sturdevant stood, hands on hips, surveying the remains of his airplane. They were all gone now, all except Mike Bain, who was still inside, rummaging among the things the rest of them had abandoned. It had been a good plane and now it was gone, like so many he had flown during the war. It was gone and Detjens was dead and not a soul in the world knew where they were. It was difficult to walk away from the plane, for now it was the only familiar thing; it was a machine and it was broken and around it stretched the prehistoric desert. He picked up the two water cans and walked away.

Mike Bain saw Sturdevant leave. He was alone. He cursed and gave up the search. He'd been looking for cigarettes. There might have been a stray pack in one of the suitcases or in some forgotten pocket. But there wasn't. He ducked through the doorway and stepped outside. He looked at the wrench in his hand and dropped it on the sand, a big open-end wrench he'd found in the end of the plane. It was over two feet long but it was well balanced and he'd used it to pry among the discarded things.

He turned and walked after Sturdevant, hurrying, trying to fix the pack that kept slipping from his back. He was suddenly afraid. He turned and ran back to the plane, picked up the wrench and then hurried after the others.

The sun went down but the heat did not go; it was in the sand and in the air and in their memory. They walked across the barren land, closer together now, talking little, their shoes grinding in the sand, crunching in the gravel. Darkness came and they were suddenly cold. Far ahead was the mountain and from time to time they would look up and study it and wonder how far away it was and when they would reach it.

It was not a night of blackness; the moon was clear and the clouds were light. They walked on steadily, stopping occasionally to rest and draw together and sip water. They were tired but they did not speak of it. They could not halt and sleep, for the sun would return and trap them on the sand and they might never reach the mountain. And whatever the mountain held for them, even if it was only shade to die in, they must reach it.

Suddenly dawn came. They looked and saw the mountain very far away and Grace Monckton's stamina gave way and she wept openly from fatigue and despair. They had tried so hard, walked so long, yet it was as if they had not moved from the smashed plane. The others saw her and looked away and said nothing. I'd cry too, Mike Bain thought; if I were a woman I'd cry.

They hurried on, faster now, for the memory of the sun came and they grew afraid. They stumbled more often, sometimes falling but always rising again and going on; and little by little the group fell apart, the unity of the night was lost; soon it was no longer a group but a mile-long line of solitary figures stumbling toward the black mountain.

When dawn came the baboons moved down from their cave and sat blinking in the light; they scratched and grimaced and yawned. Only the young were frisky.

It had been another quiet night for the clan. Back in the cave they had clustered close together in a giant ball, clutching each other in sleep to ward off fancied danger and the chill of the night. They had squirmed and pushed sleepily in the darkness; some on the outside of the group grew cold and fought others to get close to the center and the warmth; others dreamed of snakes and leopards and grew excited until they were cuffed awake.

Now night was gone. The sentinels scrambled to the high and distant posts and scanned the world that lay over the jagged slabs of rock, the sudden drops, the gravelly slopes and sudden ledges. The rest of the troop waited in the sun, happy for its warmth. The sentinels motioned to the leader. All was safe.

The leader moved forward, down the escarpment. He was old and his hairy brown body was covered with spots of white hair; he was old but he was bigger than all but two of the warriors, and stronger than even these. He led the troop down, from the point of an upward jutting rock to a smooth slab below, then along a narrow ledge to a perpendicular drop of ten feet. On down the mountainside: leaping, dropping, all without great effort. The troop followed and they were noisy now, chattering, complaining, anticipating. At last they came to where food was to be found and the group broke up. Some of them began turning over stones to look for grubs and caterpillars and centipedes. Others went to clumps of acacia trees to look for sweet gum. Some wandered looking for berries or herbs or sweet roots. Soon the troop was spread out over a wide area but they were not separated. Sentinels watched on all sides: an enemy might be near.

Gradually they moved along the valley floor, staying close to the cliffs, for the grass might shelter an enemy waiting to snatch one of the young. Once, a millennium ago, they had lived in trees but now the rocky cliffs were their home.

The sun grew hot. They had eaten well. The old leader wandered under the cliffs and then went up twenty feet. The sentinels moved around him, ahead of him, above him. The troop followed slowly. They went to where there was breeze and shadow, where they could relax and sleep, where the young could play.

But one of the young sentinels high above gave a cry and they froze with terror. It was a strange cry; they had never heard one like it. They scrambled up, saw what the sentinel saw. Far away in the hot sand where they had never gone something moved. A group of tiny figures came toward them.

The troop sat tensely, uneasily, watching. One of the figures fell and they all jabbered in wonder and speculation. The warriors bristled and boasted of their strength. The females worried, held their young close, cuffed them when they made too much noise. The old leader sat silently, frowning. He was angry. The others backed away from him, for when he was angry he was short-tempered and dangerous.

Far away in the desert below the tiny figures came closer.

The mountain was before them; there was nothing else. They walked toward it and the fears of the dawn were gone. They would reach it now. It was no more than ten miles away.

It's like a gigantic ship, O'Brien thought. A sinking ship, bow high, stern going down first. Or it was a mastless battered hulk cast upon a shore, half sunk in the bubbling surf. Or a black iceberg, an iceberg in a sea of sand. But there must be game on it; there had to be. There was life on some icebergs. And if there was life there had to be water, enough for them to exist on.

As they approached it, they began to draw closer together but there was no talking. They were all lost in their own thoughts and talking dried out the mouth and made the thirst greater. They came at last to a mile-long slope which led to a high escarpment of shale and rock and sand. Some of the rocks were great sharp chunks which had broken off ages ago from the cliffs above. O'Brien reached one of them and slumped down in the shade. Jefferson Smith came and then Grace Monckton. Then Sturdevant with the two tins of water. Then the old man and Mike Bain helping one another. They sat down in the shade and stretched out in the sand. Sturdevant measured out a little of the water in a plastic Thermos-bottle top. They drank and curled up in the sand and fell into exhausted sleep.

Three hours passed before Sturdevant stood up, brushing the sand from his pants. He kicked O'Brien and the big man rolled over and sat up, alert and ready.

"I'm going up," Sturdevant said.

"I'm ready any time," O'Brien said.

"I think it's better if you stay here," Sturdevant demurred. "I'm going up and have a look, see what's on the other side. I'll take one of your rifles. If I fire once, you bring the rest of them up. If there's nothing, I'll be back and when the sun goes down we can keep moving along the cliffs. I'll see if Bain wants to go with me. I want you here in case some of them need help getting up."

O'Brien nodded, ran his hand over the thick black stubble on his jaw. He was the strongest of them, stronger than Sturdevant and smarter too, but they listened to the pilot because he had been in charge of the plane and because he was an African. The rest of them worried him. Jefferson Smith was soft with easy living, a city man. Grimmelmann was in his seventies; it was a miracle that he was still alive, that he had made it across the desert. And Mike Bain was worse than any of them, slowly dying without his booze and tobacco; a big hulk of a washed-out man who had stayed too long in the tropics. And the woman was on the verge of hysteria. All of them would need help from now on. He might have to push them up the mountainside.

Sturdevant bent down and shook Mike Bain, talked quietly to him until Bain got up and staggered out of the shade, trying to shield his sleep-stunned face from the sun. He followed Sturdevant and they started up, picking their way through the Gargantuan boulders, walking carefully on the loose shale. The heat burned through their shirts and through the soles of their shoes, but there could be no turning back. Both of them knew that and pushed the thought from their minds. They had to go on. It was like the crash and the walk across the desert; for them there was only one direction: forward. They had to climb in the sunlight because there would be no visibility in the cool night; they had to climb up the hot shale, reach the mountaintop. From the top they might see something, a town, a ranch.

The boulders grew smaller, flatter, not as high as the ones below. The footing became surer as the loose shale gave way to rock. They leaned forward now, picking up each foot with a studied and conscious tempo, trying to maintain an even pace. And gradually Sturdevant realized that Mike Bain wasn't going to make it. It had been foolish to take him along; there had been no need for it except his own desire not to be alone.

They reached the end of the slope. The escarpment rose above them, a gigantic black wall shimmering in the sun. Sturdevant rested in the shade and finally Mike Bain joined him. They sat and looked at each other and said nothing. After a long time they were breathing normally. Sturdevant staggered to his feet.

"You wait here. I'm going up now." He waved to the break in the steep wall.

Mike Bain nodded, and Sturdevant moved away and after a time vanished in the break. It grew cool in the shade of the overhanging ledge. Bain cleared away the larger stones and stretched out, rested. He should have gone on with Sturdevant; maybe the pilot needed him this very moment. But it was the same old story: he'd flopped again. The drink and all the years had broken him. He wasn't really Mike Bain any more. The old punch was gone, the old snap. And he didn't give a damn. He failed and people looked at him as if it didn't matter, just as Sturdevant had looked at him when he didn't get up. He didn't deliver any more and people shrugged and walked away. It had been like that for years now but he still hurt. He was a guy stuffed full of pride but all out of will power.

He fell asleep.

Later, the sound of a shot came to him as it came to the others below: far away, casual in the loneliness, echoing over and over and over. He didn't move. He was comfortable. Sturdevant had found something. They'd be saved now; they'd have food and water and cigarettes. It had been a bad dream; now it was over. The others would be coming up and he'd wait for them, help the old man, the woman.

Two hours later they all joined Sturdevant. They stood on a wide ledge of ink-black stone and saw what the pilot had first seen. Opposite them, perhaps many miles away, was another steep, jagged ridge of equal elevation. It ran parallel with theirs until both ridges met miles away in a severe peak. Together the ridges formed a V-shaped cul-de-sac, a deep valley. There was grass, sun-browned, dry. Trees. And far away, close to the cliff, there was a patch of green.

They began the descent.

CHAPTER II

ALL at once Grimmelmann became the leader. Sturdevant had led them across the sand desert and up the escarpment and they had followed and admired his intelligence and stamina; now his authority diminished as the old man's wisdom emerged.

When they had crawled down the cliff and huddled in the shade, breathless and dizzy, he walked off several hundred yards and returned with five melonlike objects. The others sat wordless: O'Brien with the rifles across his knees, Jefferson Smith sipping from the tin cup. They sat and watched him take out an old penknife, cut into one of the melons and drink from it. He cut it open and began to eat the wet pulp inside. He smiled at them.

"Tsamma melon," he said. He cut the one he had into four slices and handed them to Grace Monckton. "Pass them around," he told her. "This is the sweet kind. The other's bitter but you can eat it too. If there are enough of these we can last for a long time; men, and horses too, have survived weeks and weeks on them. It's the mainstay of everything here; even Bushmen need them." He stabbed another one from the pile in front of him and tossed it to Sturdevant. Bain came and picked up one and soon they were all busily drinking the juice and eating the sweet pulp.

"They show you something about adaptation and survival," said the old German. "When it matures, the rind gets tough as you can see, the older the tougher, protecting the water inside, the water and the seeds—eat them, too, they're good—and then when the growing season's about to start and the rain comes, it rots and lets the seeds go. Perfect timing."

"They're good," O'Brien said. "But how many are there around here?"

"I saw a big patch out farther," Grimmelmann said, waving his hand out into the valley. "We'll just have to see. If we decide to stay here for a while, we should pick them all and store them out of the sun." He had a heavy German accent that people found pleasant. His English was almost perfect.

They all nodded.

"Where'd you learn all this?" Sturdevant said. "You sound like an old Boer, like my grandfather, full of all the stories of the old days."

"I was in South-West Africa long ago," said the old man. "The Herero War, all of it desert fighting. We learned much then about living. I think we're in *Süd-West* now. You think the Kalahari. It does not matter. It is all the same. A line on the map."

"That was a terrible war," Smith said. "I've read a little about it."

"*Ja*," Grimmelmann said. "A terrible war as all wars are. I will tell you. I am ashamed to say I was in it. The Herero were good people, but the settlers wanted their land and cattle and their labor. They would not submit. Most of them were exterminated. Sixty thousand. It was much like your Indian wars in America." He got to his feet slowly, helping himself with his heavy cane. All the melons were gone, their rinds scattered in the stony sand. Grimmelmann began walking up the valley. O'Brien got up and walked after him and one by one the others followed.

O'Brien caught up with the old man.

"You mentioned rain," he said.

Grimmelmann nodded, stopped for a moment and using his cane turned over a flat stone the size of a dinner plate. Two mottled lizards fled from the light.

"Yes, the rain. It does rain of course in this part of Africa. More than you would think. More in some places than the official figures say. But there is a catch, my friend. It rains but the rain hits the sand and within a few minutes it vanishes. There is nothing to hold the water. It comes down in torrents and it runs through the sand. If you dig down far enough in the right spots you will hit water. Pits they call them here. But there is no surface water. If you had surface water in most of the Kalahari the land could support great herds of cattle, but there is none. Here and there a shallow pond after a good rain, pans they are called, but they dry up and grass grows in their place. And the country is getting drier all the time, do you know that? A lake that the famous Doctor Livingstone discovered, one that you will see on old maps, it is gone now. Gone. It dried up and now you can drive a truck across it and raise dust. The curse of Africa is aridity, my friend, not jungle."

"Is this the dry season here?" O'Brien asked.

"Yes," said the old man. "It is the dry season. Don't wait for it to rain or you will wait for a long time. But there must be at least one spring or source of water around here. Coming down the cliff I saw traces of baboon."

"Let's hope so," the big man said.

"The last great rain was in nineteen thirty-four," the old man said. "I was in Germany then but I read about it in the papers. It caused the Swakop to run to the ocean and it brought so much rubble with it that the coastline moved out to sea. It was the greatest rain in recent times. It took the railroad bridge along with it. There has never been a rain like it since."

They came to a cave, passed by it and found a pool at the base of the towering cliff. It had a diameter of six feet and was five feet deep. There was no runoff but the water was not stagnant or brackish. There were small trees around it and tracks of animals and birds.

"I think we will all live now," Grimmelmann said. "With water we have a chance. For a while."

They knelt down and drank with their cupped hands. O'Brien dipped his deep cowboy's hat into it, backed away and let it run over his head and down his face. He began laughing. Grace splashed it into her eyes and on her neck. Bain lay still and pressed his face into it. Grimmelmann borrowed the tin cup from Sturdevant and began pouring water on top of his head. Smith poured it all over himself with cupped hands and Sturdevant submerged his head completely under the surface. Sturdevant took off his shirt and filled up one of the water tins and then raised it over him letting the water shower over his dust-blackened body. He began singing "Waltzing Matilda."

They went back a quarter of a mile to the cave they'd passed on the way up the valley. It was ideal: high and broad with a white sandy floor. They stood in the entrance, which Sturdevant thought large enough to back a truck into.

O'Brien took a flashlight out of his pack, and they followed him into the semidarkness.

"Over here," Grimmelmann said. He pointed with his cane to strange designs on the flat wall near him. "Bushman painting."

"They're beautiful," said Grace Monckton. The others nodded as their eyes followed the beam of light. The rock paintings had movement and life. Bands of tiny men with bows and arrows chasing nimble gazelles; an imprint of a small hand; a scene of people dancing and another that looked like a battle scene: large men with spears fighting tiny bowmen.

O'Brien turned away and walked on. The others followed, their minds still filled with the primitive drawings. Other people had lived here long ago; perhaps they could survive too. The cave narrowed and the sandy floor tilted upward, became rock and then ended abruptly. O'Brien turned the light upward and they followed it. The ceiling veered upward, spirelike, jagged, boring up into the mountain.

"A *kloof*," Sturdevant said. "A chimney. Way back in geologic time water came down this hole and ate through the softer rock and made the cave."

"For the Bushmen," Grace said.

"Or maybe people before the Bushmen," Smith said. "Maybe people lived here tens of thousands of years ago before any of them. I bet if we dug deep enough in the sand here we'd come across old campfires and bones and neolithic tools and flints."

"Maybe Bushmen still come here," Grace said.

They turned in the darkness as if an intruder had spoken. For an instant they were uncomfortable, vulnerable.

"Is it possible?" O'Brien asked.

"Where's Bain?" somebody asked. The flashlight moved from face to face. No Bain. All the faces were suddenly taut.

"Bain?" The shout echoed in the *kloof* above them.

"Let's go back," Grimmelmann said. "Perhaps he is back near the mouth."

They walked quickly through the fine white sand and passed the wall paintings.

Bain was lying in the sand, resting, trying to sleep. They stood around him. "I thought I'd wait here," he told them. "Anything wrong?"

"We figured you were with us," O'Brien said.

"I turned back after the pictures on the wall," Bain said. "I've got a fever, I think. From the cut on my hand. I'm beginning to feel lousy."

"I'll get a blanket," Smith said. "If we're going to stay here we can untie the stuff we're lugging." He looked around. "Are we going to stay here?"

"Yes," Grimmelmann said. "This is perfect. We are very lucky. If this were higher it would be a place for baboons, or leopards if there are any around here. We should stay here." And without waiting to hear from the others he went outside. The others broke up. Smith brought his belongings in and got out the blanket for Bain. Grace and O'Brien left to look for melons. Grimmelmann began collecting sticks and piling them inside the cave, close to the mouth. Sturdevant walked back toward the pool with the rifle O'Brien had given him. There were bird tracks around the water.

It grew cold with the coming of dark and some of them put on extra clothes. Grimmelmann made a fire against the wall close to the rock painting where the wall curved inward and the heat was reflected. One by one they came close to it, watched the flames dance and blacken the wall, listened to the pops and cracks of the wood.

They had eaten melons that O'Brien and Grace Monckton had found. Sturdevant had fired at a large bird but it had flown away uninjured. He described the bird and Grimmelmann thought it was a bustard; he did not tell them it tasted like turkey when roasted.

But they were not hungry, for their stomachs were filled with tsamma melon and good water. They were alive and they had a cave and fire. Grace looked up from the fire to the Bushman paintings. Smith followed her gaze, knew that Grimmelmann had built the fire so as not to destroy the primitive art but to be close to it, see it. The flames danced and the tiny figures seemed to come to life, to run and jump and dance and fight.

"Will they come back?" Grace asked. Smith turned and saw that she had spoken to him. He was surprised. Despite everything they had gone through, the blond girl was still reserved, almost haughty.

"Come back?" he said. "Who can say? These paintings are probably a hundred years old. But there are still some wild Bushmen around according to what I've read." He turned to the old man for confirmation.

"*Ja*," Grimmelmann said, nodding his head. "A few hundred perhaps if you speak of the pure wild Bushmen. There are others, mixed breeds, half wild and half Western. They are neither one thing nor the other."

"There were Bushmen in Rhodesia," Grace said. "My grandfather used to speak of them."

"I have known Bushmen," Grimmelmann said. "In South-West Africa. Fifty years ago, when it was a German colony. *Standlopers.* They were the ones who lived along the coastline. Beach runners. Then others inland. Tiny men. Under five feet. Fantastic when you think of it. Stone Age people in a world that is reaching out into space with rockets."

"How the hell do they survive?" Bain asked.

"The same way all people do," Smith said. "They understand their environment and adjust to it."

"You make it sound easy," Bain protested. He had wrapped himself in a blanket and joined the others at the fire. An hour before he had been violently cold.

Smith laughed. "Okay, so I sound like a professor now and then, but it really is the answer. Grimmelmann will agree with me."

"He's right," the German said. "They live in the Kalahari and in South-West Africa now. They are still neolithic. Hunters. Like the Australian blacks and the true Eskimos and the Congo Pygmies. Still hunting after all the ages of agriculture and towns and cities and empires and world wars."

"But why *here*?" Bain said. "Why do it the hard way?"

"They were chased here," Smith said. "The books say that they were forced out here by stronger people. It's the old story. A powerful people invade a place and the original people are either killed, enslaved or driven into the local swamp, mountain, desert or what have you. No choice. The invader takes the good soil and the easy life."

Sturdevant tossed a small stick and they watched the fire take it. "Maybe the Bantus killed off most of them," he said. "They were supposed to have come out of central Africa, maybe Nigeria or thereabouts, and come south. This was about the same time van Riebeeck and the Dutch started coming into the Cape. We killed or made slaves of them too, so they were caught between two fires. The Boers and Bantu. More and more they were forced into the Karoo and the Kalahari and the other bad places. I'm Boer descent and I'm not ashamed of it but we did some terrible things to the Bushmen and Hottentots. Hunting dogs, poison, all of it. They were hunted like vermin. I think the reason for it was that they couldn't comprehend tame cattle or sheep. They'd kill stock, couldn't grasp the idea of pri-

[27]

vate property, ownership of dumb animals who wouldn't run from them."

The others looked at the tough redheaded pilot and realized that he was an educated man, a tolerant person. Since they had known him he had been curt, ordered them about, spoken sharply to them. But he was relaxed now and they all felt better, safer.

"And even in the desert we pursued them," Grimmelmann said.

"There's a parallel, too," Sturdevant went on. "I mean being caught-between-two-fires. Later on it happened exactly the same way, only this time the Boer was in the middle. The Zulus came down from the north and the British started putting on the pressure. And so the Boers fled to the less desirable country only to make the mistake of finding gold and diamonds on it. Then the English wanted that too."

"There might be some Bushmen around here," Bain suggested. "Maybe we could make contact with them, get them to take us out."

"I've seen no signs of them," Grimmelmann said.

"What signs would they leave?"

"Bones at least," the German said, sweeping his hand around to take in the cave. "Signs of fires. Something. Perhaps I am wrong but I have a feeling about this cave. I think the last men were here hundreds of years ago."

"They could be watching us now," O'Brien said, staring into the fire. The others turned, not to him, but to the mouth of the cave and saw the total primeval blackness of the night. Grace Monckton shivered.

"We came to the cave out of an old instinct," O'Brien went on. "If Bushmen were chased here, they might not have brought the cave instinct with them. They slept in different spots each night in the open."

"They are like that," Grimmelmann said. "A good point." He kept nodding to himself as O'Brien went on.

"They could have passed this cave last week. Drank from the pool. Killed an animal, eaten it and moved on. Why would they set up housekeeping in this godforsaken spot if they can move around the desert without fear of dying of thirst? We are thinking of them in our terms; of how we would act."

"Maybe our painter is a contemporary then," said Smith. They looked at the rock painting and the shadows leaping over it. It was a thing of great beauty.

"How the hell do they live in the desert?" Bain said. "How do they stay here?"

[28]

"They are the world's best hunters," Grimmelmann said. "They are almost animals themselves in their manner of hunting. They have bows and tiny arrows and make great use of their secret poisons. They crawl close to springbok, shoot one, and then track it, for hours, days even; once they are tracking an animal they cannot lose it. The Australian black is like that too. All Stone Age hunters have to be, for life is so hard for them. Their weapons are very rudimentary and slight against any kind of game. A good wound is about all they can inflict; that's the importance of poison. When there is no game they eat melons such as you and I have just eaten and other things: roots, tubers of various kinds, berries, certain resins and bulbs, lizards and snakes and insects and honey, ant eggs, eggs of all birds, especially the ostrich, yams, seeds, grubs, anything and everything that can be digested. . . . And do not make faces, my friends. These things may soon be on our diet. I for one hope so. Tomorrow we must see what else the valley holds."

"Tomorrow will be our last day here," Sturdevant said. "I'm going up that peak and look around. We'll fill the water cans and head for the next likely-looking spot. We can't sit still."

"You might see something and you might not," Grimmelmann said.

"We've got to look," O'Brien said.

"Of course," the old man said. "But do not build your hopes too high. The Kalahari is a world in itself. The Great Thirst, that's what they call it."

"Why did we have to crash here?" Bain asked. He spoke quietly as if to himself, a childish question from a feverish brain, but its simplicity made them all start. It had been in their minds too but they had not voiced it.

O'Brien snorted. "The gods are angry, I guess." He winked at Grace Monckton, startling her. She blushed and turned away.

"I wonder," Sturdevant said. "I wonder."

The others turned to him. He had been toying with a stick and now he tossed it into the fire. Sparks flew upward, into the blackness.

"I sometimes get the feeling that I don't belong here," he said. "In Africa, I mean. When I'm up there in the plane all alone looking down I feel like a vulture coming in to feed. None of us belong here; we all know it; it's not our land. It belongs to the black man."

"You were born here," Grace said, defensively. It was true of her also.

"We don't have the right," the pilot said. "It's wrong. Terribly wrong. If it's right to enslave men on their own land, then nothing is wrong. And we've got to pay for it sometime. Suffer."

"I agree," Grimmelmann said. "We owe a great deal to Africa. The terrible things we have done. If we must suffer let it be here where we have caused so much of it."

"Don't be crazy," O'Brien said. "We're here because we're here. We're going to beat this place too. We got in a plane and it went the wrong way and that's why we're here."

"And we've suffered enough," Bain said. "All of us. Just by living. It's hard to survive outside of here too, remember that. And you suffer enough just doing that."

"I am religious," Grimmelmann said, quietly. "I am old now; I've been involved in evil; I've done many things I should not have done."

"So have I," Bain told him, "but knowing it is punishment enough. Living with it."

Smith pulled himself closer to the fire. "We all feel guilty about something," he said, staring into the flames. "And I suppose it's one way to explain the suffering we might have to experience. We rationalize it. Sturdevant feels guilt because he is Boer descent, a South African. Grimmelmann has other reasons, and all the rest of us perhaps. You know something? I feel guilt too here in Africa. A reverse kind. I see the appalling things here, all that my race must endure, the subservience, the humiliation, the peonage. And I am ashamed that I never knew it, that I was born free, not equal, but still free. I didn't have to suffer . . ."

"Until now," O'Brien said.

"I guess I've still got a lot of old-time religion in me," Sturdevant said. "An eye-for-an-eye."

"Don't apologize," Grace said. "We all feel the same way, I think. We are wrong. But what can we do?"

Grimmelmann nodded. Grace sat watching Mike Bain who hunched forward, eyes closed, wrapped in his blanket. He looked very sick but there was not much they could do for him. It was quiet now except for the wind outside in the black night. O'Brien got up and began to make a bed for himself inside the circle of warmth created by the fire. One by one the others followed. Smith helped Mike Bain, brought water to him, made him comfortable for the night.

The fire died down. The cave grew colder. They slept.

Finally the sun rose and brought warmth. They waited for it in the darkness, watched it rise, saw its redness tint the gray-blue horizon. They understood now a little of the sun rites of prehistory, the sun gods, the sacrifices. Without the sun the world would be a sterile frozen ember aimless in black space.

The sun rose and brought light and heat; the night creatures shunned it and found deep crannies in the rock. The sound of the insects came; birds stirred; the baboons came from their den on all fours, lazy and sullen, half-awake. The east wind came: night air seeking the warm sea.

Then the long day with the sun supreme, merciless in triumph, beating down upon the sand and rock, on the withered trees, the desert plants. Rock sometimes crumbled and stones split when one side became hotter than the other or when there was a sudden change in temperature. The sun ruled. All life adjusted to it or perished.

Over the eons, the sun and the wind and occasional rain. The soft rock became pitted from the wind-borne sand; it crumbled, fell, turned into sand and helped batter the chalk cliffs, carve gorges, scour the tougher crystalline rock that stood defiant and alone in growing sand belts. Through long geologic periods the land rose, formed high plateaus, sharp mountain chains. Long rains came, and the cascading water wore knifelike ravines in the earth and stone as it raced to the sea. One element fought the other and in the end it made a land that was hard and pitiless and unrelenting.

When light came they found it difficult to leave the cave. It was still cold and they were exhausted. The excitement of the first day had worn off; the terrible fatigue had caught up with them. They knew they would have to climb the peak before they could move on but for another day they would rest and drink water and eat the wonderful melons.

O'Brien and Sturdevant got up and walked off across the canyon. They came to a place where many of the thorn trees had died and the pilot crouched down and started a fire with a few handfuls of dried grass and bark.

They built up the fire, adding to it everything and anything that would burn or smolder or make smoke. The roots of many of the dead trees were weak and rotten and the two men pushed them over, dragged them into the fire.

A great pillar of smoke rose from the canyon reaching for the clouds; the air was almost still; the smoke column grew thicker, mushroom-shaped. The two men continued to carry broken limbs and decayed tree trunks. They were black with soot and filth, their clothes torn, their eyes watery from the intense heat. In time they became too exhausted to work and they found tree shade and rested, watched the smoke, speculated on how far it could be seen.

They rested for an hour and walked back to the cool cave.

There were lizards in the canyon. Later in the day Grimmelmann killed one with his walking stick, cut off the head, tail and feet, cleaned it, roasted it and ate it. The others watched him, scowling, disgusted. They could not bring themselves to eat a lizard for breakfast or for dinner; yet each of them knew that it was inevitable. They would do it if they had to close their eyes and stuff it down their unwilling throats. The tsamma melons were tasty and filling but six people could not live for long on the available supply. Unless they moved on or found other food they too would eat lizard.

"It is not the first time," Grimmelmann said, looking up at them. "With me it is not difficult. The first time, yes. But you get used to the taste. This one is like chicken." He licked his fingers and rubbed them in the sand.

"Let's climb the peak," O'Brien said.

"Not today," Sturdevant told him. "I'm still groggy. And so are you. We need the rest. Eat the melons and drink plenty of water and sleep. Maybe tomorrow . . ."

"I did not eat the lizard to disgust you," the old German said. "You will have to adjust to this place. To survive is to adjust."

"We'll get out of here," Sturdevant said. "From the top of the peak we'll be able to see a hundred miles."

"But we can't walk a hundred miles," Grace said. "I don't think I could reach the plane again."

"But I could," Sturdevant said. "Walking at night with water I could make a hundred miles. More."

"But it might not be enough," Grimmelmann said.

Another night. They gathered around the fire.

"When will it rain?" Smith asked Sturdevant.

The pilot thought for a while. "Six weeks, five weeks. A long time for us. It rains in February and March and then the rest of the year is dry as hell. Two months maybe of greenness and that's in the good parts of the country, not here. When the rain stops, everything starts drying out again and it's the best part of a year before any more rain falls. The sheep and cattle get along on the dry stuff or they starve to death."

"Sometimes there are great grass fires," Grimmelmann said. "And when the grass is gone nothing comes back to replace it until the rains come again. It's terrible for the animals."

"I can't get used to the cold nights," Smith said suddenly. "I keep forgetting we're three thousand feet or so above sea level."

"I wish now we hadn't burned up all that wood," O'Brien said. "We should have had sense enough to go farther away from the cave."

Sturdevant nodded. The American was right.

"Are we going to stay here?" Grace asked.

"I don't know," Sturdevant said. "We'll have to see how far this mountain runs. I've got to get up that peak and have a look and see what I can see. We were lucky to find this place, the water. It was one chance in a million . . ."

They knew this. They had survived the crash and by some miracle had stumbled upon a fountain in the desert.

But it was not enough. They had to move, go on. The cave was but a temporary refuge. When Sturdevant found out which way to go they would fill the water cans and leave.

It grew colder. They wrapped themselves in their blankets and clothes and fell asleep.

In the morning, the sound of birds.

They brought the dead coals to life and heaped wood on the fire, shivered over it for half an hour eating tsamma melons and drinking water warmed over the fire.

"Let's climb the peak," O'Brien said.

Sturdevant spat a melon rind into his cupped hand.

"I was thinking the same thing. We'll take turns carrying one of the water tins. It'll be hot up there. I can tell you that."

"With the binoculars we should be able to see right into Windhoek," O'Brien said.

"Don't say funny things," Sturdevant said. "I have a feeling we flew to the moon."

They moved out of the cave into the weak sunshine.

They looked at the far peak. Sturdevant stretched, yawned.

"Okay," he said. "Let's start getting ready."

The others were relieved; they had been thinking about it for two

[33]

days now, wondering what they would see from the top of the jagged peak.

Mike Bain sat in the warm sunlight and silently pleaded to go with them. He had never wanted anything so much in his life and he wondered if he was losing his mind. But he wouldn't go. He was too weak, too sick. In a few minutes he would get up and go back to the cave and rest. Somebody would bring him water; then he would drift off to sleep and dream terrible dreams. He was dying; his whole body was a glowing pain, his throat, his mouth, his stomach. He needed cigarettes, cigarettes and some real food. Bread. Meat that was not from disgusting creatures that crawled in the sand. If the pain did not go away he would take one of the rifles and kill himself.

He got up and went inside to his bed. As he did so the blond girl came to him, knelt down beside him.

"Are you better now?" she asked.

"No, it's the shock of going off liquor and cigarettes, that and the hunger, the exertion, the cut thumb and the sun. That's a hell of a lot for a guy like me. I've been out of shape since the war."

"You were a soldier?"

"I was in the American navy. But not on ships. An outfit called Seabees. We built airfields, camps, harbors."

"You liked the war?" She'd always believed that men did.

"I liked building," Mike said. "We did fantastic stuff with bulldozers and cranes and rock crushers. You have no idea . . . no idea . . ."

"You liked it," Grace said. He was talking; it was a good sign.

"Yes, I liked it. We built roads through swamps and jungles and paved them with crushed coral. I wonder about those roads sometimes, and the bridges and buildings. I wonder if they are being used or if the jungle has taken over again, the rot, the time. I like to think that people are taking care of them, using them."

"What were you doing in Nigeria and all those other places?" Grace asked. "The same?"

"The same," Mike said. "Whatever needed building. I'm a knockabout, roughneck type of engineer. I've got a knack for improvising and getting by with half of what you need for a job. You learn that in out-of-the-way places and in wars. They send you the wrong material and half of that is stolen for the black market. They send you the wrong men and you end up doing most of the work yourself and train-

[34]

ing the guys under you. It's a tough life if you're honest and you like working."

She got up and brought water to him and he drank and felt better. She left him and he dozed off dreaming about her. . . .

While he slept the others left: Sturdevant, O'Brien, Jefferson Smith and Grace Monckton.

Grimmelmann walked slowly down the canyon. He looked everywhere for honeybees, for signs of game, for indications that people had been in the valley. They were in the Namib Desert. Sturdevant kept saying they were in the Kalahari but he was wrong; they were in South-West Africa. But it mattered little; it was all the same, sand and sun and desolation.

But it smelled like South-West Africa. . . .

It was getting so that he thought of nothing else but his first months in Africa, those bad times he wanted to forget. The Herero War and the chase over the desert and all the boys who had died that year. All his life he'd been trying to forget it, drive it down into the bottom of his mind, and now it was with him again. Fate had returned him to this place. The land had been waiting for him.

January, 1904. Wilhelmshafen. It was right after Christmas, a clear, cold day, and they had stamped their feet on the cement pier waiting to go on the ship, a long line of them in their short blue jackets and high yellow boots, stiff with newness. They were going to Africa, South-West Africa, and they were going to avenge the poor colonists there, Schlesians and Bavarians for the most part. They were going to Africa and wipe out all the blacks who had committed the awful outrages they had read about. They were going to save a German colony; they were going to restore German honor.

There was never a day like that. They marched through the streets to the docks and the band led the way and their boots smashed against the cobblestones and the people pressed around them, cheering and clapping and waving and singing with the music.

They got on the boat and they sailed away. On the third day they had been issued new uniforms. Light brown khaki and light brown tropical helmets. They had fun with the strange helmets, strutting around admiring one another, clowning. Then an officer bawled them out and they tried on their uniforms and found them all too large.

They reached Swakopmund, dropping anchor and rocking in the heavy swells. They crowded close to the rail, trying to see the shore, but there was heavy fog. And then the fog lifted and they fell silent, for there was nothing but a few other rusty ships and behind these an endless strip of reddish-white sand. Nothing more. They had expected palm trees and monkeys, straw huts and swamps and jungle. But there was only the sea and the sky and the endless sand. They saw some long, low buildings that looked like barracks and a lighthouse sitting on the sand. Swakopmund.

The next day they disembarked. They hurried through the sand with noncoms hollering and their rifles sliding off their shoulders.

There was no one to greet them. It was as if they had landed on the moon. They formed into their units and marched to the railroad station. The tiny open cars were used for hauling. At first they thought it was a joke and stood without moving. But the noncoms shouted and they crawled in and squatted in the metal cars and after an hour the train pulled out, into the interior, through endless sand dunes.

Later in the day the grade grew so steep they had to jump out of the tiny cars and push. The grade was uphill all the way and not until evening did they reach the summit of the giant rise. Then they looked back and saw Swakopmund behind them, twenty-five miles away, saw the sea and the vast stretch of sand between them. And they turned and looked ahead and saw a wild and terrible mountain range. For some it was the first mountain range they had ever seen and it frightened them. Even the few Bavarians among them were amazed by the coarseness, the wildness, of the jagged mass of stone that rose before them. It was dark now and cold and all of them unrolled their white woolen blankets and tried to get comfortable in the rolling, squeaking cars. And some of them down the line were singing:

> *"Doch mein Schicksal will es nimmer*
> *Durch die Welt ich wandern muss.*
> *Trautes Heim, dein denk' ich immer . . ."*

In the morning the sun came. They rolled on into a narrow valley of the mountain range and above them the cliffs threatened. They stopped at a string of sheds and boiled some rice and coffee. They scrubbed their utensils with the rough sand and moved on. They were short on water now and were supposed to drink only when ordered. In the afternoon they emerged from the mountains and found themselves on a wide plain.

They felt relieved. The earth was reddish yellow and there was a sparse growth of rough grass which looked like rye. Here and there were thick bushes. They saw birds and then a gazelle. They began to relax and talk more.

They came to a farm which had been burned and saw graves near the charred walls. Toward evening they stopped at a large station. They slept on the ground that night and it seemed like a luxury after the cramped cars swaying and creaking and men kicking in the cold night.

The next day they saw their first river bed: a band of clean dry sand running through the barrenness. The country was softer; in the distance were the green slopes of new mountains.

They reached Windhoek at noon. They marched through the streets of the spread-out city and saw smiling faces and other soldiers and women. Up the hill they marched to the fort, broke ranks and wallowed in the water which ran from rusty faucets in the courtyard wall.

The other soldiers were men and boys who had been simple settlers and now, since the native uprising, were in the home guard. They wore wide-brimmed hats and high boots. They had been in the country for years and were quiet and superior. They would act as guides. Some of them were wounded; the barracks were filled with the sick.

And there were prisoners. Proud Negroes, men and women, and they did not look like defeated people. Some of the girls were strangely beautiful; many of the older women looked like witches and some of them smoked pipes. . . .

Grimmelmann bent down and studied a mark in the sand. Baboon, probably. The cliffs were full of them. He straightened up and walked on, swinging his heavy cane. He had to clear his mind of the past and concentrate on the present. It was getting so that all he thought about were the old days, half a century ago when he was a very young man.

The heat shimmers along the dead rock; nothing moves.

Now a glint in the air: a female wasp. She hovers close to the ground, searching among the stones and pebbles, the parched grass. She finds an ant colony and flies away; she explores another hole. A lizard's tongue licks at her from the blackness. After a long hour the delicate insect finds her enemy, a great tarantula.

The big spider comes from his hole in a rush. He is hungry and the thing that flies over him is tasty; he will catch it and bring it deep into his burrow.

The fight. The spider is a monster, hairy and powerful. The wasp

[37]

is fast and desperate with an urgency that must be appeased. The great jaws of the spider come at her and she feints and weaves away. A heavy leg hits her, she is stunned; for a moment the spider has her but in a final instant she dodges away. The sparring goes on. The wasp's stinger is ready, a black rapier glinting in the sun. Now, without warning, she allows the giant spider to run over her; she rolls and jabs upward at the great soft belly as his jaws seek her. When the spider shudders and shrinks from the pain she escapes.

And she is back again, fighting. The tarantula lunges heavily, groggy from the poison. The rapier punctures again and again; paralysis hits the giant's body. The wasp rests, watches her victim stumble and lie totally paralyzed, completely helpless.

The wasp drags the great body across the stone and gravel to a sandy spot. She digs a hole, pushes big pebbles out of it until it is large enough for the tarantula. She pulls the living body into the tomb-nest and begins to bury it. Then she stops, rests again, lays an egg on the spider's warm body. She finishes the burial and flies off.

In time the egg will hatch, the larva will feed upon the tarantula's body, will survive and come forth and fly away.

Sturdevant led the way. O'Brien and Grace Monckton walked together and Jefferson Smith was last. The peak dominated their thoughts but they did not talk about it; it was too important. Their lives depended upon what they would see from the highest point.

"What do you do in Rhodesia, Mrs. Monckton?" O'Brien asked the girl.

"Cattle," she said. "Cattle and sheep."

"And you came down from Nigeria?"

"Yes," the girl said. "We flew up last month to visit an uncle. My father hadn't seen him since the war. He had to get back but I stayed on for another two weeks and then started out on my own."

"And your father didn't know you had started home?"

"No, we just left. Flew to Leopoldsville. Missed the plane to Livingstone. Took the Impala plane with the rest of you. If we'd all waited for the scheduled plane we'd have been all right."

O'Brien was silent. He'd missed the flight too and gone on the Impala plane. It was a small South African airline with good pilots and good planes but they'd been forced down in Angola with engine trouble. They'd spent the night in an ancient Portuguese hotel and in the morning Sturdevant was there, eating breakfast with them and offering to fly them to Windhoek. He was an ex-fighter pilot with a shiny new plane and he was obviously getting rich flying chartered runs and hauling equipment and mine boys. So they got in his plane and flew away, south and eastward. Night came and then a sudden storm. By dawn they were lost, flying low over endless sand and rock, running out of gas.

He turned to the girl again.

"Did your husband stay back in Nigeria, Mrs. Monckton?"

She hesitated for an instant. "I'm divorced."

O'Brien nodded.

"I came back to Africa last year," she said. "From England. After my divorce. I've been staying with my father."

"I see," O'Brien said. He wondered what sort of a man her husband had been, what she had been like as a wife.

"Do you think that Impala pilot will put two and two together?" she said. "He knew we left on Sturdevant's plane."

"Yes," O'Brien said, "but he doesn't know that we got lost and crashed. A guy like Sturdevant is always on the move. He leaves one place, flies off into the blue, and that's it. Nobody waits for him. His flights aren't logged. The Impala pilot figures we got to Windhoek and went our separate ways and he figures that Sturdevant is now chartered out to some mine in the Katanga maybe or working for the South African government if he's got the right connections. Nobody knows we're down."

"Have you decided where we are?" Grace asked.

"Sturdevant says we're in the Kalahari."

Jefferson Smith caught up with them. "It reminds me of Nevada," he said. "Or California, the desert part. The stark bare mountains and the shale and sand and scraggly bush. It's like the Southwest." His voice was pleasant, deep and unhurried.

"I'm from California," O'Brien said. "You hit it right. It is like the Southwest. You get the idea back in the States that Africa is all jungle and maybe some veldt. You're amazed when you find out that a hell of a lot of it is just like Arizona or West Texas."

Grace Monckton turned to Smith. "You're a professor, aren't you? I thought somebody said that back in Angola."

Smith nodded. "I'm an assistant professor, really, working on a doctorate. I got a grant from the Ford Foundation to come here, for a year. I'm trying to unify what we know about Africa before the European penetrations, especially Negro Africa."

"Where do you teach?" O'Brien asked.

"Harvard."

O'Brien whistled. "You make me feel like a barbarian. I managed to get through college by playing football and having an uncle on the board. And I came over to hunt. Sounds simple as hell now, doesn't it?"

"Yes," Grace said. "You could have stayed in America and hunted."

"And you, Mrs. Monckton, could have stayed in England and raised cattle," O'Brien said. She smiled. Why didn't he call her Grace?

"And as for me," Smith said. "I should have had sense enough to stay put after all my ancestors went through to survive the slave ships and all the rest of it."

They all began laughing for the first time. Far ahead Sturdevant stopped, turned around, and waited for them to catch up.

Grace Monckton had been on her way home. She had been born and raised on a farm as had her mother and grandmother before her. Her people had been in the eastern Cape Province for a long time, descendants of the 1820 Settlers who had been organized and sent to South Africa by the British government after the Napoleonic Wars.

She was wealthy. The family owned several sheep farms; they bred horses and blooded rams and bulls. The first ancestor had stayed on the land and fought it. The hundred acres that had seemed fabulous in Britain was actually pitiful here because the land was dry and hostile and not suited to the plow. Most of the settlers quit, moved to the frontier towns and found other means of making a living. But some others stayed. They took over great tracts of land, grazed it with sheep and cattle, a handful at first, and then as the years passed they prospered and in time they were established on great manorial holdings of several thousand acres.

She had grown up in the open, on horseback. And she was not quite a lady despite the schooling and the special tutors and the protocol of the local society. There was an urgency in her, a seeking, which worried her father. He was a busy man and he wondered sometimes if he had done wrong by keeping her at home and letting her grow up on the farms among the workmen and animals. Her mother had died when she was two and there had been thoughts about sending her to a convent school or boarding school but he could not bear to part with her and so she had grown up at his side. A colored woman servant had looked after her, grown to love her and become almost a mother.

They climbed the peak carefully, stage by stage, resting each time, for the sun was on them. It was not a difficult climb nor dangerous but it was long and only O'Brien had ever climbed a mountain peak before.

They reached the top and stood on a flat wind-swept ridge that veered up another fifty feet to a final pinnacle. Below them was the canyon; far away, almost at the end of it, was the pool. Next to it was another canyon and then a third; and to their left, on the other side of the ridge, another spur of rock running off enclosed still another narrow gorge. Sturdevant guessed that the two farthest ridges were ten miles apart.

And there was nothing else. They stood on the top of a great black stone island in a sea of sand.

"I thought this would be the end of a mountain range," Smith said, voicing all their thoughts.

"We still have all the water we want," Grace said. "That's all I was hoping for, the water."

O'Brien took his binoculars from Sturdevant and studied the gorges below them. "It's like a big hand," he said. "Five ridges running and enclosing four canyons. Let's hope a plane comes soon." He handed the glasses to Smith and sitting down, took off his boots.

They sat down with O'Brien. His feet were bare and he was wiggling his toes. They looked around them again and wondered how the top of a peak that looked so sharp could be so flat. It was a platform, acre-sized, of black rock. And it was hot from the sun.

"What'll we do?" Grace asked. She was not frightened as she had been when the plane crashed. They had survived. They had found things to eat. They were intelligent. Sturdevant had been born and raised in the bush; he was smart and tough. And so were O'Brien and Smith and the old man.

"If there was anything to burn we could start a fire up here and keep it going full time, plenty of smoke and all. Maybe somebody would see it." Smith was thinking out loud. But they had all thought of it. There was nothing to burn.

"We'll just have to stick it out," O'Brien said. He began putting his socks back on carefully; now they were free from sand. He tapped one of the scuffed boots on the rock. "We can stay here. We've got water. Somebody is sure to spot the plane and investigate. It's just a matter of time."

"You're wrong," Sturdevant said. "You have no idea of the Kalahari. It's endless. That plane might rust away before anybody flew over it; and it wouldn't be a search flight so they might not even see it. I'm a pilot. I know. If we sit here and wait we'll never make it. There are too many of us for the food supply, for one thing. There is an end to sand hens and lizards and melons."

"What about the baboons?" O'Brien asked.

Sturdevant made a face. "I never heard of anybody eating baboon." The thought disgusted him, more than the thought of eating rock python and yellow lizards.

"There's always a first time," O'Brien said.

"But there's a limit to them too," Smith said.

"I'm going to get help," Sturdevant said. "I'm going to take the two water tins, make a good pack out of them and walk out of here."

"No," Grace said. "Don't go. Let's all stay together."

"I think she's right," Smith said.

"Suicidal," O'Brien said. "You said so yourself. This place is endless. Bigger than most countries in Europe. What chance would you have?"

"A good chance, I think," Sturdevant told him. "Those two cans hold quite a lot of water if only one is drinking. I'd walk at night and get out of the sun in the day. I'm in good condition. I know a little about deserts. And I'm responsible. I'm going."

"The compass was broken," Grace said. "It's nobody's fault. I say we should stick together. You said that yourself at the plane."

"I'd go in a straight line," Sturdevant said. "Eventually I'd have to hit something, a railroad, a ranch, a road, something." It wasn't really true and he knew it. It was possible to walk hundreds of miles and see nothing but scrub and sand. But there was nothing else to do. They'd all die unless they made contact with the outside world.

"I'm against it," O'Brien said. "We've survived this long. We can hold out. Maybe natives come here. The Bushmen old Grimmelmann was talking about."

"I don't think so," Sturdevant said. "There are no signs. If there were any real wild ones around they wouldn't come near us anyway. Or if they did it might be dangerous for us. I've heard stories of them taking hunters out into the desert and then abandoning them."

"I could go with you," Jefferson Smith ventured.

"No," Sturdevant said.

O'Brien stood up. "Shall we start back?" He held his hand down for Grace Monckton and helped her up. She felt the power in his arm and stood close to him for an instant, aware of his maleness.

Sturdevant and Smith groaned and got up and they began to make their way down the cliff. They did little talking on the way down. Instead one and all thought about what they had seen from the peak. They had stood at the point where the two sharp ridges came together, an arrowhead of black rock rising out of the sand. And between the rock walls the valley with a strange abundance of living things, the Biblical garden in the wilderness, narrow under the peak and then growing wider until the cliffs that enclosed it fell away and the sand started again.

When they reached the cave it was already late in the afternoon. They stumbled into the darkness and drank from the pool and slumped to the white sand. Grimmelmann sat by Mike Bain, who was asleep, wrapped in a blanket.

"Our friend Bain has a fever now," said the old man. "I think from the cut hand."

"I can look at it later," Sturdevant said. "Maybe we can do something for him. We've got to watch infections and cuts."

"There's nothing but sand," Grace Monckton said. "Everywhere there's sand. . . ."

Grimmelmann nodded in the gloom.

"We didn't see anything," Jefferson Smith said. He too was beginning to doze off; the sand was so soft and it was cool here, unlike anywhere else in the canyon.

"I think we are farther west than you think," Grimmelmann told Sturdevant. "In the Namib."

"It's possible," Sturdevant said. "I told the others so I'll tell you. I'm going to walk out of here, tomorrow maybe or the next day. I'll take the two water tins and I'll go out and tell them that we crashed. I'll be back in a nice big planc . . ."

"You'll die in the sand out there," Grimmelmann said.

"Maybe," Sturdevant said.

"The desert is a terrible thing," the old man said.

"I think I might go with you." O'Brien stretched out in the sand now, hands in back of his head, eyes closed.

"I didn't invite you," the pilot said.

"It's a free country," O'Brien told him.

[43]

"Listen," Sturdevant said. "I'm going alone, carry my own water and set my own pace."

"I could go in another direction," O'Brien suggested.

"You haven't any water tins, anything to carry water in," the pilot said. "With those two tins I can make it. All a matter of endurance. If you want to help, let me have one of the rifles. And that big hat of yours with the wide brim. Once you beat the need for water it's all distance."

Grimmelmann cleared his throat and in the semidarkness they turned to him. "Listen to me," he said. "Stay here. Do not try anything so foolhardy. The desert will kill you. The sun will get into your head and boil your brains. You will get tired and you will lie down and pray to die. You are a pilot, you are used to speed. The desert is no place for men; our bodies are not made for it; we are too small and weak for it, too slow."

"He's right," Smith said. "It would probably be impossible to do it with anything short of another plane. Remember when we were coming down? All that space . . ."

Outside the sun went down and the canyon was suddenly dark. The noise of insects grew louder and a baboon sentinel barked from somewhere on a sheer slope. The troop moved higher, out of danger. It became cooler.

Mike Bain stirred in the sand and opened his eyes. The rock overhead seemed far away in the gloom; the daylight glinted dully on it. He closed his eyes. He was dying.

And he didn't care. When he died all the pains in his body would stop; the crawling, scratching rawness of his throat, the stomach nausea, the constant headache, and above all the terrible hunger for tobacco and liquor. Death would be a welcome end.

Someone was bending over him; someone sat in the sand beside him.

"Feel better?" It was Sturdevant.

"I'm dying," Bain said. "Dying happily. It's going great."

"Don't talk like that or you will," the pilot said.

"We haven't got a chance, any of us."

"I have," Sturdevant said.

"I hope you make it," Bain said.

"Where were you heading?" Sturdevant asked.

"Me?" Bain said. "I was going to Lusaka. Looking for a job. I know

[44]

some guys from the old days who are with the big copper outfits there. Was going to hit them for a job."

"What do you do?" Sturdevant asked.

"I'm an engineer. I've knocked around. Bridges, dams, mining, construction. Anything . . ."

"Well, get rid of that fever. We can use you."

"Don't be silly, Sturdevant. We've had it."

"Where were you working before we got together on the plane?"

"Nigeria. We were messing about with a railroad in the back country. I got sick of the place after a year so I told them good-by and headed south."

"What's wrong with the U.S.A.?"

"I went back there after the war," Bain said. "I got a nice job with a big construction company. I bought a dozen white shirts and cut down on the booze and started to reform. It was tough but I was winning for a while there. Then trouble. I was fired. I went to Pakistan on a government deal, and I haven't been back to the States since, I'm the original Point Four boy; I'm half-civilized, that's why I go over big in the underdeveloped areas as they call them now. What the hell, the money was always good and if you made a mistake who the hell knew or cared? I mean we worked like bastards when we had to and when we played it was hard, too. I was sort of a bum in one way, or maybe I just felt like that being out of the country so goddamn long, kicking around, drinking too much. . . ."

"You want a melon?" Sturdevant said. "We got some cooling."

"Maybe later," Bain said. "How about some water?"

Sturdevant got up and came back with a canteen cup. Bain emptied it in one gasping drink, spilling it on his face, his chest, not caring. He pretended for an instant that it was good liquor.

"Thanks," he told the pilot. He was weary again.

He felt Sturdevant putting one of the blankets over him as he slid off into sleep.

In the night Grace awoke. She lay still for a time and the sounds came again and she knew it was Bain.

Nobody moved. She got up slowly and stood over the almost-dead fire. She added a few pieces of wood to the glowing coals, shivered in the cold night air. She went to Bain and knelt down next to him. His teeth chattered; he groaned from the cold that follows a fever.

She held his face, spoke quietly to him. Other dark forms turned and moved in the darkness, O'Brien perhaps or Smith. There wasn't anything more they could do for him. They brought him food and water; Sturdevant had given up his sleeping bag. And during the night they were all cold, waiting for the dawn and the sun.

She wanted to cry. There was no medicine, nothing.

Bain's teeth chattered. He was trying to double up in the bag, make himself smaller, conserve his warmth. But it would do no good; the cold was everywhere; there was not enough wood to keep a big fire going all night. He would have to suffer.

She began to shiver. A tear ran down her cheek and she brushed it away.

She found the zipper of the sleeping bag and pulled it down. Mike recoiled from the rush of cold air, came fully awake. She worked herself into the bag, wiggling, pushing, sliding her body deep into it, feeling Bain enclose her, seeking her warmth and softness. She turned and pulled the zipper up, sealing off the cold world.

When dawn came, Bain was against her, warm but without fever. He had survived the night-cold, the despair. She worked free from him and the sleeping bag and returned to her own bed.

Hours later, when Bain awoke, he lay and watched the girl move around the cave. She brought him a canteen cup of heated water and a piece of melon. She seemed so familiar . . . should he ask her?

"You had a fever last night," she told him. "But you're cooler now. You're getting better."

Bain looked up at her, studied the soft mouth, the warm neck, the heavy blond hair. . . . It had been a feverish dream, all of it.

After he had eaten melons with the others, Sturdevant took his map case and walked away until he found a place where he could be alone, where he could work, think. And he found such a place a quarter of a mile down the canyon. In the shade of the towering cliff was a thick, smooth slab of rock that reminded him of a table. He put the leather carrying case on the rock, unzipped it, and then carefully unfolded a large map, placed small stones on the edges to keep it flat.

He stood looking at the map for a long time, scratching himself, shifting his weight from one foot to the other, rubbing his bearded chin.

They were here on the map, somewhere, somewhere . . .

The lettering on the big map was of various sizes and types. The largest and most ornate was reserved for SOUTH-WEST AFRICA, BECHUANALAND PROTECTORATE and CAPE PROVINCE.

Then came DAMARALAND and GREAT NAMA LAND and BRITISH BECH-
UANALAND followed by the smaller letters for Windhoek, Keetman-
shoop, Luderitz, Gobabis. And there were various colors on the map
indicating altitude above sea level. Dark green for the lowest, then
light green, tan, orange and brown for the high places over five thousand feet. It was a vast region, filled with great empty spaces. There
was the railroad running up to Windhoek and there were some first-
class highways and many roads but they were like a broken spiderweb
spanning a wide window.

He found a pencil and turned away from the map. He began figuring, calculating, estimating. There was the gas load and the distance
from Mossamedes in Angola; there was load and wind and the features
of the land he had seen before the crash. He took a ruler and began
placing it on the map, from one point to another. He began to whistle,
to hum. He had to figure out their general whereabouts, to narrow it
down. They were certainly south of Windhoek, say at least a hundred
miles. And figure a hundred miles from the sea at a minimum. He
put the ruler on the map and drew a line that started a hundred miles
from the sea and ran eastward five hundred miles; it cut the railroad
a hundred miles south of Windhoek almost on 24 degrees latitude.
The line crossed into the Kalahari Desert at a tiny spot named
Lehututu. He made this line the top of a rectangle, five hundred miles
long, two hundred miles wide. They were somewhere inside of it.
Both sides lay in pure sand desert, the Kalahari and the Namib on the
west. Most of it was at an elevation of three thousand feet; but there
were vast areas much higher. There were rivers but in this part of the
world they were without water except during the brief wet periods
after a violent rain. The Nosop, the Elephant, the Oup.

A hundred thousand square miles . . .

Two thirds of it was east of the north-south rail line. But there was
no way of cutting down the area—nothing on the map or in the landscape that hinted whether they were east or west of it, nothing that
indicated that the black mountain was in one part or another. It could
be anywhere, in the Namib or in the bleak stretches of the Kalahari, in
some sand pocket along the fringes of the jagged mountains between
the railroad and the distant sea.

He folded the map and put it away with the papers. He would walk
westward. There was nothing north and east except more of the Kalahari. He'd go west and maybe hit the railroad or a recognizable watercourse, a road.

He walked back to the cave.

CHAPTER III

STURDEVANT left the next day, two or three hours before the sun set. He would travel by moonlight, in the night, whenever the sun did not dominate the world. But for the first leg of the trip he would give himself a head start. He wore the big wide-brimmed hat that O'Brien had discarded and he carried the other rifle. He looked strong and able, almost casual—tall and lean, red-bearded. He wore a pair of American Army-surplus shoes, twill trousers and a tattered shirt. On his belt was a small hunting knife that he'd kept in the plane to open beer cans.

But the pack was the most noticeable, most unique feature. He had taken the two light water tins and fastened them to a makeshift packboard. They set high on his shoulders after much adjustment, filled with water now, heavy. The packboard was an ingenious affair of light pieces of wood, an old belt, a short length of copper wire, bits of cord and string from the things they had carried from the plane. It was covered now with his light windbreaker. He would need the jacket, Grimmelmann warned, and it would keep down the water evaporation. The old German shook hands with him now and patted him on the back.

"Walk at night," he said. "Look for *vleys* first of all. Build fires from high spots . . . do you have some of the matches?"

"Yes," Sturdevant said. "And I'll make it. I've got enough water here for a long time."

"Good luck, now, Dutchman," O'Brien said. They shook hands.

"I'll have the rifle cleaned before I give it back," the pilot said.

"And the hat too," O'Brien told him.

"What can I say?" Jefferson Smith told him. "What can any of us say except thanks . . . as long as we can't keep you here. You're a brave man."

And Grace came. "Take this," she said. It was a bundle made from a piece of her clothing, bulky and mysterious. It contained many melons, more than they could really spare.

Sturdevant looked around at all of them for the last time, up at the black cliffs, at the far peak.

"I'll be seeing you," he said and he turned and walked off down the canyon, toward the sand and the far horizon. In a little while he was no longer visible.

They carried armloads of wood to the top of the cliff up a zigzag trail that O'Brien had discovered and improved until it was relatively safe. It was close to the cave, close to the tiny fire that the girl kept going throughout the day. The wood was piled carefully so that once ignited it would flare quickly. There were four special piles of tinder at the bottom of the big pile. If any of them saw or heard a plane at any hour they were to seize one of the torches, light it and race to the cliff top. And perhaps the burning pyre would be seen and reported and they would be saved.

For a few nights Grimmelmann had made a fire each evening and in the morning it would be cold and they would have to start another. They had only a few dozen matches left, most of them in the old man's tobacco can. A large permanent fire was impossible due to the scarcity of firewood, but in the end they decided to maintain a small fire—a bed of glowing coals in a cleft a dozen feet from the cave entrance. It was left to Grace to keep the fire alive by feeding it scraps of tinder and wood. In the evening she scooped it up in O'Brien's mess kit and brought it into the cave and kept it alive throughout the night. And in the morning the glowing embers were again brought outside. The daily routine of carrying the fire back and forth became almost ceremonial; somehow the old man took it upon himself to do the job although the mess kit was O'Brien's and the responsibility of keeping the coals alive was the girl's. All of them carried firewood and never returned to the cave without a few dry sticks to add to the supply.

"It's easy to see why primitive man worshiped fire," Smith said that night as they sat around it.

"And why he feared the night," Grace added.

"And the sun," Bain said. "Don't forget the sun. If it had been me, I'd have made the sun a devil." He lay in the sleeping bag close to the fire.

"It was," Smith said. "A god and a devil all rolled into one. Something that could be good and bad depending on the quality of human sacrifices."

"Like all gods," O'Brien said.

"And all devils," Smith added. He threw a twig into the fire and they watched it curl up and snap.

"You're so vulnerable here," Grace said. "The sun burns you, the hot sand too; the night makes you shiver. Stones hurt your feet. When shadows come you imagine things, you see the goblins and spooks and ghosts that you laughed at in your easy chair."

"And you wonder about the next day and the next week," O'Brien said. "I mean you're conscious of living and dying. You see a scorpion or you bruise a finger and you know you might not be around too long if luck runs against you."

Jefferson Smith stared into the fire.

They were cut off from the world outside, not so much by sand and distance as by aloneness, fear, wanting. . . .

O'Brien needed excitement, risk, challenge. Bain had almost lost the will to live. And what of Grimmelmann? What of Sturdevant? Himself? Yes, what of himself, Jefferson Smith?

He tossed a chip of wood into the fire. His back was cold, his face and arms warm. He had really come to Africa to find himself, to see himself totally. He was not a scholar as much as a self-seeker; the Negro past was his past, his searching had become personal.

Africa was his home, perhaps the home of all men. He had been drawn to it out of some desperate need to see it, to look upon the face of his people, to smell, to feel, to touch the great land of his origin.

"I'd like to dig down in this sand," he said to the others. "I bet we'd find fossils, old bones, skulls, tools maybe." He held a fistful of the fine sand and let it run through his long brown fingers.

O'Brien grunted. "If you feel like digging, dig up some lizards for us."

"The earliest men lived around here," Smith said. "All over this part of Africa. They've found bones and skulls of men and of those who came before men."

Grimmelmann nodded. He had seen fossil bones.

"Missing links?" O'Brien asked. He lay prone in the sand, head toward the fire, eyes closed.

"No," Smith said. "Real links. Man-apes or ape-men; something between animal and true man."

"Like the Java man maybe," O'Brien said. He had a vague memory of something he read in a college textbook.

"No," Smith said. "The Java man and the Neanderthal and the rest were men. Real men. These African skulls they've found represent something in between. They are only part human."

"Brains like ours?" Bain asked from his bed.

"No," Smith said. "Bodies like ours."

"I thought intelligence came first," Grace said.

"It couldn't come until we had hands," Smith told her. "Until we stood upright and used tools. The brain developed afterwards."

"I always thought it was the other way around," O'Brien said.

Bain worked himself closer to the fire. "One thing that I've wondered about," he said to Smith, "is this: Why didn't some of these in-between characters survive, why aren't some of them still around? What happened?"

Smith smiled. "Remember, I'm no expert. But I'd say that they were killed off, exterminated by the earliest men."

"Why?" Grimmelmann asked.

"Because they were close enough biologically to inhabit the same area, compete for space and food. They fought and man was the victor."

"In most cases," Bain added.

"In most cases," Smith agreed, smiling. "It's possible that in some localities whole groups of early men were wiped out by the wilder and more vicious man-apes."

They were silent for a few moments thinking about it.

"That's one explanation," Smith said. "It might account for the great gulf between man and even his closest living relatives, the apes, say, the other anthropoids. All we have left of our past is a few bones and skull fragments, and some of the really important ones were found not too far from here."

"This is an old place, then," Grace said.

"Yes," Smith told her. "Very old."

Bain cleared his throat. "According to you, our real edge over the baboons, say, is physical rather than mental."

"It's the big difference," Smith said, nodding. "The decisive difference. The brains, the intelligence of the baboons, is stymied by their bodies. They have no real hands so they can't use tools, fire, weapons.

They went up a biological blind alley. We didn't. We kept getting smarter."

"And then turned on the forms we evolved from and wiped them out," Grimmelmann stated.

"How terrible," Grace said.

"It might have been necessary," Smith said. "We had to fight our way up, fighting and destroying anything that stood in our way. That's how we became human."

"And inhumane," Grimmelmann broke in.

"Exactly," Smith said. "The paradox called man. The terrible aggressiveness that created us might soon destroy us."

They were silent for a time, each lost in private thought.

"These early men," Grace said. "And later ones. How are we different from them?"

"We're smarter of course than the real antique boys," Smith said. "But no smarter than people in the last Ice Age. The important difference, unlike the one with the animals, is not physical as much as it is cultural. We have laws, codes, ethics. We are concerned with one another."

"Some of the time," Bain said. He thought of Sturdevant.

"Some of the time," Smith repeated in agreement, nodding and smiling.

"Hell," O'Brien said, sitting up. "I'm going to bed."

He stood up and yawned, moved into the darkness.

O'Brien trapped a lizard and killed it with a long stick, a hard dry limb from one of the thorn trees that grew in the sandy part of the canyon.

He picked up the dead reptile by its long tail and studied it for a long minute. There seemed to be different species and the one he'd killed was the most common. The head and body were together only two or three inches long but the tail was closer to six inches. The back and upper parts were light brown, mottled with a deeper hue, and four narrow lines of reddish-orange ran down its back. Its sides were creamy yellow. It was the kind Grimmelmann had roasted on a splint and eaten.

It was snakelike. He flung it away from him and it fell and lay belly-up in the sand. He couldn't eat one now; he wouldn't eat one. The melons and the water were enough and with any luck he might shoot something soon. There were big animals somewhere, animals that came to the pool and drank, gemsbok and zebra probably. It was just a matter of time. . . .

He walked away toward the pool, tried to find some of the tracks that they had not obliterated. Zebra were supposed to prefer drinking at night. Maybe he should come back and wait in the darkness. A big animal would give them enough meat for several days, all they wanted —thick, juicy steaks grilled over the fire.

A knot of hunger gripped him. He walked to the pool and drank as much as he could, lying face down, drinking the water from his cupped hand. He felt faint; his head ached. The dull hunger pain was still with him and he cursed silently.

He stood up and checked his rifle, began walking toward the opposite ridge. They had to have meat or die.

Hours later, in the middle of the afternoon, he climbed out of the canyon and walked along on the ridge. He could look down on the canyon now and across it to the cliffs they had descended a few days ago. He thought of the view from the peak and saw himself standing on the middle finger of the great black hand that stretched across the sand. The ridge was two hundred yards wide here, a difficult maze of upended slabs and loose shale that was dangerous near the edge.

He made his way across the ridge and studied the third canyon. None of them had been down into it; there was this canyon and yet another that they had not been in. And they had not yet explored the base of the central mass or the desert side of the most distant ridge.

Something moved below. He reached slowly for his binoculars and focused on it. A baboon was scowling at him, jabbering excitedly. He swung the glasses around and saw more of the dog-headed, apelike animals. He had frightened them; they looked toward him and although the distance was too far for human eyes O'Brien knew that they saw him easily. He waved his hand and they scowled and moved around and jabbered to each other.

He found a place to sit and studied them for a long time. They did not forget him. They watched him too but they gradually relaxed and went on with their foraging. They dug in the ground under the dead grass and turned over loose stones. One of them pulled something from the ground that resembled a carrot. What did baboons eat? He would have to ask Grimmelmann. Did they eat tsamma melons? Was the carrotlike thing fit for humans?

He counted them several times but they were in constant motion and he knew that his figure of twenty-five was not correct but only close.

He got up and walked along the ridge toward the peak, looking for a way down. Within a half hour he decided against it; it was too late in the day; he was too tired. He turned back, found the way down into the home canyon and walked across the wide dry plain.

Grimmelmann was sitting in the shade in the cave entrance.

"Why are there baboons here?" O'Brien asked. He walked past the old man and put his rifle in the niche and came out again. He sat down and took off his boots and let the sun dry his sweaty feet.

"Why are we here?" the German asked.

"Because of an accident."

The old man nodded. "The same, perhaps, for the other things here. It is not an ideal spot for baboons. The food supply is limited. But it might have advantages too. I do not think there are leopards here and they are the worst enemy of the baboon. Perhaps it is a good place after all. . . ."

"What do they eat?" O'Brien asked.

"Anything and everything. And I should imagine the ones here eat what baboons in better areas would not touch."

"Do they eat melons? Those cucumbers you showed us? The tubers?"

"*Ja*," Grimmelmann said. "All of those. They eat what we can eat and many things we can't. They are better adapted."

"The hell they are," O'Brien said. "We're smarter, tougher."

"In what way?"

"I've got a gun," O'Brien said. "They haven't."

"They don't need guns," Grimmelmann said.

"They do now," O'Brien smiled.

"I do not understand . . ."

"I'm going to kill them," O'Brien said. "Wipe them out."

The old man rubbed his chin and nodded to himself.

"Sturdevant told me that you can't eat them," O'Brien said.

"I suppose he must be right," Grimmelmann said. "I never thought of it. They are so human-like . . . but of course people eat monkeys. I do not know. I do not think I could eat one; not at this point anyway. I see it as something close to cannibalism."

"My idea is just to shoot them," O'Brien went on. "If they eat what we eat they are competitors. I figure there's only so much food and we might as well have it. Why let the apes eat it when we can

[54]

stop them?" He looked sharply at the other man. "I can see you don't like the idea."

"I don't," Grimmelmann told him.

"Why not?"

"I do not like to see slaughter. I have seen enough. All my life there has been killing . . . I am sick of it."

"But this is self-preservation," O'Brien said.

"All killing is."

"Do you want to die here because the baboons ate what you could have eaten?"

"No. I want to live. I want to survive and die on my brother's farm. But I do not want to kill these animals. It is murder."

"It's war," O'Brien said.

"I do not approve," Grimmelmann said.

The big man got up and went into the cave.

Grimmelmann watched the evening come, felt the cool air. There was something wrong with all of them, some hunger within them that was unappeased, some weakness or shame. They had somehow failed as people and the hand of fate had given them a chance to find themselves in the purity of time and space that was the desert, the black mountain.

O'Brien. There was a terrible thirst in him for something he had never found, a seeking that had driven him to Africa. There were reasons why all of them were on the plane. Bain was an alcoholic despite his good brain and good manners, a wandering, homeless drunk. Sturdevant was part of the whole dirty mess of South Africa, a transporter of black flesh for the new slavery of the mines. The young Mrs. Monckton was unhappy; she was alone, unhappy, without love. They might find what they sought here, away from the distraction of civilization; there was nothing trivial here, nothing to divert.

Evening came and they ate around the outside fire. Grace Monckton had made a soup. She filled Sturdevant's copper kettle with water and added, with Grimmelmann's approval, various things that they had found during the day of foraging. A smooth oily root that the old man tasted first, a half cup of grass seed, a withered narras cucumber. She boiled this and when it cooled it tasted better than warm water. They ate melons and took turns drinking the weak soup from the kettle.

O'Brien told them about the baboons, about his plan to exterminate them. The others listened and nodded.

[55]

"Whatever you decide won't change things," Grimmelmann said. "You will not bother them too much."

"How's that?" O'Brien asked. He saw the old man smile and it made him angry.

"You *can't* wipe them out," the German said. "They are too intelligent, too fast. When they learn that you can kill them at long distance they will stay out of range. You will only wear yourself out. The baboon is too smart to allow himself to be exterminated. Do you know that the Egyptians used them to perform menial tasks such as gathering wood? That they were only replaced when war prisoners became easier to secure? Their intelligence is almost human. One of the Egyptian gods was a baboon."

"You better forget it," Bain said. "Save your energy and the ammo for something better."

O'Brien smiled and let the subject drop.

When Pearl Harbor came he was halfway through college, restless, failing two subjects, playing football. It was a big, mediocre university which had been founded in the closing years of the last century by a half-dozen self-made intellectuals and scholars backed by some of the big mining fortunes of California. It was a success. In the raw, half-frontier days of the early 1900's it instructed, educated and refined two generations of Western elite and they had gone forth enlightened and proud.

But the First World War ruined the university. The anti-Boche propaganda found a target in the core of the school and dozens of the best teachers were forced out. A few years later many others were harried and forced to resign because of the Red Scare. The complexion of the institution changed; liberalism and inquiry fled, to be replaced by regionalism and rote. When football came it achieved national recognition for the first time.

He went there for two reasons. His grandfather had donated a quarter of a million dollars to it in the early days, and he wanted to play football. There was no need for him to study because his family was worth twenty million dollars; they owned newspapers and ranches and urban real estate and a small percentage of Standard Oil. And he didn't want to go east. He hated cities and good clothes and books. He hated other rich people. He stayed in California and went to the big university and played football; he took all the snap courses and wore dirty sweat shirts and old slacks. He sometimes went for days without shaving. He was a fine athlete.

He enlisted in the Marines the day after Pearl Harbor.

They shipped him east: to boot camp on Parris Island and then to Quantico, where he was turned into an officer. For the first time in his life he lived in an environment that was all-satisfying because it was totally competitive, wholly physical; where the weaklings were weeded out and sent away; where the hardest became leaders. He finished OCS at the top of his group and was sent to the Solomons.

He had a rare quality for a junior officer. He was a creative soldier. Within the framework of authority he exercised a special autonomy over his men; he saved them and protected them. They mistook it for love and returned it with a fanatical devotion. He sensed when an order to advance was ill-advised and doomed to fail and he held back until the edge of danger had been blunted. At other times he acted on his own intuitions and once probed so deeply into the enemy area that a general advance was ordered, resulting in a great saving of lives and time.

He was wounded once and spent a restless week in rear echelon sitting in a makeshift hospital, staring at the sagging green canvas overhead. He went back and led a night patrol to the edge of a Jap airfield and won the Silver Star. In the final big battle he became company commander and was wounded again by a mortar shell.

There were other campaigns, other islands, long years of dazzling white sand and spidery mangrove roots and tender coral. He remembered some things more than others: dead gyrenes floating together with the gulls flying overhead, Japs in the jungle night yelling obscenities about Babe Ruth and Roosevelt, the first prisoners who looked pathetic and silly, the Jap officer he'd shot who turned out to be an ex-Californian.

A world of light and dark, dead and living, retreats and advances. He turned down a promotion, a staff job. He stayed where he was until the war ended. Company commander. The best in the division.

Long before dawn, while it was still cold and black, O'Brien got up silently, took his rifle and walked out of the cave.

The old German was a fool. The baboons had to be wiped out. They were competitors.

He was a hunter and they did not understand him; they did not

[57]

know what hunting was, the waiting, the planning, the thinking. They did not know. . . .

The rifle reassured him in the darkness, the wonderful feel of it, the balance, the potency. A beautiful rifle that he had cleaned carefully the day before, loaded now with clean bright ammunition waiting to seek out and kill at long range.

He was going to shoot a baboon and eat it. Smith's open disgust at the idea did not make sense. If one ate lizards to survive, then one could eat baboon meat. This was no time to be squeamish.

There was an excitement in him, something he did not fully understand but which exhilarated him. The mountain was a great challenge; it could kill him. Everything else had been easy. Football, the Marines, everything; even the war had been easy because you weren't alone, your fate was tied up with too many others and the element of luck was too great. Here it was all in the open. There was the mountain and the desert and him.

Light streaked the sky. Perhaps thousands of years ago men walked across the valley at dawn with throwing sticks and flint-headed spears; the men who had made the flints they found, they were hunters and then the land must have been different, fertile and filled with game as the Sahara had once been. Prehistoric men. But that would be the wrong term, for all the men who had ever lived and hunted in the valley were without history—the flint makers and the Bushmen and the Bantu if they had ever come. They were all wild hunters without a written language or the time to toy with symbols and invent one, savage men who spent all their time gathering food. Like them.

He'd given his hat to Sturdevant but his hair was long and thick; now he didn't need the hat. It was an artificial thing which would not help him hunt; his black beard and long hair blended with the obsidian rock.

He stayed close to the cliff face until he reached the first break; then he began the difficult climb upward. He was sure of himself, sure of his strength; he was twenty pounds lighter than he'd been when the plane crashed and despite the diet he knew he was stronger, quicker, his senses sharper. The sun rose.

He rested for a few minutes on a ledge. He took off his binoculars and swept the jagged rock world around him. A lone baboon sat on a rock high above, a sentinel. It would be a useless shot; he had to get closer and get the sun out of his eyes. He put the glasses away and began climbing.

He reached the top and stood for a long time looking out over the sand sea; Sturdevant was there somewhere, reaching out desperately to contact the outside world. If he failed they might be here forever. He walked to the end of the cliff and looked down. It was a straight drop of hundreds of feet, perhaps a thousand. He backed away from it and found his glasses, looked for the sentinels. He found none.

He made his way down the ridge, away from the peak, eyes alert for anything: for bees that might lead him to honey, for fat lizards, for new plants to take back to Grimmelmann who knew the poisonous from the edible, the good from the bad. The steep cliff on his left ended; it was broken now, shattered. He studied it for a while, found a way down and began the descent.

The smell of baboon came to him; he stopped and looked around but none of them were in sight; it was as if they sensed his purpose. He moved on and the way became easier and he sat down and rested, his back against the warm stone. He took off his boots and switched his socks; they were full of holes.

He stood up and started down the slope and ahead of him something moved and cried out. A sentinel, perched on a needle of rock, called out in alarm. Somehow they had lost him and he'd surprised them. He swung the rifle up and found the big doglike primate in the telescopic sights; he held his breath; he fired.

The baboon leaped backwards into the air.

He moved forward carefully, for the way was suddenly dangerous again—a fifty-foot drop on his left. Then ahead of him, level with him, the troop appeared, shooting up the escarpment to the dizzy heights above. Never in their memory had they known such a noise; never had a sentinel died before. They fled in terror.

O'Brien came to the high rock and worked down around it. He found the dead baboon. It was bigger and heavier than it had appeared; its arms and neck and shoulders made his own look puny. It was an ape with a dog's head; its great jaw was filled with terrible teeth. He looked up and around him in sudden fear. Grimmelmann was right. A big baboon was dangerous; this one could have killed him, torn his limbs off, bitten great chunks from him. It was easy to understand now how two or three of them could kill a leopard.

It was too big to carry back to camp. He found his knife and began cutting into the warm body; the body was human-like and he wondered if he could eat it. He would. It was meat and he was on the verge of starvation.

Then a sound in the rocks around him. He froze, knew what made the sound. He reached for his rifle and spun around.

A baboon was twenty feet from him, creeping, baring its big teeth in sudden surprise, reaching out with long hairy arms. He shot it through the head. A second bounded at him screaming and he pumped three bullets into it before it collapsed almost at his feet. Two others fled, bounding over the rock jumble like rubber balls.

He stood up. His legs shook and he wondered if he could make it up the cliff. It was like the war. On Okinawa a crazy drunken Jap had come running out of a cave waving a sword and had died the same way the baboon had. Hunting was war. Three dead baboons.

He retreated to the shade of a tall slab of rock. There was no fuel here, nothing to burn. He'd cut the best meat from the three bodies and carry it back up the escarpment and down again to where there was wood. And then he would cook it and eat it; he was slowly starving to death and he would eat anything to stay strong, stay alive. If people ate snakes and lizards and insects, then baboon meat was edible too.

He got up and went into the sun again and began cutting pieces of meat from the stiffening carcasses. He was hungry.

Jefferson Smith took his fountain pen and his diary and left the cave. He and Bain were alone. O'Brien's rifle was gone and the girl and Grimmelmann were out after lizards and firewood. He couldn't sleep any longer; he had to write.

Outside he sat down with his back against the smooth cliff wall, opened the book and propped it against his upraised legs. The urge to write was an old urge which he understood and welcomed; it was a link with the life before, a time of long ago when he lived among books, studying, reading.

He turned the pages, studied the words which he had written, read scraps of it. It was familiar. He was glad that he had taken the book; it was better than the new socks and the saw and the copper wire. He found the last pages on which he had written.

Last day here. Next stop: Windhoek. Angola has an old sadness about it, a heaviness. Most of the Brazilian slaves came from here and it was a short trip across for them. Try to get figures on this on return trip. See Orteza. Ask Brill about his sources for the Institute report.

[60]

He had written this in the hotel in Mossamedes the night before Sturdevant flew them out. Angola wasn't too bad; there had been no trouble, no color problems. The Portuguese were old-timers in Africa. Brill was the Englishman in Windhoek, a wealthy eccentric who had made a fortune in the rare book business and had become a scholar in the process, an expert on ancient Africa. Brill had invited him to Windhoek and he had looked forward to the visit as the most important aspect of his journey. The Englishman owned some of the only known Arabic writings on the slave trade and had translations of them made at his own expense. It was a chance of a lifetime. His own book could not be written without them.

What should he write now? A record of the crash and what had happened since? No. He was not in the mood. He unscrewed the top from the fountain pen, touched it to the edge of the page to see if the ink was flowing. He would try to piece it all together later, find out the correct dates; the others could help him. He leafed through several blank pages and then selected one. A Monday. He wrote, finding it strange, almost difficult. His hands felt large and he had to concentrate to keep the letters small and neat.

I am hungry. All of us are always hungry. We eat but we do not think of it as food. This is my first entry since the crash. We are in the canyon now, in the cave, waiting every day for a rescue plane to come. Sturdevant left with cans of water to find help. Grimmelmann thinks it was suicidal to attempt it. The sand is terrible. Sturdevant is no fool. He must have known what he was attempting.

Why don't they have camels here? Somebody said they have some in Bechuanaland. Used for police patrols in Kalahari. We might be near them now. Always hope. Camels came from Arabia. Did slavers use them at all? Check this. Did British bring them into Kalahari? Work on importance of camel to the Saharan slave trade. Impossible to cross Sahara without them; from Black Africa to Morocco, etc. . . . Blame camel for slavery.

Where did it come from? Central Asia. Turks? I wish I had all the hamburgers I could eat and French fries with plenty of salt. If we get out of this I'm going back to U.S.A. and eat. The hell with history. Buy a huge strawberry shortcake and eat it with my bare hands. Steaks. Baked potatoes. Bread. Stop.

We are not sick. Bain was; recovering. A nice fellow. Detjens died after crash. Buried near it.

[61]

He sat for a while and then closed the book, put the pen away. He should have brought a book from the plane. It would be good to read again.

Sturdevant got to his feet, fixed the pack until it rested comfortably on his shoulders and walked off. The sun was touching the flat horizon far away. It was time to move.

He walked on, westward. The water sloshed in the tins and he liked the sound of it. Since he had left the others four nights had passed, long quiet nights of the sky and the stars and the flat desert devoid of any living thing, like a great sea. He walked all night and when the sun came again he sought refuge from it. He dug a trench in the sand the first day and covered it with the pack and the jacket and he had spent the day there, almost suffocating but out of the direct and brutal rays. Never had a day been so long and the cold night so welcome. The next day had been better; the land became a little more irregular and he came to a long rock whose base had been scoured and worn away by wind-blown sand so that it afforded some shade. He found an arrowhead in the sand and a broken jar with a pointed bottom. Bushman.

He walked on. . . .

It was all one big gamble and it was best not to think about it. Walk, move, keep going. Cover the space, the distance. He began to think about all the great blank spaces still left on the map, places where men could walk for weeks and finally die. Australia, Brazil, Arabia, Libya, Canada—so many places in Asia and Africa and even in the United States. The Great American Desert. Nevada and Arizona and New Mexico and all the rest.

He had to keep going and reach some place or they would all die. Nobody would ever trace them. They were all on their own, six people.

Two hours later he stopped and rested, ate another melon and sipped some of the precious water. So far, so good.

When dawn came he found himself on the top of a long sloping rise; as the light improved he saw a blur of thornbushes below. He walked toward them, rifle ready. Bush provided shade and cover: perhaps a bustard here, a fat zebra. Deserted anthills, some of them ten feet high, rose out of the bush, insect castles, almost indestructible.

He found no game. An hour passed and he grew tired and hot, for the sun was rising. He found a suitable anthill, one that would provide some shade, and put his pack and rifle down. He searched the base carefully for scorpions and snakes and then drank from one of the tins.

He wedged himself close to the concave anthill and closed his eyes. It was better to be here than back in the canyon; better to escape, to get out, to try. He could not endure waiting, hoping for time to pass, sweating out a rescue.

The sun rose but he was safe from its direct rays. He felt the relief in his legs; he was tired, so tired. . . .

The prison ship.

The intense blackness of the stinking hold, the jammed bodies, the voices whispering. We're ready now, another hour and we'll start. The voice of Allister trying to find him in the darkness.

He got two in the air and one on the ground before they brought him down in Libya. He bailed out and ended up in an Italian PW camp in Bangazi. Everybody had an escape plan but the camp was well guarded and nobody made it.

The word came down: they were being shipped to Italy. That night two Australians were shot dead on the free side of the wire.

A week later they were on the boat, packed in like animals, pushing and fighting each other for space to sit. In the night Allister found him. They had bribed someone, a door would be open, a guard would be missing. Did he want to go?

Yes. Anything to get out of the darkness. It might be a trap and there might be a sudden light and a machine gun but he would risk it. A night's freedom from the hellship was worth anything.

You're a fool, someone muttered. A cockney voice.

There's somebody waiting for you out there, said another. Somebody said the two Aussies bribed somebody back at the cage.

But he went. He and Allister and several others he never knew. He found the door and then another, went down a line and into the secret water and paddled away in the darkness.

He made it. Ten days later he was flying again.

The prison ship was torpedoed. There were no survivors.

At dark he stood up, his legs stiff from fatigue. He drank some water, fixed the cans on his back and walked on across the great level land, white and unreal when the moon came.

In the deepest part of the night he began to laugh. At first the sound of it terrified him, for it made the dead world seem more spectral and the aloneness more acute. Then the noise seemed familiar and comforting. Walking became difficult, then impossible. He sat down still laughing, a part of his mind telling him that he was over-tired, perhaps on the verge of complete exhaustion.

It was so funny. . . .

Looking for water. Seeking and questing for water. It was the core of the *trekboer* life and now he was part of it after all the long years of struggle. His great-grandfather, his grandfather, all those before whose whole life was a search for water with the bellow of thirsty cattle in their ears and the hot dust blowing in their faces. Water, water, water . . .

The burden was his now, the wheel had turned full cycle. But he was alone, all alone, and if he did not find water he would die. And yet it was funny.

After a while he stopped laughing. His stomach hurt. He worked the water tins loose and drank a mouthful. Somebody had played a great joke on him. He fixed the cans on his back and got up and walked on.

He came to low dunes which rose into somber hills, desolate and strange. Rock replaced the sand he had struggled through and his feet felt strangely light. When dawn came he was an hour from the highest point and he headed toward it, excited for the first time.

But there was nothing to be seen from it except the faint outline of a dry stream bed which wound snakelike to the south and west. He would follow it. It was dry and insignificant and probably vanished into some great sand bed miles or days away but he would stay with it because it was something. It might lead to the sea.

He worked down the slope and felt the sun on his face. There was a cleavage in the stone with a slight overhang and he decided to make it his sleeping place. He put the water cans in the shade and counted his matches. Seven left. He'd make a fire.

He walked off with the rifle and came back an hour later with a long brown lizard that had studied him too long from the flat rock where it sought the sun after a night in the clammy rocks. He skinned it carefully, removed the entrails and buried it all immediately to keep the flies away. He gathered dead thornbush branches, picking many of them individually from the bushes, raking up the remains of others with his hands. It took a long time and he was sweating and thirsty when he was finished.

He roasted the lizard meat over a small hot fire, cooking small chunks of it a piece at a time. He had two melons left and he ate one of them along with the meat and allowed himself some water. It was a good meal and when it was over he buried the remains of his kill, crawled under the outward-jutting rock and fell asleep.

When the sun went down he would follow the river bed.

He went on, walking by night and sleeping where he could during the long day. He followed the dry stream bed and on the second day it grew wider and stonier. But there was no water. He dug in several places but found nothing. He hurried on as his water cans grew lighter.

He talked to himself at times during the night walks; he would tell himself not to quit, to keep going. There was salvation for him and the others he'd left back at the mountain; he'd make it, he'd make it. . . .

And he would sing. The noise was welcome and it proved he was alive and there was always the chance that somebody might hear him. Sometimes his voice grew hoarse, his throat dry, and he would have to drink more water but he was willing to pay for the singing with a few extra sips of water, for the loneliness of the desert night was oppressive. If he did not despair, if he kept control of himself, he might well make it to the coast.

The country began to change, to slope downward. Then on the far horizon one dawn he saw a great blur of mountains. He walked on until the heat drove him to dig a burrow under a protruding slab of gray stone. He spent the rest of the day there, faint from hunger. Night came and he staggered on, talking to himself of the deep pools of water and the game he would find in the mountain ahead. And people. There would be people. A ranch run by an eccentric old German . . . natives herding sheep . . . a hunting party . . .

He went on through the night, falling many times from the dizziness of hunger. The last time he went down he stayed down, curled in the gravel, and when he awoke it was light. He got up and walked carefully out of the river bed. He had to eat within a few hours or he would die. The rifle was too heavy to hold level. The country was rough, mottled with thornbush and scattered trees.

He came upon a strange phenomenon—a big, dusty turtle lumbering across his path. He stopped and watched it, knowing that he would kill it and eat it and live for another day or two.

The eating of it did not worry him. He had eaten turtle before in civilized places with white tablecloths and silver; his hunger was such that he could eat anything. But the killing bothered him. He could

[65]

not shoot it and waste another shell and he could not smash its shell with a heavy stone as one could kill a lizard or a snake; he did not know why, but he knew that killing it this way was beyond him.

He caught up with the turtle and it hissed and pulled in its head and feet. He rolled it over and sat down. He tapped the shell with a stick and the head shrank farther into the reptilian folds. Turtles were creatures that no one should kill. They were too old and slow and helpless and dignified; if he lived and made it to the coast and safety he would never again eat turtle soup.

He stood up and began to gather wood. He could eat it raw but it might be better to cook it. He would make a great fire and someone might see it and come to investigate. There was a lot of wood here, more than he had seen.

The turtle was gone when he came back with his first armload of thorn branches. He threw the wood down and ran around until he found it lumbering off with uncanny speed. He caught up with it and picked it up. The shell was over a foot long and it was much heavier than he had supposed. The head and the legs had been sucked inward but as he walked back to the pile of wood the head came out and two orange eyes studied him. Like all turtles it became tamer as it was handled.

"I'm sorry," Sturdevant told it. "I am sorry I have to kill you and eat you, but it is your fault. You walked the wrong way this morning. It is your fault . . ."

He could not smash it with a rock and he could not shoot it. He put it down again upside down but he knew he could not leave it for it was able to right itself and run off. It might somehow escape and if it did he would probably die in the night.

He selected a strong straight thorn branch and cleaned it with his knife, taking off the thorns and minor branches. He sharpened the thin end of it. A miniature spear.

He went to the turtle and bent over it. This is how one murders, he told himself. Now I have done all things . . . I have killed men in the war with no feeling but this is truly murder. Or am I mad now from the sun and the guilt and the yearning? I cannot shoot you, Turtle, I cannot waste a bullet on something so slow and helpless. I will not crush you. . . .

He drove the sharpened stake into the wrinkled folds of the neck, felt it penetrate deep inside. He groaned and looked away, then ran from it as it writhed and flopped and bled to death. He ran across

[66]

the sun-baked land and stopped at last and found that he was crying, shouting wildly. He slumped down and rested, telling himself that he was sick and half-mad from hunger, that he must eat and find some shade and sleep until the sun went away. He could make the mountains now.

After a time he got up and gathered an armload of sticks and went back to the turtle. It was dead and flies crawled on the bloody spear that protruded from its neck.

Another night. Another fire against the wall of the cave. They huddled close to it, watching the progress of a flame on a gray stick, anticipating the crumbling of an ember, the slow disintegration of a favorite piece of wood.

"I think story telling began this way," Jefferson Smith said. "In front of a fire. A fire is alive; things happen in it if you watch for them."

"The television of the Stone Age," O'Brien said.

"It soothes and relaxes," Grace added. "Your imagination takes over." O'Brien was close to her; she could smell him; she brushed against him. She'd never been alone with him yet.

"Yes," Grimmelmann said. "A fire is good. It brings people together, all of them seeking something basic such as food or warmth or companionship. There is too little companionship left in the world. We all live too much alone, afraid to draw close to others."

"I keep thinking about the Bushmen who lived here," Bain said. "I see the fire and I look over and see the rock paintings and I go back in time and see some little guy standing in the sand with his paint pots."

"They carried the paint in the hollow ends of little horns," Grimmelmann said. "I saw a set of them once, eight or ten woven together in a sort of apron, with wax plugs to keep the paint covered."

"I read somewhere that they don't paint any more," Smith said. "Another lost art gone to hell."

"Tell me," Bain said. "Where did they come from? Were they always here in Africa? What's the story on them?" He turned from Grimmelmann to Smith and back again.

Grimmelmann smiled and Smith let his hands fall into a gesture of hopeless ignorance. "Who can say?" Smith said. "When you start talking about the origin of Bushmen you get into the origin of mankind. Some claim that Bushmen came from the north, from the Mediterranean, that they were pushed down here to the only place nobody else wanted.

"There is another theory that appeals to me," he went on. "We know that until recent times the Chinese were great seafaring people, greater than is supposed. In the sixteenth century I believe a junk turned up in England, an amazing event, to my mind. We know that the culture base of Madagascar is not African, not Negro, not Bantu, but Malayan. There must have been considerable intercourse between the Far East and South Africa. Chinese objects have been found in some of the old gold mining spots, at Zimbabwe and elsewhere. Perhaps the yellow Bushman type is an offshoot of the Chinese and the pre-Bantu types. It would explain the Mongoloid look of the Hottentot, too, and the curious pointed hat one sees him wearing in the old prints and the way he rides cattle. Something happened to the Chinese settlements on the east coast when the contacts with home were broken off. I think they were absorbed by the pre-Bantu stock and merged into what we now call the Hottentot and Bushman."

"I keep hearing Hottentot and Bushmen," Bain said. "What's the difference?"

"A great difference," Grimmelmann explained. "The Hottentot are pastoral people; they raise crops, keep cattle. The Bushman is a primitive man, wild, a hunter. People confuse them because they are both small and because they live in overlapping areas. They are quite different in skin color and speech and all other ways."

"How big are these characters?" O'Brien asked.

"Under five feet," Grimmelmann said. "They might average four feet ten. The women smaller. Once, long ago, I saw a woman who was four feet two inches. An adult."

"There's another theory about the origin of the Bushmen," Smith said. "An idea that they came from somewhere in Asia, say India, and spread both ways. There are tiny neolithic people everywhere, people more or less like the Bushmen. In the Andaman Islands, in the interior of the Philippines and Malaya. They might have all come from some original stock and changed a bit over the tens of thousands of years. The early people in Ceylon and India were supposed to be a small Negrito type. It's not difficult to imagine that they came to Africa and were pushed into the desert by waves of dominant races."

"I think the man or the men who painted those pictures on the wall were part of a hunting party," Grimmelmann said. "Perhaps they came here to seek game and then moved on."

[68]

"Did they fight among themselves much?" O'Brien asked. "Wars? That sort of thing? Maybe they wore themselves out."

"They had nothing to steal from their own people," Smith said.

Grimmelmann nodded. "They raided other people on the edge of the Kalahari, all around them. Cattle raids. They would go off, a party of them, and the women would follow behind with water carried in ostrich eggs. The shells would be buried at various spots along the way for the men and cattle to drink on their way into the waterless desert. The raiders would come upon a herd, slaughter the watchmen and run off with the cattle. The alarm would be given and the pursuit would start. The Bushmen would poison the wells and pits if there were any and subsist with the cattle on the water the women had left for them. If the pursuers got too close the raiders would shoot the beasts with their poison arrows and melt into the landscape. Or they might wait and ambush the owners of the cattle."

"And the cattle would be butchered and eaten in any case," Bain said.

Grimmelmann nodded. "Nobody could follow them across a hundred miles of sand. There would be a great feast which might last for days and days until the last cow was gone."

"So they never settled down to raise cattle and plant crops and live in houses," Bain put in.

"People never do," Smith said. "No group of hunters has ever, in all of history, given up the chase, the hunting life, for the farm. People turned to farming out of sheer necessity; it was either that or perish."

"Why is that?" Grace asked.

"Hunting is too much fun," Smith said. "It's one of the basic urges, I think. The stalking, the matching of wits and skill, the killing. Farming is hard, unromantic work. Until very recently it was done by serfs and slaves. Men never turned to it because they loved it."

"War is hunting," Grimmelmann said.

"Which explains why people like it," Bain said.

They sat for a time, quiet. Grace threw a new piece on the fire and the sparks swirled upward to die in the blackness above. They could feel the cold outside now; a cold that had suddenly replaced the heat of the day.

"Why did you come back?" O'Brien asked.

Grimmelmann looked up from the fire.

"To escape," he said. "I came back to find my brother. He has a

[69]

place here, a great farm. I had planned to stay there with him and his family, his five sons. I wanted to die there."

"What did you escape from?" Grace asked.

"From Europe," the old man said. "Europe is sick. It has been sick since 1914."

"Why did you wait?" Bain asked.

The old man turned to him. "I will tell you. I was caught up in the first war like everyone else. It was terrible, more terrible in many ways than your war. There were no ideas, only blood blood blood. . . . All through it I dreamed of coming back to Africa, to the peace, the great spaces, the freedom. But the war ended and South-West Africa was taken from us at Versailles. Then came the bad times for us in Germany. My brother and I worked when we could and tried to keep ourselves and the family alive. It was impossible to save. Money was worthless. The years went by. The old people died. We managed to save a little and one night we decided that one of us would leave. We tossed a coin and my brother won. He managed to find a boat to Swakopmund. It was the last I saw of him. This was in 1928."

Bain reached for a piece of firewood, a deformed and half-rotten branch that he remembered picking up a few days ago. It was strange to remember, to recognize small bits of wood, but they were important now.

"And the next year was '29," Smith said.

"Yes," Grimmelmann said, staring into the flames. "Germany went to pieces. There were no jobs, no money. I couldn't leave. I went to Bremerhaven and somehow got a job. I started to study English at night. Do not ask me why; perhaps I thought it would be useful in South Africa. I met a girl in my classes. I am in my forties now but suddenly we are married and life seems wonderful again to me as it was before the war. We are very happy and a baby comes. I hear from my brother and he tells us he has managed to get land in Africa; he convinced the authorities somehow that he was Dutch and they gave him some great tract of barren land. I start to think of going there and joining him but first we need more money and the baby must grow a little."

"And then Hitler comes along," Smith said.

"Yes," Grimmelmann said. "Adi comes and we do not make it to Africa; we do not try to flee from Germany. He sets us on fire, that man, and before we know it the gates have closed on us. Oh, I will not tell lies here, my friends. I was with him from the start; my hand was the highest. I was in the SA until the murders began and then I saw things and gradually worked my way out. I cultivated an imaginary ailment and in time they forgot about me. So I became an air raid warden and survived while the others went on and became Waffen SS heroes and occupation officials. Somehow I live through it."

He was silent for a long minute. The others waited.

"But my wife and child do not. They are killed in one of the big air raids. My little girl . . ."

Bain cleared his throat.

"That is the price we pay," Grimmelmann said. "The terrible price. I think I went bad for a while, I do not know. I left the city and wandered about working on farms, trying to forget. It got worse after that. The Russians began pushing us back and suddenly there are Americans in Europe and planes over Germany day and night. I am rounded up and forced into the *Volkssturm*. Old men and boys. It is no longer war now; it is national suicide. We are sent to hold back the Americans and when the regular army leaves us to defend a village in the Rhineland I manage to gain control of the situation and surrender. There is no more killing. The Americans are just. They laughed at us but it did not matter. And we were glad to be prisoners for a time. The food was very good, that I remember."

"Don't mention it," Smith said.

Grimmelmann smiled. "The war ends. I am an old man now and I am tired. I can speak some English, however, and I get a good job working with the Americans. The years of occupation go by and suddenly I get a letter from my brother. It is three years old and has been passed from hand to hand by those who knew me in Bremerhaven. I decide to leave Germany for good. It takes two years to arrange even that. And now I am here with you."

"Your brother will be surprised," Grace said.

"Yes," said the old man. "He will be surprised."

Bain yawned. "Another day." He was feeling better.

Smith looked at him. "Is that good or bad?"

"Bad," O'Brien said.

"Good," Grace said. "We are a day closer to being saved. A plane will come soon . . ."

Smith nodded to himself. It would be such a waste to die here, starve to death waiting for help that would never come. And he couldn't die: he was too young and had too much to do. And he was a rare bird too, a Negro professor in a great university, a scholar, a symbol. He was needed.

He held his hands out, palms facing the flames. Hope. It was the drug that kept them all going. Condemned criminals carried hope with them to the steps of the gallows and beyond. Life was so uncertain that people invented all sorts of myths to bolster their fears. And he was guilty of it too, thinking of himself as more important than the others because he was a success symbol, a needed person.

Perhaps he was important but if he was it had nothing to do with being a Negro. Being a Negro had not mattered much in his life; he had never been seriously harmed by prejudice and hate. During his boyhood there had been embarrassments and experiences that had left him shaken but they had been uncommon.

He had been born into a family of substance. His father was wealthy and respected, a physician on the staff of Lincoln Hospital. His mother was genteel and bookish; she had been a teacher in a southern school and had drifted into magazine work in New York. He had grown up in a busy and stimulating home, filled with books and alive with music and conversation.

He went first to a small private school in the city and then to Stony Brook on Long Island. There had been no shock or pains connected with his moving into an almost-white school. His background was equal to that of most of the other boys; he was witty and gracious and good at sports, especially tennis. He was accepted. There were other Negro boys at the school, upper-class and refined, and in the free society of adolescence there were few distinctions or penalties.

It was a good time in a life of good times. He spent most of his weekends in the city with his parents and as he grew older he drifted into another world of party-goers and play-seers. He grew tall and lithe and opened an account at Brooks Brothers. He wore glasses now and read constantly.

They had a water-front home farther out on Long Island where he spent the summer with his mother while his father came on weekends. He played tennis and swam and dug clams. He made new friends among the white neighbors and read late into the night. His father bought him a secondhand car and he learned to drive on the endless back roads of Suffolk County.

He graduated from Stony Brook and went to Cornell. Then the Korean War came; he registered for the draft but he wasn't taken. For a time he was a premedical student; everyone had assumed that he would follow his father's profession. But medicine did not excite him. He had been too close to it. Or perhaps he associated it with death and dying and chemical smells and frantic calls in the night. And he was not driven by the vision of wealth and security. He switched his major to history with a vague idea of going to law school or into foreign service, finished Cornell and went on to Harvard for graduate work. Everything was easy and comfortable. The world was good. The fact of his race rarely entered his head; he didn't think of himself as a Negro and it bothered him, made him feel guilty at times. He felt that he owed something to his race, that he should become a spokesman, a fighter against all that was wrong, a political leader. But he remained in the academic world, staying on at Harvard as an instructor, then as assistant professor.

When they left the fire and went to their beds, Grace Monckton lay for a long time watching the fire. She wanted to go to O'Brien; she was empty and alone and she wanted him.

She had waited for him to return in the late afternoon. He was always gone from the cave before she awoke and the days seemed endless now without him, waiting for him. And then he came striding down the canyon, big and yet graceful, naked except for the old tennis shorts he wore. She watched the muscles ripple across his chest, his hard stomach. He was so different from the boys she had known a few years ago in her girlhood, so different from her husband who was her ex-husband now, the good and gentle Andrew Monckton, journalist and mama's boy.

O'Brien had come and stood before her, showed her the lizards he had found and killed, the meat that would be their supper. But there was a greater hunger in her. She moved close, brushed him with her bare shoulder, pretended to examine the dead lizards.

He leaned close to her and she no longer knew or cared what he was saying; she wanted him to reach out and hold her, kiss her, tell her that he loved her. . . .

Unlike most men he looked better with a beard than without one, looked better half naked than fully clothed. He reminded her of something out of antiquity: a victorious gladiator, a corsair, a wild Celt.

Then he was gone, moving away into the cave, and she stood trembling, aching with her great need.

Now, in her bed, watching the fire, she knew that she wanted O'Brien more than anything else she had ever wanted or dreamed of wanting. She was a delicate creature in a relentless world of rock and sand. She could not be alone any more; she had to have a mate. O'Brien was alive and hard and vital; she wanted him physically as she had never wanted her husband. There was a ruthlessness in him that she both feared and hungered for, a violence that she knew in her dreams, that left her shaking and sweat-covered in the darkness.

She couldn't go on much longer without him.

There was an eagle's cave on the outside of the peak, facing the desert, the north. O'Brien discovered it one day searching for baboons. It was just visible from a spur on the short ridge, the one he some-times thought of as the Thumb Ridge. He saw the big bird glide down from the cloudless sky and vanish into the great cliff face; he went farther out on the spur and studied the cliff, saw nothing. Then he noticed a whiteness on the black stone, bird droppings. He aimed the rifle at it and saw through the telescopic sight a break in the stop above the whiteness. It was a cave, a wide slit, and he could see move-ment inside. Later the eagle appeared, thrust itself into the air and flew away over the desert. O'Brien moved and found a spot where he could rest the rifle and observe the eyrie. It fascinated him; the idea of an inaccessible place, perhaps a deep cave, which no man had ever seen. How long had it been the home of eagles? How many lived there, were able to find carrion in the empty world on all sides?

Some days later, on the other side of the peak, he discovered a way down to the desert floor. It was a dangerous descent but he took his time and moved down the hundreds of feet. None of them had ever been here; they had dismissed it as a source of food but he knew that it should be explored.

He rested at the bottom, in the shadows of great fallen slabs that had once been part of the massif. He killed a long yellow lizard and ate it uncooked. It was a reward he was entitled to, he told himself. He needed more food than the others. He was the hunter.

He remembered the eagle's cave. It was two or three miles from where he was; hundreds of feet up. He began to walk toward it, around the bulge of the cliff. The sand was extremely fine here, desic-cated granite with a large proportion of mica. His feet sank into it and after a quarter of a mile he was forced to rest and drink some water. It was more desolate here than in the most remote parts of the canyons; the desert closed in, pressed against him; the sun gave no quarter; above the sheer rock threatened.

But he kept on. He had told himself that he was going to locate the cave and stand beneath it. He would go on if it consumed the rest of the day and all his strength. . . . He walked on through the heavy sand and after a long time he located the white splash high on the cliff overhead, saw the great bird fly away and vanish in the distance.

The unspoken thought that he had toyed with, the idea that he might climb to the cave, would never again enter his mind. No human could climb the glasslike rock. The cave above was safe from all wingless creatures.

He came to the base of the cliff and started. There was life here, strange gruesome plants growing in the granite sand, fertilized by eagle droppings. From one rock a stalagmite of white dung rose. A thick-leafed plant grew near it, finding life somehow in the impossible environment. And everywhere there were bones and splinters of bones, the debris, the garbage from above. There were prints in the sand, of hyena and jackal perhaps, of land scavengers who came to investigate and steal from the scraps. The sand was covered with ants too, strange white ants, slow-moving, disgusting. And there was a smell that penetrated the very rock, a smell that seemed ancient, poisonous. But yet, in the dung and among the decay of old feathers and ancient filth, there was life. The dung had altered the chemistry of the sterile soil and brought alien seed to it; things lived here now, alone but alive.

He turned and walked away.

The desert was quiet except for the hum of invisible insects. There was a beauty here, O'Brien thought, a wildness that stirred him: the sharp cliffs, the great black peak, the jumbled rock piles and the stunted grass that grew in the hard soil and heavy sand. It was a sparse and difficult place which reminded him of the family ranch in California where he'd spent the first winter after the war. It was high in the sierra and the snow came early and stayed until spring. He'd spent four months there, alone except for the workmen, hunting deer and roaming the great timbered slopes. Once he'd tracked a mountain lion, shot it through the head and brought the skin back to show the cow hands who worked the place. He liked the snow and the silent places, the cold wind in his face.

After that winter things had gone wrong. The two terrible years of his marriage, the fights and brief reconciliations and the long bitter divorce proceedings which spilled over into the newspapers and caused another rupture with his family, his staid brothers and quiet sisters. He had simply married the wrong girl; a girl who did not love him and was at once puritanical and rapacious. Correcting the mistake had left him bitter and humiliated. He could not trust women afterwards. He saw them as a breed apart, willing to destroy themselves for the symbols of luxury and status.

He went to South America and tried to forget it all in wild living and constant movement but he grew weary of the Latin temperament and came back to the States. There was nothing for him to do. He refused to work. He considered it absurd for the son of a millionaire to work: it was needless pretense. And politics annoyed him. He did not believe in democracy; he found compromise unbearable; he did not enjoy popularity. Boredom finally drove him to New York and he became involved in Society and stock speculation. He lived wildly, squeezing each day like a lemon and tossing it away. He kept two mistresses, each unknown to the other, and spent his days in dubious transactions. He was not repelled by the idea or fact of hoax and fraud. It was all a monstrous joke. He did not understand poverty, remained unimpressed by wealth, and the whole idea of buying and selling invisible shares of ownership of invisible and drab business seemed like some adult game. And it was simple to win. You made sure you would win, you removed the gamble and chance and made your own luck. He had capital and boldness and others had the connections and knew the loopholes and legal tricks. He made money. He had fun.

He went to Europe a couple of times, spent a winter in London tasting a new environment. One summer he went to Italy and met a girl who claimed to be from Vassar and he took her to Cannes and Biarritz. The years passed. He was handsome and rich and secure but he was not happy. It was all so easy. . . .

CHAPTER IV

GRIMMELMANN was falling asleep, lying on the soft white sand in the cool cave. He thought of Sturdevant and the desert; he thought of the Herero War again. . . .

It was shameful like all wars the white man fought against the simple peoples of the world. And the guilt was on him, not on the Fatherland. He'd killed men for no reason.

All the fighting, all the campaigning; it was all mixed up in his mind now, fragments of days and nights of thirst and fear. There was one time when they went out to make a wide swing toward the Bechuanaland border to try to cut off the retreat of many hundreds of Hereros with their thousands of cattle. That time they hadn't seen one of the enemy. Five weeks in the bush and not one sign of them. Then one of them had sighted some native homes, giant beehivelike huts made out of thorn branches and dung. They had set fire to them and moved on but the heavy smoke followed them and made them sick and they had all vomited in the hot sand, trying to get away from the smoke.

There was never enough to eat. If they'd had the proper food the campaigning wouldn't have been too bad, for they were all young fellows, eager and strong. With the proper food many of the sick men wouldn't have died and the rest of them would have lasted longer. Instead the pancakes were made from flour and water which was milky with lime or bitter with the salts in it. Now and then when an ox collapsed from pulling the heavy wagons there was fresh meat. The animals were slaughtered and eaten before the meat went bad but nobody enjoyed it because it was too warm, too fresh.

A strange war with the enemy almost always invisible. Even the militia and the Boers on horseback never saw much of them. They were always stumbling through the sand, chasing men they never saw, men whose crime was that they were black and owned fine cattle and would not part with them. The German government had claimed all the land and told the Herero they had to pay taxes in cattle. The Herero refused. The war began.

In the morning it was still cool and they marched through wet grass. Then the sun came up and they fought through hot sand, three or four hundred men usually and twenty or thirty Cape wagons pulled by half-mad oxen fighting the flies and the heavy load harnessed to their dumb backs. Thornbushes reached out and tore their uniforms; their cheap boots cracked and dried out and began falling apart. The men all looked alike now: scraggly beards on young-old faces that were gaunt and yellow. Their coats grew greasy. They began to neglect their rifles. They were all infected from the thorns. Now and then a man started to cry and nobody could stop him. There were suicides.

The war finally narrowed down to the possession of a single water hole. There was a real battle with the Herero firing at them with captured rifles, charging them with spears and clubs. They won. The natives retreated to the east with their women and children, their cattle; a whole nation fleeing through the wilderness like the Israelites escaping from the Pharaoh's wrath.

They slumped to the sand and slept among the dead and wounded. Officers and noncoms bellowed but they lay in the sand and pretended to be dead. In the morning they dug a mass grave and ate breakfast. Then they collected all the horses and the strongest of them became mounted infantry. They followed the Herero.

It was not difficult. The path of the retreating nation was a hundred yards wide. They followed it on the sick horses and soon they began to come upon the refuse of the flight: blankets and women's trinkets, utensils, broken weapons, iron pots and all sorts of tools which had been looted from German farmers. They came upon men dead of wounds they had received at the water hole. They began to find live men who sat and stared at them uncaring—men and women and children dying of thirst and despair. And everywhere dead and dying cattle, some of them wild from the heat and thirst, crazy and dangerous. Dead dogs. Dead horses. Goats. Babies. And worst of all, women sitting in the sand or lying in it, some alive, others dead with their living young clasped to them. . . .

A dying nation. Stink and flies and calves bellowing for their mothers. In the middle of the day they came to the first watering place but the Herero had filled it with corpses and slaughtered cattle. They pulled out the bodies, one by one, but in the end there was only a little bloody water in the bottom. They dug deeper in the sand. Nothing. The sand was too hot now to lie on. There was no pasturage. So they moved on and came to a group of the oldest women he had ever seen. They sat in a circle and stared blankly at some bone objects before them. One of them was trying to chant a prayer but no sound came from the moving lips.

Once a young boy with a spear stood in their path. They began shooting at him but mounted as they were, too weak to hold a rifle properly, they could not bring him down. A dozen shots, two dozen, and still the boy stood waiting, unharmed. The men began to laugh, cheer. They put their rifles away. Then one of the officers dismounted and walked toward the boy with his pistol. He aimed carefully and fired. The boy fell. They stopped the crazy laughing and went on.

They came to another water hole and this too had been spoiled by the enemy. It was a deep well and it was filled to the top with dead oxen. Somehow he had found a way down through the great warm bodies, slippery with blood. There was water at the bottom, bitter with blood and salts. He filled some canteens and crawled upward through the wedged bodies, praying that they would not slip and trap him forever in the stifling hole.

They made coffee. Other men crawled down into the well. Someone found a great nest made by weaverbirds and they tore it apart and fed it to the crazed horses along with cow dung and thorn branches.

They started back along the path they had followed; they were in no condition to pursue and fight the enemy. Now they were as weak and terrified as the Herero. Horses dropped dead and men pitched forward on the sand; every half mile cost a horse. The walking men gathered in a group and tried to stay on their feet. The night went and morning came; the unit was a long line of stumbling men, none of them quite sane, fighting the terrible lethargy within them, occupied with the greatest of all ambitions—to put one foot ahead of the next and to go on. Vultures followed them. The last horse died. The last rifle dropped in the sand. Most of them got back to the main party but none of them remembered the details. When they recovered they learned that the war was over. . . .

It was a world of extremes, a lost place of antique plants and people, of primordial things; to enter the desert was to go backwards in time.

Here were plants without leaves, misshapen, hoarding their precious moisture in thick, spine-armored stems, in bitter roots and deep tubers, behind poison thorns. They had become deformed and ugly but they could thrive and reproduce.

Grotesque beings: tarantulas and giant beetles, spiny lizards with horns and armor, leftovers from the age of dragons and giant insects. As one goes deeper into the desert the softness of nature vanishes; the plants become fewer, armed with spikes and thorns; the insects become more virulent; savage baboons watch from their rock castles and the vultures from their vantage points. Time does not matter.

There are exceptions.

The gemsbok has grace and beauty. It is a horselike antelope, fast and noble, the oryx and the unicorn of fable. It can live and grow fat without ever seeing surface water. It is a gentle grazing animal but its long horns are saberlike and when it is aroused or at bay the lion backs away.

One of them came to the canyon, remembering the pool and the strange open water; once, some summers ago, a great herd had passed here on the way south. Desert creatures do not forget forage or water.

It came to the canyon and O'Brien shot it.

A strange and wonderful thing: all at once they had a seemingly unlimited supply of meat.

O'Brien had come upon it suddenly close to the water hole in the uncertain light of dawn, a great and beautiful animal standing under one of the withered trees. Its head was turned so that the two arched horns seemed as one. His first shot killed it and it fell heavily on the stony ground.

The others came. They examined the sleek hide, the white legs which reminded them of spats, the overlong horns. Grimmelmann took O'Brien's hunting knife and cut the animal's throat. Fresh blood gushed forth.

"Shall I butcher it?" he asked the big hunter.

"Go ahead," O'Brien told him. "I wouldn't know what to do really. Cut it up."

"Go, bring some coals," the German told Smith. "We're going to have a feast, eat the things that are best eaten while we make biltong."

"Are we going to dry it?" Grace asked.

"It's the safest way," Grimmelmann said. "We can hang the strips in the tree and let the sun work for us. We can keep the fire going.

Some of us can remain here overnight with the meat to keep the carrion birds away."

Smith hurried away and the others wandered far off over the flat canyon floor picking up dead branches from under the scattered trees. The sun rose, and vultures came and circled above in the clear sky.

Grimmelmann skinned the big animal and then, with O'Brien's help, butchered it. The entrails were drawn and they began cutting the carcass into large manageable chunks which O'Brien wedged into forks of the nearby acacia trees. The two men were soon drenched with blood and sweat but they were hardly aware of it; they had to put the meat where the blood would drain off.

They stopped and rested and ate, using the bloody hide as a table top and searching the entrails for tidbits, which they roasted over the fire or ate half-raw. The liver and heart and intestine. Grimmelmann smashed the heavy skull and put the brain away for his evening meal.

The meat made them thirsty and they made frequent trips to the pool. They cut steaks and settled down to eat leisurely. The frantic gulping, the trembling, the tearing at the raw meat, was behind them. They groaned now, watching the meat curl and sizzle on the ends of their charred sticks. Now and then they would drop a piece and then rush off to the pool to wash off the sand. They would finish one piece and cut another; they stuffed themselves and after a time they drew away from the fire and found refuge in the shade, close to the meat.

"What do we do now?" Bain said. He lay like the others on his back, lazy and hot and sleepy. He felt wonderfully bloated.

"We'll cut the meat into slices and let it dry," Grimmelmann said. "We can speed up the process if we squeeze it first between flat stones."

"Dehydrate it," Bain said.

"Yes," the old man agreed. "We let it stand in the sun. One of the big problems will be the flies. Look at them. They are laying eggs in the meat. We must build smaller fires around the carcass, fires with lots of smoke to drive them away."

"Yes," Bain said. "But let's rest awhile. I'm too full to do anything right now." He closed his eyes. A fly settled on his bloody hand. He shook it away.

"If we could only shoot more of these," Smith said. "Do you think there are many around? Off in the desert?"

"I've seen herds of a thousand or more," Grimmelmann said. "But who can say where this one came from or whether we'll see another one?"

"I'm glad O'Brien is a good shot," Bain said. "Think of all this meat running away."

"It came here for water," Grace said. "Why don't we move to some other place, another canyon? We might be scaring others away with our noise, our fire, our scent."

Grimmelmann shrugged. "Perhaps, but I do not think so. The big herds are not here, deep in the desert, at this time of year. When the rain comes, when things grow again, they will return. This animal came to water. Danger and strange smells would not have turned him back. I think we should stay in the cave. It might be wise to have someone stay near the water each night with the rifle. I would be glad to."

"It's a deal," O'Brien said. "We've got the water and they've got to come to it. If we could get one of these antelopes once a week we'd be doing okay. Plenty of meat."

"There might be zebra," Grimmelmann said.

"Anything would be better than the melons," Grace said. "They fill you up but there's no strength in them. For the last few days I've had dizzy spells. I've felt so weak . . ."

"We all have," Bain said.

O'Brien got up slowly, groaning. "Let's get going before the flies carry it off."

They moved the fire under the low trees and the smoke drove off large numbers of flies and insects that all but covered the raw, bloody meat.

Grimmelmann began cutting long thin strips from the big chunks of meat, handing them to the others who hung them carefully from the branches. The sun would dry it, shrink it, suck the moisture from it, and it would become tough and hard. It would not rot. They could save it, hoard it.

They took turns cutting. The scraps were collected and wrapped in the hide, away from the insects for the night meal. The sun grew weak and they worked on. Bain carried off the bones, scattered them far away downwind from the meat. Flies swarmed after them; the vultures wheeled closer. Then the last long slice of meat hung drying from the tree. Grimmelmann and O'Brien decided to spend the night under the tree with a small fire; they went back to the cave to get their beds and while they were gone the others tried to find firewood for them.

Evening came. The tree stood in the cooling night festooned with the drying slivers of meat. O'Brien and the old man settled down to rest and keep watch. The others returned to the cave.

It was the best day they had seen.

Jefferson Smith wrote in his journal.

The gemsbok meat saved us. Bain is getting stronger now. Told me he was an educated roughneck. Apt.

How long can we stay here? Five of us. O'Brien hunts but gets little. He tries to kill baboons now. They're clever. Stay out of range. I think it is doing something to him. He doesn't talk to us as much as he did. Grimmelmann is fine. He's a wonder at his age. Requires little. Tough. Good outlook. Grace is O.K. I am fine. I wish we could get another gemsbok. Raw meat. We all complain of headaches and dizzy spells. We need salt.

Jefferson Smith, B.A., M.A., Ph.D., is barefooted. Pants are now Bermuda-length, ragged. We get dressed at night, all we can wear. Nights are cold. O'Brien wears only filthy old tennis shorts. No shoes. No hat. He has never shaved, cut hair. Says it protects skull from sun, keeps his brain below boiling point when he must be in it. He's right, I suppose. He brings in most of the small lizards in a small bag, all cleaned and ready for the fire. I am the worst hunter here. Grace is better. Out-door girl. I have a bad eye, no patience. Grimmelmann is owl-like: waits for them to come from hole, sits for an hour, then strikes with his cane. He digs them out from the ground too. O'Brien throws rocks at them, hit or miss—he doesn't care.

Civilization is a membrane stretched over the dark abyss of barbarism. Florid sentence. We've broken through. If this place was bigger, more food, if we all had women, the resulting kids would be born into a stone age. O'Brien's gun would use up last bullet, all clothes would wear out. Kid's vocab. would be basic. We might teach them something but after we went it would be meaningless to them (math., history, philosophy, etc.) and they would not pass it on. Toynbee's twenty-some civilizations did it. H-bombs will again maybe. All for now.

One afternoon, sitting in the shade at the mouth of the cave, Smith became restless with the speculation, the idle talk. He got up and found his flashlight, discovered that it still worked and stood before

Mike Bain and Grace. Grimmelmann was inside the cave resting from his forage in the morning's hot sun. O'Brien had been gone since dawn.

"I'm going to have another look at that *kloof,* as you call it," he announced to them. "You want to come? I'm curious about it."

"What's there to see?" Grace asked. "It's just a hole going up through the rock."

Bain got up. "You going to crawl up it?"

"Yes," Smith said. "There's a bend in it, I think. I want to have a look. I think I can climb it if you hold the light for me."

Bain nodded. "What can we lose?"

"You can fall," Grace said. "Break a leg."

But Smith went and Bain followed him back into the cave. Grace joined them.

Smith's flashlight cut through the blackness of the interior cave; the light in back of them faded, then vanished as they turned a corner. The sand became deep, softer. They had the feeling that they were entering another place far away from the others, a place where they did not belong. And then they came to the end of the cave, to the place where the floor veered upward, where underfoot were rocks and shale mixed with heavier sand. They watched the beam of light go up into the wide, chimneylike hole overhead, saw it wander over the jagged sides. It did not go up straight as they had imagined; there was a slight angle to it which only Smith had seemed to notice, an angle which made it climbable.

"See where it veers off?" Smith said. He held the light steady and they saw that far up, the slant became more pronounced; one wall veered over and became a ceiling and the other vanished into the mountain.

"I've been here a couple of times," Smith said. "I got to wondering about where that hole went. We should find out. Remember what Grimmelmann was saying about flash floods? Maybe this thing drains off water when it storms. If it does we'll be in a hell of a fix; we could all be drowned or washed out of the cave."

"It's good you thought of it," Bain said.

Smith handed the flashlight to Bain. He walked around the wall and then began to climb, his big hands reaching up and straining on smooth knobs, searching overhead for narrow fingerholds. He was barefooted and the others watched his toes seeking the places that the hands had found and used. He moved upward and they backed away so that if he fell he would not land on them.

He made it. They saw him stop fifty or sixty feet above them in the rock tunnel. He had climbed easily. After the first twenty-five feet, he was in no danger of falling. Bain had followed him with the light, keeping it ahead of him, helping him find his way up the jagged wall. But Smith vanished now without a word into the blackness. They waited. Bain held the light and wondered what they'd do if it suddenly went out. And then Smith came out of the hole, feet first, and he began to descend. Within a few minutes he was with them, sitting on the sand, bathed in sweat, laughing to himself.

"I'm going up again with the rope," he said. "I crawled ten feet or so along the tunnel. Couldn't see a damn thing, of course, but it must go somewhere. I'm going up again and toss the rope down and haul the flashlight up and explore the place."

The others were excited with him.

"I'll go back and get the rope," Bain said. "I can walk back in the dark. Why not turn off the light before it wears out?" He was gone.

Smith pushed the button and they were drowned in darkness. Grace shivered next to him. "I'm afraid in the dark," she said. "If I were alone I'd be hysterical."

"This is total darkness," Smith said. "It seems to weigh down on you, press down. I didn't feel any air movement up there, but it's difficult to tell. I'm willing to bet there's a back door to this cave. I bet the Bushmen used it."

"I'm afraid of Bushmen too," Grace said. "I dream that they'll come here and watch us from the cliff and then in the night come down and kill us."

"I hope they do come," Smith said. "They wouldn't harm us. They're not wild men or savages, remember that. I think they'd help us get out of here, help us get across the desert. I'd go with them if there are any left, any around; I hope they do come."

Noises in the darkness came toward them. Smith turned on the flashlight and they saw Mike Bain with the coil of rope.

Smith took the rope, tied a loop in one end and tied the rope around his waist. "I might be able to tie it up there," he told them. He went to the wall and began to climb, faster this time with Bain lighting the way with the flashlight. He reached the top of the *kloof* and halted at the horizontal tunnel.

"You want to come up, Bain?" he shouted down. "There's an elbow of stone up here. I can make a few turns around it with the rope and hold it too. What about it?"

Bain didn't want to go. It was pointless, and he wasn't agile or confident of himself. But Smith seemed to want him to come.

"I'll come up," he shouted. He found the rope and tugged on it.

"It's safe," Smith said from above in the darkness. Grace held the light and Bain climbed slowly upward, pushing against the rock with his bare feet, leaning out above them, moving up the rope hand over hand. He reached Smith, and Grace Monckton let out a sigh of relief.

"Tie the flashlight on the end of the rope now," Smith called down. Grace did and called back that it was ready. They watched it bob upward in the blackness, swaying and throwing an eerie light, showing her face turned upward, strained, taut.

Mike Bain followed Smith down the tunnel, holding the flashlight so that the man in front of him could see. The tunnel sloped upward and became larger until the two men walked upright. The stone closed around them and they walked on, wordless and awed by the sense of discovery.

The floor tilted upward at a sharper angle and the tunnel narrowed. Smith took the flashlight and went on and Bain followed as close as possible. The stone around them and underfoot was a deep dull obsidian black, smooth and glasslike; they began reaching out and touching the sides of the tunnel. The ceiling suddenly went up and Smith stopped for a moment and explored it with the beam of light and they saw that far above them the walls of the tunnel closed.

And all at once the slope ended and the floor underfoot flattened out and they stood in a wide corridor. The ceiling was even higher here; the light did not find it as Smith raised it up and up over the tapered side of the fissure.

The light came down and they went on. Smith stopped suddenly and Bain bumped into him. Smith grunted and Bain looked to see a skeleton curled against the side of the passage.

"Bushman," Smith said. "Look at the size of it."

They went to it and bent down and studied the small skull and the time-worn bones. The remains of a tiny bow were near it, and four arrows from which the stone heads had long since dropped. Bain touched the wood and it crumbled.

"Don't touch the arrowheads," Smith warned. "They were probably covered with poison once and it's supposed to be one of the most powerful in the world. It might still be dangerous."

Bain nodded and they stood up and went on. They came to another skeleton and then two more beyond.

They knelt by the last two skeletons and studied them. One was obviously a child and the other one a woman. Smith picked up a few beads: ostrich shell, uniform and perfectly made. And there were the powdery remains of the clothes they had worn. Why had four Bushmen died here so long ago?

Near the smallest skeleton were a tiny bow and a few arrows the size of pencils, curls and mounds of leather. Smith touched one of them and the ashlike decay crumbled.

The flashlight blinked and for an instant they were alone in the darkness. It frightened them.

"Let's go on," Smith said. Bain felt the excitement in his voice.

They moved on, away from the skeletons, down the black tunnel. Smith pointed the light upward and they saw that the ceiling was still out of its reach.

Something white ahead. More bones perhaps. They went on without speaking. The white objects were giant eggshells. A neat pile of them against the black stone. Some were broken. Smith stopped, reached out for Bain's arm.

"Ostrich eggs," he said quietly. "There must be twenty or thirty of them." He reached down, picked one up, hefted it, handed it to Bain. "The Bushmen use them as water containers."

"Are you thinking what I'm thinking?" Bain asked. The shell was rubbery-hard with a small hole in each end.

"We can go out into the desert now," Smith said. "These might save us."

"Let's get back to Grace," Bain said. "I'll carry a couple of them with me."

Jefferson Smith nodded, played the flashlight over the pile of dirty white shells. "Be careful. Don't break any."

They worked their way back down the tunnel, Bain first, now walking in the path of Smith's flashlight.

O'Brien came back from hunting as the sun went down. He was tired and short-tempered, flushed from the sun, with nothing to show for hours of tense waiting and stalking. They ate melons and some of the dried gemsbok meat and talked again of the ostrich shells Smith and Mike Bain had found in the *kloof*.

"We could create water stations," Grimmelmann said. "I should not speak, really, for I would not be able to walk so far as would be necessary. In any case, with so many shells it would seem possible."

"How would we do it?" O'Brien asked with sudden interest.

"We have plenty of water and plenty of shells and nothing else to do except wait for a plane to fly over and see us. Let us say that Bain here and Smith walked off into the sand with all the water they could carry in the shells. They walk all night. When they can no longer go on they stop and Bain buries his load where it can be found again. The next night they go on and do the same thing with the remaining water. They come back leaving two water points in the desert. They rest for a few days and regain their strength. They set off again with more water but now they can walk for two days without depleting the supply they carry; they drink from the two stations they created. They walk on and set up two more stations, the last four days from here. Eventually they would have a line of stations across the desert and there would come a time when one man could set off with no water weighing him down and walk for days finding, let us say, two shells of water and food too perhaps at the end of each night's march."

"It sounds possible," O'Brien said.

"I'm not sure I could last that long," Bain said. "It's a good plan if you overlook the human factor."

"We could take turns," Grace said. "I could go out the first time. That would be the easiest trip."

"I'll volunteer to be the last one," Smith said, "the one who makes the final run."

"It's not necessary to do that," Grimmelmann said. "You would just throw away your life. With these shells it's possible to *explore* the area around us. We might very well find another permanent source of water or a road. There is no point in anyone walking off the way Sturdevant did. None of us has the right to ask anyone else to do that."

"I agree with that," Bain said. "No heroics. If Sturdevant didn't make it none of us can. Let's use the shells to set up water stations for the purpose of searching the area, not to shoot somebody out there in hopes that they'll find help before they die of thirst. Unless that is agreed upon I will not help."

"You are right, of course," Grimmelmann said. "I was only speculating on the uses the shells could be put to. We might well be two or three days' walk from a small town, closer perhaps. I think we shall soon be out of here."

"I can't believe it," Grace said. "It seems as if I've been here half of my life."

"You have," O'Brien said. "From the standpoint of your emotions and experiences." He spoke slowly and carefully and the others looked up and nodded vaguely.

"We are more *alive* here," O'Brien said. "There are the basic elements around us. The sun, the air, the darkness of the night and the heat shimmering over the rocks at noon. We live because we are so close to death; we are all more real here than outside."

Smith nodded and looked at Bain. Grimmelmann understood and smiled to himself as if someone had discovered something in him that he had not known.

"That's the trouble," Bain said. "We're too damn close to nature." But he understood too, for he'd spent half of his life apart from the mainstream of civilization. And Smith knew: the feel of time about you in the lonely canyons, the smell and taste of the game they ate, the sweet water, the wonder of dawn.

"What do you think about using the ostrich shells?" Grace asked O'Brien. "You didn't say much."

"We have no choice," the big hunter said. "It seems to me that it would only be a matter of time before we hit something. Go out two or three days in all directions. Two guys carrying all the water they could in the shells leaving two behind every six hours or so. Go out and come back the same way carrying nothing except the empty shells. Only one thing: be sure we put them where we can find them, where they'll be safe from some animal."

"Mark each place with a pile of stones and maybe a piece of rag flying from a stick," Smith said.

"The desert is not really featureless," Grimmelmann said. "Once past this sand desert the country would change, that I am sure of. It will be just as dry but with trees and some grass and you would find landmarks to go by."

"We can start tomorrow evening," O'Brien said. "I'll go with one of you guys." He turned to Smith and Bain.

"I'll go with you," Smith said.

"Okay," O'Brien said. "Maybe I can come back with fresh meat. If nothing else, this will widen our foraging area."

"Take a bag for melons," Grimmelmann said.

"And build a big fire every day," Grace said. "Lots of smoke."

Suddenly they were all alert and expectant. Smith had chanced upon the cache of ostrich eggs and they were going to expand their world. They were going to be saved.

"I'm going to bed," O'Brien said and he got up and vanished deep in the cave. Grace followed him.

And the others found their beds. Sleep was an escape from the hunger and the reality of their surroundings; sleep was dreaming. Bain was the last one to go. It was the best day so far; the eggshell expeditions might save them. They could be back in civilization within a week. . . .

It no longer seemed impossible.

Days went by and all of them were busier than they had ever been. O'Brien and Smith had made one trip into the desert, to the north. They found only endless stretches of bushveld with no surface water. The trip had taken six days, three out and three back along the same route, drinking the water they had left on the way out. They found nothing but O'Brien shot a gemsbok on the last day. They went no farther. O'Brien butchered it and Smith wandered over a wide area and brought back armloads of dead bush. They cooked huge steaks for themselves and wished the others were with them, for there was no time or fuel to attempt smoking the meat. They ate all they could hold and fell asleep exhausted, feeling bloated and half-sick. The fire went out but they started it again when they awoke in the early evening. They cooked big chunks of meat and then hurried back the way they had come. The night was ending and they had to reach the last water station. They had found nothing, but the trip was worth the effort because of the meat. They slowed down on the last leg of the trip and O'Brien almost shot a gazelle but it was too far away and vanished as he raised his rifle.

Grimmelmann found a spearhead buried in the sand of the cave floor, seven inches long, narrow and balanced, chipped from a heavy black flint. He held it in his hand, studied the honed edges, the clever groove that some Bushman or Herero craftsman had fashioned to hold its wooden shaft. It was an artifact, old, an elemental tool. He dropped it into the deep pocket of his windbreaker.

He would keep it, bring it back to the outside world and send it to some museum. He had killed Herero and Bushmen and it was something he could do now; a good deed to place with all the bad deeds. The guilt was on him. He had seen but he had not acted; he had known but had not spoken. He was the base on which everything rested, good and bad, the *kleine Mann.*

He'd come back to Africa to hide, to escape Europe and the shame; he'd come to see the places of his youth again, the land he'd seen as a boy with good dreams, so long ago. . . .

He showed the spearhead to the others and they all agreed that it was a rare thing of great beauty.

Entry in the diary of Jefferson Smith.

The desert is a place beyond description. The real desert where there is only the great dry earth, the sky and the terrible sun. It is so alien to me, to most men. We have always shunned such places as we have shunned mountain peaks, caves, the depths of the sea, swamps. Before that we were afraid of the night, peopled these places with spooks, goblins. Fear of unknown. Most feats of mountaineering, cave exploration, desert crossings have occurred in memory of those now living. (New techniques, scientific advances.) Strange that we were so late in conquering these places. We had television and A-bomb before Everest was scaled. Stone Age people in Brazil stand in ruins of lost city and watch Sputnik. This part of the world seems as remote as the far side of the moon.

O'Brien is magnificent. I cannot picture him outside of this place. He would seem strange in a business suit, tie; I can believe he is extremely wealthy. Has unlimited assurance, adaptability, leadership. Better born in another time. Elizabethan. An officer of Alexander. Hard to picture him at stockholders' meeting. He keeps us all on the ball, fighting. We might all be gone if it were not for him.

Trip seemed so long. Got a gemsbok, ate until we were sick. Too far out to bring any back. O'Brien says we relieved pressure on canyon's food supply for the time (lizards, honey, melons). *I was happy to get back to mountain.* Strange feeling. Slept better in cave. People can adjust to strange ways of living. Read of convicts who regret leaving their cells. Understand. If only we had more to eat this wouldn't be too bad to take for a while. Our problem an old one. Overpopulation.

Difficult to determine how far we went on this hunting-exploration trip. Walked at night. Barefooted. Water heavy on our backs. O'Brien impatient with me. Six nights of slow walking. How far out? Fifty miles? Pointless for me to go if I can't come back with a load of meat. I could go alone, look for melons, etc. but would be afraid of getting lost, breaking ostrich shells, dying out there on the Great Thirst.

Bain seems better since before we left. He made a net from all manner of string and wire. Catches birds with it somehow near the pool. Not bad. Is working on lizard trap. Deadfall principle, balanced flat rock with bait under it. Difficult because of terrific speed of lizards. Grimmelmann and Grace Monckton are thin as we all are. Hanging on. I suppose we are all in a state of slow starvation.

O'Brien and Smith went into the desert again. They took one melon apiece, hoping that they would find new patches of them in the wasteland beyond the horizon. They carried enough water to last them six days.

"Don't take chances," Grace said.

"If I shoot anything we'll bring it right back," O'Brien told them. The melons kept them alive but they needed meat. They'd eat baboon now if he could get any, but the apes were too smart; it was impossible to get within range of them.

"A fat zebra," Grimmelmann said. "Look for them. If you find tracks follow them and they will lead you to water."

"We'll bring something back," O'Brien said. He did not want to face them again empty-handed.

They left and after a while the sun went down and the night breeze came. They headed south and after six hours they each took a waterfilled eggshell from their pack. O'Brien dug a hole in the sand while Smith searched for stones to make a cairn. They buried the precious shells and rested for half an hour. Then they rose and walked on, hurrying before the sun came to halt them.

On the third night they came to another variety of terrain. Bushveld. Dry powdered soil filled with sharp pebbles and a billion halfdead bushes. When dawn came they did not stop but continued on, for they were excited. The monotony of the sand depressed them; the bush seemed to promise something. An hour later O'Brien shot a bustard and they stopped, putting their remaining eggshells in the shade to cool the water. They built a huge fire and cooked the big bird; then they found shade and slept through the heat, feeling strengthened and revived by the turkeylike meat.

The sun waned. Smith got up.

"Let's get an early start. We can take the rest of the bird with us."

O'Brien got up and rubbed the sleep from his eyes. They ate some of the bird and drank deeply from one of the shells. Smith picked up his netlike pack with the shells in it.

"Do me a favor for a little while," O'Brien said. "Carry my water."

"Okay," Smith said. "You take the bird."

O'Brien carefully took his five remaining ostrich shells and put them in with Smith's. He made the whole pack tight with an old belt so they would not jostle each other and break.

"How does it feel?" he asked Smith.

"Good."

O'Brien picked up his rifle. He walked back a few yards and then snapped a shell into the breech.

"Just hold still a minute now," he told Smith. "I want to say something." Smith frowned but he went on.

"You're going ahead with all the water. I'm going back alone. I'll use the water at the stations and I might get lucky and shoot something and bring it back to the others. They're starving to death back there. They need meat."

"I'm not going to do it," Smith said.

"You are."

"No," Smith said. "When these shells are empty I'm done for. We decided against this the first time we talked about it."

"You'll go or I'll kill you right here," O'Brien said.

"I don't think so," Smith said.

"Try me. Come at me now. Try to take this gun."

Smith looked at him and knew he wasn't faking.

"This is pointless," he said. "We have enough water to go on together and come back together."

"You miss the main point," O'Brien said. "There are too many of us back in the canyon. With you gone there will be one less belly to fill. And I really think you can make it to water or to a railroad or a ranch. Keep your wits about you now. Build a big fire whenever you stop."

"I might circle in back of you and beat you to thc watcr stations and leave you out here with nothing," Smith said.

O'Brien laughed. The idea of Smith outwitting him and outrunning him amused him. "Let's not get silly, Professor, shall we?"

"Don't be too sure," Smith said.

"Keep in a straight line," O'Brien cautioned. "You've got a good chance. Don't quit on us now. Think of them back in that canyon."

Smith pleaded. "Don't do this to me, O'Brien. I found these ostrich shells. I can't last long without you. This bird we ate. You shot it. What can I kill with my bare hands?"

"Look for melons," O'Brien said.

"Don't do this," Smith said.

"Too many people to feed," O'Brien said. "It's best all around. In the end we might all die but this way gives us the best chance."

"But what gives you the right to decide?" Smith asked. "The gun?"

O'Brien nodded calmly. "The gun. The gun and the ability to kill with it. If I find you following me back I'll shoot you. I don't want you back in that canyon."

"I have a feeling that you're planning to kill all of them back there," Smith said.

O'Brien brought up the rifle until it pointed at the center of Smith's chest.

"Okay, let's go now. We've talked enough."

"You really mean it, don't you?"

"Listen to me, Smith. Whenever I talk to you I mean every word I say."

"I can't make it," Smith said.

"But you can try," O'Brien told him. "Just try your best. That's all anyone can expect of you."

"It's murder."

"Sure, it's murder if you don't make it. But if you find water or get lucky then you'll be a hero. You and me. We'll both be heroes. I'd deny all this and you'd be a fool to talk about it anyway. I'm going to tell the others that we got separated, lost. And then after trying to find you I headed back. Airtight case."

"I might come back with a gun," Smith said.

"Sure you could," O'Brien said. "You could come back and shoot me but you won't. You're too civilized. And too smart. If you survive the desert you'll be in no mood to throw your life away for revenge."

"I could get you," Smith said. "One way or the other."

"Wonderful," O'Brien said. "You start figuring out how you're going to revenge this. Get mad. Survive. Come back and get me. Now start walking."

Smith didn't move.

"I'll kill you if you don't go," O'Brien said. "I told you that once."

Smith looked up, saw the rifle, the face, the eyes. He turned his back on O'Brien and walked off.

O'Brien sat on the high rock until Smith was out of sight. Then he slipped down and trotted off. There was only a slight possibility that Smith would try to swing around and beat him back to the first water station but he could not ignore it. He had to act as if Smith were smarter and stronger and tougher than he was. That was the way to win.

People like Smith . . . and Bain; all of them. Weaklings. The old German was tougher but old and without the desperate will to live.

He stopped trotting. He began to walk fast. Once on an elevation he turned and swept the horizon behind him with his binoculars. He saw no sign of Smith. He went on.

Five hours later he reached the water station and dug up the ostrich eggs. They were heavy with their precious water. He drank from one of them carefully, then put them in his net and continued walking. He was not tired. It was almost light now and he'd keep walking until he reached the next station.

He walked up the valley just as the sun came up. He was very tired, and it seemed an eternity before he reached the cave and slumped in the sand exhausted.

"Where's Smith?" Bain asked in the darkness.

"He's gone."

"Gone where?" It was Grace.

"He took off. Said he was going to find a way out of here. Said he was going to save us. I tried to stop him. He fought me, threatened to brain me with a rock. This was way out where we came to real bushveld."

"You should have stopped him," Bain said.

"I know," O'Brien said. "But what the hell could I do, shoot him?"

They were all silent for a while.

"Has he got any chance?" Grace asked.

"Who knows what chance he has," O'Brien said. "I've had the same feeling out there; the feeling that it was better to keep going than to come back here. The horizon pulls at you; you start thinking about the next rise and what you can see from there." He spoke slowly, lying with his eyes closed.

"He hasn't got a chance in hell," Bain said. "Sturdevant didn't make it. How could Smith? You shouldn't have let him go."

"He's got one chance in a hundred maybe," O'Brien said sleepily. "But I wouldn't bet on it. I told him it was suicide. He wouldn't listen."

O'Brien was asleep.

Far ahead in the tricky light of dawn Sturdevant saw trees. He saw them and he looked away, to the reddish sand, to his shoes. There could be no trees, bushes perhaps but no trees. It was another mirage to trick him. It was seven days now, or rather seven nights of walking, and in all that time there had been no trees, nothing green, only a few wait-a-bit thorn and queer desert plants that could live for years without water. Grimmelmann had been right. There was no way a man on foot could get to or from the black mountain. How far had he come now? A hundred miles? More?

But they were trees. He felt the excitement build up; trees indicated water, water somewhere underground. He found himself running and stopped. Conserve energy. Act intelligently. He still had some water left and it sloshed around in the tins with each step, sometimes throwing him off balance.

A *vley*, a depression filled with withered grass and scraggly trees fighting to stay alive. He sat down in the shade, slipped free of the water tins, rested, tried to sleep. There was no surface water; he'd have to dig for it but only when the sun went down. There were sixteen skinny trees, two of them obviously dead.

He sat up and drank some of the water while it was still cool from the night; he drank all he wanted. The ground was hard under him and he scraped away a place for his hip and worked into it and closed his eyes. A hundred miles of sand and now a paradise of shrunken trees and dead grass.

In the evening he would get up and find a spot in the grass and dig. The crust would be hard but he would break through it with the hunting knife. The soil would be dry at first and then heavy with moisture and then water. There had to be water. He would fill the two cans and then drink all he could hold and walk on. And the country ahead as far as he could see looked somehow higher, stonier; perhaps the blur ahead was more trees or hills. He would climb one of the trees later and look.

He fell asleep.

The dream came. He was underwater, swimming naked through great masses of tropical fish, and he caught one and surfaced. The fish was ready to eat and he bit great chunks from it and gulped down the boneless flesh. O'Brien was there too with several great grilled steaks sizzling over an open fire; they ate the steaks alone in their greasy hands and drank big mugs of cold beer with it.

And the dream went on and he writhed and groaned and talked in stubborn sleep. He dreamed of good meals he had had, of meals that he had heard about, that others had eaten. Restaurant meals of turkey and wild duck; special wartime meals they'd had after the really tough deals; banquets, Thanksgiving Day at the American Air Base in 1944. . . .

When the sun went down he got up and found the lowest spot in the *vley* and began to dig. He broke through the hard sun-baked soil with the hunting knife and lifted out the big chunks one at a time. Then the soil became soft and he stabbed it with the knife, loosened it, then scooped it out with his cupped hands.

He thought of digging Detjens's grave. . . .

He had to find water here and get through to civilization and save the rest of them. It was his responsibility; if they all died it would be his fault. They had trusted him, put their lives in his hands, and he had crashed them into the middle of nowhere.

He rested. The hole was two feet deep. He began digging again, clawing into the soil and flinging handfuls of it away; darkness came and he continued, slow now, for his fingernails were broken and worn, his fingers raw. He dug and rested, enlarged the hole. And then he was in the hole itself still digging, clawing through the endless sand and finding nothing. He stopped and rested once more, put his head on the soft sand, made himself comfortable, fell asleep.

He awoke several hours later, cramped and still tired. He began to claw in the bottom of the hole, finding handfuls of sand and throwing it up and away. Then he remembered that he had some water in the cans and he found them and drank deeply. The sun was coming up. He ate one of the melons and went back to the hole.

It was four feet deep now but the sand piled around it made it look larger. He got in it carefully and began to dig. Fatigue set in again and his arms began to tremble. He cut his right forefinger on a sharp stone and rested for a time until the bleeding stopped.

When he started digging again the sand was moist and then the miracle: water. He began to laugh and cry at the same time. Water seeping up from the dry sand.

Two days later he came to a gnarled tamarisk stump, gray and ancient. He kicked it and it broke and fell heavily to the sand, split and bared its rotten pulp. Ants ran crazily from the new raw top of the stump that was almost level with the sand. Sturdevant saw them and was sorry; he had destroyed their home by a senseless act.

He walked on.

Long ago a seed had buried itself in the hostile soil, found rare moisture, germinated and grew. Tiny roots reached into the earth and the first leaf sucked life from the cold dew of morning. The year was good and the seedling thrived; no zebra came to eat it; it was tiny and it was not seen.

It grew; its taproot found water far below the hot sand; its branches spread and reached for the sun. It lived. Twenty years passed.

A pair of buffalo weaverbirds chanced to find it and they built a nest in its branches and reared their young. They returned the next year with other birds; the nest was repaired and new ones were built next to it. After a few years it became the nesting place of scores of weaverbirds and a great communal nest grew in the tree, an enormous clump of sticks and trash, for this is the nature of the weaverbird.

The great nest became the home of other creatures. Lizards discovered its labyrinths and moved into them; tiny mice came and built their velvet-soft nests deep inside; lovebirds and finches came and fashioned their own nests from the debris and each year more and more weaverbirds came and the giant nest grew.

A snake came. He fed upon the eggs and the young birds and the mice. He frightened the creatures that lived in the tree but they did not go; they grew used to him and warned each other when he uncurled from his slumber and began to move about the vast pile of sticks.

The years passed; the tree was mature now, its growth slowed, almost stopped. And each year the birds came and it groaned under their weight as they roosted on the heavy branches. The tree became a focus of life, of birth and homecoming, of mating; grass grew now in the shade under the great nest and little yellow flowers bloomed briefly after the rains; beetles found nourishment and their parasites followed them. The shade and the bird droppings had made the bitter soil soft and potent.

And then the nest grew too large. The myriad communal nests, all under one roof, had multiplied each year until now scores of nesting weaverbirds came. Old nests were abandoned to the other species, to the mice and the lone snake; new couples brought sticks and nesting material from far away.

Some fiber within the heart of the old tree broke; it sagged and the weight of the great nest bore more heavily upon it. It leaned sideways and the weaker surface roots broke and pulled loose from their grip in the hard soil. Bit by bit the tree bent, its trunk fibers taut and twisted; the sun found the grass that had once been shielded by the nest and burned it away; the beetles and soil organisms retreated. In the new areas of shade nothing grew: the droppings of the birds were too thick now, a hard shield over the earth.

The great flock of weaverbirds came back; they roosted on the branches and began building new nests. Each day more birds appeared and the tree shivered under the weight; it had stopped growing long ago; now its whole purpose was to endure, to fight the dead pressure that bore down upon it. Its roots shifted and sought new holds; its trunk thickened to sustain the growing weight; new branches sprouted in an effort to counterbalance the pull of the great pile of sticks to which the birds kept adding.

The rain came, a sudden great shower amidst thunder and lightning and a cold wind. Water fell upon the dry faggots and made them soggy and heavy; water fell upon the ground, made it soft around the straining roots. The wind found the tree and it began to sway. Inside the great nest, hundreds of weaverbirds huddled and waited.

The tree collapsed. The nest smashed against the earth, and crushed many of the birds. The trunk of the tree was split; it protruded from the earth like the broken shaft of a spear. All the creatures that had lived in the nest cowered close to it and under the branches. The rain stopped and the sun came out and the surviving birds flew away. The snake slid from the debris and made his way slowly across the land, bleeding, dying from the great crush of the sticks. An eagle found him a mile from the tree, scooped him up, and brought him to the sharp beaks of her young.

The stump died and the roots decayed; the ants began to devour the dried limbs and one by one the mice and lizards fled. The grass burned up without shade and the life in the good soil died or went away.

After some years there was nothing left except the rotten husk of the trunk rising from the ground. Now that was gone.

Sturdevant walked on. He did not hurry and his steps were methodical. He was five days from the place where he had dug for water and the two tins were still heavy; he had found melons and had killed and eaten a rodent of some sort.

There was only the sky and the land. His enemy was distance and the feeling that he was the only man alive, walking the earth.

The Great Thirst.

Grace waited for O'Brien to come down the canyon.

It was late afternoon and the others had come back to the cave after hours of foraging in the hot sun. Mike Bain and the old man slept. She had taken some of the bottles and quietly left them, headed up the canyon toward the pool. She had rested there for a while, filled one of the bottles and gone on. Soon, O'Brien would come. He almost always came back by climbing out of the gorges where they met the mountain and descending the path that they had climbed long ago when they scaled the peak.

She had to be alone with him. All he thought about was the hunting, the questing, food. He barely noticed her as a woman, a beautiful woman. She couldn't wait another day, another night. She had to be with him. Now. Alone.

She walked on. He would hold her soon, kiss her. . . .

She saw him coming toward her, walking barefooted and easily, shirtless, wearing only his dirty white tennis shorts. He saw her, scowled, came on. She felt her heart beating.

"Any luck?" she asked.

"Nothing," he said. They stood looking at each other.

"Where're the others?" he asked.

"Back at the cave. I went out for water and then started walking." She held up the bottle of cool water. "Want some?"

He came toward her and took the bottle, drank from it. She walked away to the shade under the black wall of rock and sat down in the warm sand. O'Brien followed, put his rifle on top of a big boulder, sat down next to her.

She leaned back against the rock, closed her eyes.

O'Brien kissed her. Her arms came up, found his shoulders, held him, pushed him away; she was dizzy.

"Why did you do that?" she asked.

"Because you wanted me to, Mrs. Monckton."

She smiled. "I suppose I did, in a way. I've never been kissed by a man with a beard." She tried to laugh but nothing came.

He kissed her again, harder. She struggled for a time and then surrendered. She no longer cared. He was hers.

"O'Brien?"

"Yes."

"Do you want me?"

"I've got you," he said.

She kissed him lightly. "I mean do you like me? I think I'm in love with you." She'd said it now. It had been easy.

"You want me like you've never wanted anything," he said.

"Yes, it's true. Do you love me?"

"No."

"A little bit?"

"Don't be silly, Mrs. Monckton." His hands were hot on her back now, his fingers digging in, hurting her.

"Please . . . you want to, don't you? You want me?"

"Not any more, Mrs. Monckton. I want what I haven't got and I've already got you." He picked her up like a child and put her on the sand. His bearded face was on hers, her neck. His hands were on the buttons of her skirt, the zipper. She was wide-eyed with fear and disbelief. She began fighting, squirming, punching, infuriated now, screaming, crying.

"I'll kill you, kill you, kill you . . ."

She was sobbing hysterically.

Grace was aware that she was alone; O'Brien was gone.

She began brushing sand out of her hair, and after a while she got up and fixed her clothes and started down the canyon. The fierceness was gone from the sun now; evening was coming; it was cooler.

She came to the pool. O'Brien was there, pouring water over his head, rubbing his face, his neck. She went to him and kissed him, standing tiptoed, and he reached down and picked her up and carried her to a rock slab, his fingers hard on her thigh.

"I'm sorry," she whispered. "The things I said . . ."

He kissed her face, her eyes.

"I deserved it," she said. "I went looking for you. I suppose that isn't wrong. I want you so much, so much . . ."

"I want you too, Mrs. Monckton. But no cat-and-mouse games."

"Why do you want me?"

"You're a woman, Mrs. Monckton."

"Stop calling me that. I'm divorced, I'm free. I just wished you loved me."

"I love all women," O'Brien said.

She lay in his arms. The great ache in her was gone. Someday

O'Brien would love her; there were things about him she feared and didn't understand but someday, when they were saved and away from the mountain, he would be like other men and he would love her and take care of her.

Bain came out of the cave and blinked at the light. His legs felt weak but he was no longer sick.

He walked up the canyon toward the pool. The air was fresh and cool from the night; soon the sun would blister down but there was a morning freshness now which he enjoyed.

He reached the pool and frightened some small shrill birds. He drank and then took off his clothes. He took the coffee can and washed himself methodically, using the fine sand as an abrasive. He did not get into the pool or allow the dirty water to run into it, for it was one of their rules. He sloshed the water on his body and rubbed sand on it. He was filthy, bestial. And his body was strange and new to him: thin and anatomical; the bulk gone, the fat gone, the heavy bones visible. Suddenly he envied O'Brien, so big and powerful and healthy. O'Brien fitted in with the cliffs and gorges and the sun, walking around barefooted, shirtless, hatless with the thick black hair protecting his skull and his skin already tanned deep mahogany.

He dug a hollow in the hard wet sand, threw his clothes in it and began to fill it with water; next time he'd bring a container of some sort (Smith had had one) and boil his clothes. The hollow was full and the dirty pants and shirt and socks and underclothes floated for a time and then the water sank into the sand and he repeated the process.

He was hungry and in all the days he'd been here he hadn't contributed to the food supply. Grimmelmann and O'Brien were carrying them all; but they were on the verge of starvation, an arm's length away from death. The melons and the dried meat couldn't last forever.

The hole was dry again. He picked the clothes up, squeezed them and spread them on the rocks, already warm from the sun. He sat down near them, the sun pleasant on his back and arms.

The coffee can glinted in the sun; parts of it were already rusty. American coffee. Maxwell House. The can was still wet; globules of water hung to the sides. A bee circled and settled on the knife edge, drank from one of the drops, flew away.

He reached for the shirt and turned it over. Almost dry. The sun was hotter now.

Where was the bee going?

To its hive. Honey. Once when Grimmelmann was talking about the Bushmen he'd mentioned honey. Somewhere there had to be a hive and honey.

He got up and put on the clothes, which were still clammy. He took the coffee can and dipped it into the pool, scooping up two inches of water in the bottom. He was excited now and he noticed that he was barefooted. The hell with the shoes, he'd come back for them.

He walked up the canyon, concentrating on the flight of bees. There seemed to be more than he'd noticed before but it was probably because he'd never bothered to look. He came to an overhang and rested in the shade. A bee-loud glade . . . some poet wrote that once.

He went on, stopping every few yards to look and listen. It seemed that a lot of bee traffic was headed down the canyon, past him. It might mean he was going the wrong way and it might mean that the bees were flying away from their secret hive. There was no way of knowing.

At last he found a place that suited him. A head-high niche in the smooth rock protected from the sun. He found a flat stick and placed it in the can, a landing place for the honeybees. He set the can in the niche and backed away. A new watering place for the bees. He should have filled the can to allow for evaporation but he would come again and fill it with a canteen.

There was nothing to do now except wait and there was plenty of time. He turned around and headed back for the cave. The sun was high now, the sand and the rocks burning his bare feet.

Grimmelmann spotted a big lizard in a pile of debris on the far side of the canyon. He moved toward it slowly and it flashed away to its underground lair, which he located some ten minutes later when it reappeared.

It did not see him this time, for he was hidden in the rocks above, motionless. The big reptile came out of its hole slowly in sudden jerky motions. It was three feet long. Grimmelmann knew he must catch it somehow. He had eaten one long ago with another soldier. They had come upon some wild *Klipkaffirs* and the natives invited them to sit and eat and they did so because they were lost and hungry. The meat, he remembered, was firm and white, tasting almost like salmon.

He sat in the sun and the lizard vanished into the rocks. It too was a forager, a hunter, a scavenger, a dwarfish dragon living in a world without men or history, a scaly antediluvian whose form was the same as it had been millions of years before, a creature that could live in the black mountain and survive with almost no effort. He almost envied it.

They would have to devise a way of catching and killing it. O'Brien would have been able to think up a plan perhaps; he had the hunter's instincts, a strange man to be an American in the twentieth century. He seemed to belong to another place, another time. But the others were clever too in their own way. Smith had a scholar's mind so that nothing was really new or strange to him; he was inventive and discerning and far-ranging. Bain was smart too; he just wasn't trying hard enough.

He sat in the sun enjoying the glare, wondering where the lizard was. Maybe Sturdevant was alive, maybe he'd been wrong. . . .

Trapped in a sea of sand. Condemned to a slow death of starvation. Perhaps it was justice . . . maybe they all deserved to be here. It could be a final punishment for them all, an old way of death by abandonment.

It would be just for him to die here. He had done nothing for the outside world, added nothing to it. All that he had ever done was to obey and obey and obey and it had led to nothing except futility and now, at the end of his life, a profound despair. The world would be better without him; it would have been a little better if he had never been born.

Ten years after the Herero War ended, the First World War was under way. Of that period he had spent one year recuperating from the ills and wounds of the African War and the rest working at nondescript jobs in the Ruhr. When the war came he enlisted and became a sergeant almost overnight. And it was a relief to get back into uniform; everyone had known that a war was coming and when it started, a great wave of relief and happiness flooded Europe for a few months. It was the end of one century, one time, and the terrible beginnings of another.

On the Russian front he had murdered three men: wild-eyed peasants wearing the rags of their uniforms who had been caught by a patrol, stealing frozen potatoes from a battalion wagon. They were brought to the company commander and the young captain had called to him.

"Sergeant Grimmelmann, take these looters and shoot them."

He would never forget those words. His whole life had started there or ended there, he never knew which.

"Sir, the prisoners are Russian soldiers. They are war prisoners, not civilians."

"Are you questioning my orders, Sergeant?"

"Does the Captain wish me to shoot war prisoners?"

"They're looters, the uniforms are probably stolen. I'm ordering you to shoot them."

He had taken the three men into the woods and shot them as they knelt in the snow, crying and begging. He told himself that he'd had no choice, that a superior had ordered him to shoot the men, that he himself might have faced a firing squad if he had refused. Ever since he had told himself these things but he never believed them.

The physical act of killing the men had been easy. Blood and horror and brutality had been the order of the day in Africa, and it was for this reason that the captain had singled him out. He was a veteran. He had walked in back of the kneeling men and shot each one through the head with his pistol. They were left there in the snow, in the gloomy forest, their pockets still bulging with the stolen potatoes.

To have resisted the order was beyond him. One did not argue with superior officers even when they were wrong, even when they used you to sin. The soldier obeyed. The soldier was exempt from good and evil.

The war went on. Europe became very old and very sick from the plague of killing. He lived through it, winning an Iron Cross, Second Class. He did his duty.

Bain returned to the coffee can that he had filled with water and left for the bees. They were drinking from it. He sat for an hour and watched several of them come and go. They went up the canyon. He got up and began following them until he was far from the can, too far to be sure what bees he followed. He went back and got the can and brought it back to where he had lost the bees. He found a place against the cliff wall, out of the sun, filled the can with water from the canteen and walked slowly back to the cave. He had told none of the others about the bees. He wanted to find the hive and the honey alone.

O'Brien was at the pool, sitting on one of the flat rocks, naked in the sun. His ragged tennis shorts were spread carefully nearby, drying. Bain sat down next to him.

"We've got to go back to the plane," O'Brien said after a while. He yawned.

Bain thought about it. There were things in the plane they could make use of. Clothes, tools, almost anything they could carry back.

"When do you want to go?" he asked.

"I'm ready as soon as the sun gets weak. We can sleep until then if you want to. Fill up on melons. Take a bunch of ostrich shells."

"I wonder how far Sturdevant got," Bain said.

"You think he's dead?" O'Brien asked.

"Yes. Both of them."

"The Dutchman's a tough guy," O'Brien said. "Lots of guts. And he had plenty of water, remember that. I think he's still out there, myself. And Smith too."

Bain said nothing. He watched O'Brien get up and put on his half-dry shorts. The sun would dry them completely within minutes.

"Shall we go in the evening then?" O'Brien asked.

"Okay," Bain said. "We might as well go. It'll take all night to get out there."

"Maybe longer," the big man said. "Hard to compare it with the last time. The others slowed us down."

"I slowed you down," Bain said. "I wanted to die that night right out there in the sand."

"You were sick," O'Brien said. He began to walk back to the cave. Bain got up and followed.

"We'll sleep most of the next day and then take off when the sun goes down again," O'Brien said. "Three days for a couple bags of stuff. But there are things we need out there, things we didn't think we'd need. Containers and basic tools and lenses from broken flashlights and cord for making snares. If the trip took ten days it would be worth it. Let's be thankful that we have a place to get it."

"I'm with you," Bain said. The idea of the trip was distasteful; he did not like the sand, the hours and hours of hard walking, for he was still weak. But he would go because O'Brien was going and there was no one to go with him.

When they got to the cave they told Grace and Grimmelmann and then tried to sleep in the back of the cave. It was about noon now and they would rest until sunset. Then they would take the water can and some melons and climb the escarpment. When night came they should be miles out in the sand that surrounded them.

Bain and O'Brien reached the plane an hour after dawn. They rested for a time and then ate one melon apiece and drank all the water they desired. They made beds and fell into a deep dreamless sleep; the night trip over the sand had exhausted them. The sun rose higher and burned down on the twisted metal but they slept through it. When the cooler air of evening came O'Brien stirred, opened his eyes and shook Bain.

They got up sleepily and began a systematic search of the plane. Detjens's sleeping bag was where they'd left it. O'Brien took it and began to fill it with odds and ends that would be useful: a coil of copper wire, a hammer and an ancient saw, a handful of nails, a heavy sweater that had been Detjens's, a reading lens of Grimmelmann's that would be valuable to make fire with.

Bain found a coil of rope and a canvas water bucket. He put them together outside in the sand and soon found other things: a hand mirror of Grace's, dirty socks and soiled shirts, extra belts, and three empty whiskey bottles flat and sturdy, which would make good canteens to carry on melon hunts and walks around the cliffs. He went through the tools and selected the metal shears and some files and the copper and zinc scrap. He found a camera in one of the bags and unscrewed the lens. In a battered suitcase he found six sugar cubes wrapped in paper.

They made packs as large as they dared and carried the rest in their hands. Bain fixed a large suitcase so that he could carry it on his back and O'Brien rolled up the heavy sleeping bag and did the same. They left as the sun went down.

They walked off and it seemed now that they had been a long time in the canyon; they felt as if they were going home.

They reached the cave when it was still night, stumbled inside and fell asleep in a few moments.

Later, they undid the pack and opened the bag and the suitcase and marveled at their new treasures.

"It's like Christmas," Grace said.

Grimmelmann nodded. There was nothing that would change their lives too much but it might help for a time; the lenses were important, the whiskey bottles, the clothes. Perhaps the trip had been worth it.

Bain returned to the coffee can he had placed for the bees and found it almost empty. As he stood by the shaded nook a lone bee came, buzzed past his ear and landed on the flat stick protruding from the can. The insect had been here before. It did not hesitate but walked quickly down the inclined ramp and drank deeply. Then it flew away.

Bain nodded to himself. A few bees drinking from one tiny pocket of water; it was not enough. He took the paper-covered sugar cubes he'd found in the suitcase in the plane from his pocket. He removed the paper from each one carefully and dropped them into the inch of water, watched them slowly dissolve. Then he walked back to a shady place, sat down and closed his eyes.

He came back two hours later. There were three bees on the landing stick and as he watched, one flew away and two others came. He stood and watched five bees fly away and began following them. He found himself moving along the cliff, toward the peak. He started with his first bee and waited in the spot where he had lost it. Another came and he followed for twenty more feet. He did not hurry; there was enough sugared water to last all day. He followed each bee until it flew out of sight and then waited for another. A half hour passed and he became aware of the fact that a line of bees was flying past him from the opposite direction. He assumed that these were insects returning to the coffee can for the second or third time or that they were new hive members who had joined the rush to the new bonanza of sweetness.

He moved along under the black cliffs which bulged out over him, jagged and threatening. The opposite cliff grew closer and higher and the valley floor started its upward tilt. It rose in some places in sudden, waist-high granite steps; again, hard graveled beds sloped upward in long swells, and there was one place where the black stone had split and a sheer ten-foot wall had to be negotiated by leaving the shadows and going out into the valley where the wall fragmented. He had never been here before.

Another half hour. The buzz of flying bees was always in his ears and he realized that he no longer stood and waited. There was a continuous line of bees, some going, some coming, a visible line which anyone could follow. He smiled to himself; he'd show O'Brien and the old German; he'd add to the larder by using a little common sense and some sugar cubes.

A few minutes later he located the hive. It was twenty feet above the canyon floor, a yard-long, half-a-foot-wide slit in the black cliff. He found a place to sit down and watched the stream of bees issuing from and returning to the lair. The shadows grew long. He built a cairn with flat stones directly under the hive opening and walked back to the cave.

Sturdevant slept, dreamless and satisfied. It was late afternoon. A fly crawled on his face and he brushed it away without waking. Next to him a small fire burned weakly. The crudely butchered carcass of a zebra lay between him and the fire. Flies and tiny gnats crawled over it.

A few vultures wheeled overhead, high above the cliffs in the narrow band of sky. The boldest one had flopped down minutes ago and sat now on a slab of rock viewing the carrion, the fire and the sleeping man.

The carrion birds and the scavengers had come almost as soon as he had shot the big zebra. It had happened very simply. He had come to a turn in the gorge and suddenly in front of him six motionless zebra were staring at him. He unslung the rifle and aimed at one of them but the weapon was too heavy for him now and the front sight wavered over a wide arca. He sat down. The zebra stood facing him, strangely unafraid. He braced his elbows against his knees and aimed at one of them and fired.

They vanished but he hurried after them. The water swirled in the tins and threw him off balance but he followed their spoor. The bullet had hit something, and the sand and shale showed blood spots. Twenty minutes later he found one dying. He was tempted to shoot it again in the head but he did not. He waited for it to bleed to death.

He took off the packboard and, setting the water tins in the shade with the rifle, began to collect sticks and bits of wood that lay half buried in the white sand. After a while he took a precious match and started a small fire. He was trembling with a terrible hunger and the first few morsels of meat he ate raw, for he could not bear to wait for them to cook.

Another fly landed on his matted hair and crawled down his face to the blood-smeared lips. He grunted and rolled away, exhausted from the meal he had eaten, filled now and sluggish from the zebra meat. He looked up and saw the cliffs and the sky and the circling birds. He closed his eyes again. . . .

The dream came and he shuddered in his sleep; he knew at the very start what was going to happen, for the dream never varied. He'd had it almost every night since he'd left the mountain.

He saw buildings before him on the horizon, a town of some sort, and he stumbled toward it, falling and calling out. And from the town came people, little boys and girls at first, ragged and skinny with the bright eyes of the malnourished. He sat in the sand and they stood before him. He smiled and waved to them; they looked at him without emotion. From the town now, others: men and women, hurrying to see. Someone helped him up, a big black man in a dirty coat. He hung onto the man and the crowd moved toward the buildings. There were no white people in the crowd. It must be some outlying slum town. The Negroes were quiet but there was an undercurrent of excitement in them and they began to talk in quick sentences in a language that he had never heard before.

They stopped and gave him water from a dirty tin can. He was able to walk alone now; the crowd grew as more Negroes came from the bleached and misshapen huts, from the narrow trash-littered alleys. He tried to talk to them but they seemed unable to understand English—a queer, impossible situation. They could not hear him and they did not seem to care. He smiled and nodded at them, grinned, waved. They had rescued him and he was thankful.

The excitement grew. More people came and he was surrounded by a wall of black faces, wide-eyed, calling out to each other, laughing now. Somewhere the beat of a stick against a tin; the crowd picked up the rhythm and they bore him through the narrow cluttered streets that stank with refuse. The crowd pressed in on him now, hurting him, carrying him along. Somewhere a woman screamed, a high-pitched wild scream that made him cringe, made him afraid.

Then he was alone, dizzy and weak. He slumped to the ground and when he looked again he was in the center of a great circle of black men, festive now and happy. He looked around and saw the pole that protruded from the hard-packed dirt. Chains hung from it, and hand-cuffs. They were going to torture him, kill him; he understood the silence of the children now, the dumb faces of the others, the woman's scream. They were going to lynch him.

He got up and ran and they threw him back into the lonely circle. He fought them and they laughed and flung him away. He prayed. On his knees with uplifted hands he cried out to them for mercy and forgiveness. He made promises to them, he begged them to spare him. He was a good man, a friend. He began to sob. They were going to burn him.

Four men carried him to the pole. They stood him upright and bound him with the chains and went back to the circle and he was alone again. Then an old man broke away from the others and came toward him. He carried a dry gray stick, crooked and canelike. The old face came close and looked at him, studied him with sadness and contempt. He threw the stick down and it fell between his legs. The old man turned and went away. And now a younger man, bent and crippled from some accident. He dropped his stick near the pole and stood for a moment, sullen and dangerous. He went away and a child of ten came, a girl, her body covered with malignant sores, her thin face bright with fever. She too carried a stick and dropped it on the others.

He called to them. It was not his fault. He was white but that was no reason to burn him; evil was evil but a man's skin should not condemn him. They would let him go. They would not burn him. He was a good white man who had always been a friend of the black man.

But they kept coming with their accusing eyes and their dry sticks which they threw near him. Old men who had once lived where their fathers had lived, bitter now and alone in an alien compound without pride, without hope. Young girls, slum-poisoned, degenerate. And thin boys in castoff clothes, torn from one life and barred from another. They all came and looked at him and dropped their sticks.

He began calling for help. There were white men nearby, police. They would come and save him. The crowd would dissolve and they would free him from the chains and the growing pyre of dry sticks. He would be saved.

Day became night. A thousand torches burned; the people began cooking and eating, drums began to beat. A thousand faces came before him and he looked into them and saw the terrible tragedy written on them. He saw now what he had never wanted to see; he looked into the eyes that he had always avoided. And he knew that he was wrong.

He struggled against the chains. If they freed him he could help them; he saw it all now. But he was in chains and his language was not theirs and they did not want to listen. The pyre was waist high now, pressing against him.

A hush fell over the people. Then, directly in front of him, a figure broke from the crowd, the old man who had been the first to stand before him. He carried a torch. A great animal roar arose from the mob.

He threw himself against the chains and the packed sticks, screaming and kicking, sobbing . . . don't burn me, don't burn me . . . please. *O Jesus Christ don't burn me.*

[111]

But the old man came toward him and he struggled and screamed. Then the impossible: he was standing in the center of a pyre that was already on fire and the smoke was in his eyes. He could not breathe. The flame found the bare flesh of his legs and began to cook it.

He sat up, soaking from sweat, terrified, sick.

The big birds sat around him. Four of them already; soon there would be a dozen, then a score, sitting in a ring, growing bolder, closing in on him. It would be best to cut what he could carry from the zebra and move on. If he remained with the meat he'd have to defend it. Stay awake. The birds would grow bolder as their numbers increased, they'd be all around him, disgusting, dangerous.

He got up, groaning, heavy from too much eating. He looked at the rotting fly-covered meat and turned away quickly. The carrion birds could have it. He walked to the water tins and got them on his back, picked up his rifle and moved on. He had all the water he wanted and enough meat in his belly to last him a week. He was going to make it, going to make it. . . .

He walked down the gorge through which the dry river bed squirmed and crawled like a white snake, a gorge that sliced through two hundred feet of black rock but never grew wider than forty feet. It was cool, for the sun came only half an hour each day, a strange place that sheltered him from the sun, where he walked in the soft sand and on the loose shale, looking up constantly toward the band of blue sky above, half afraid that the black walls would crumble down upon him.

When the sun came he slumped down as usual in a shaded spot and slept until the sour fatigue faded into the numb exhaustion that was normal now. He rose and walked along in the white sand that the river of long ago had robbed from the soft uplands. When darkness came a few hours later he found that he was unable to go on; the moon's light made almost no impression in the deep slit of rock.

He had to keep walking. The gorge ran to the sea and along the coast there were towns, ranches. The river bed was his road; he could not leave it.

Two hours later the canyon walls spread apart somewhat and the ground became rockier, firmer, with a narrow band of sand in the center. And then a strange thing that he could not believe: he came upon a small quiet pool of water hidden from the sun, close against the cliff wall that leaned out and protected it. He drank and filled his water cans. He took off his clothes and sat in it, a tiny pocket of water trapped in a stone pit; water that had been part of the river when it was last running. After a long while he got up and moved on, down the widening gorge. The water cans hadn't been so full and heavy since he'd filled them so long ago from the well he'd dug with his hands. The idea of dying from thirst fled from his mind. He had been very lucky finding the *vley* and he'd been lucky stumbling on the watercourse; before the cans were empty he would reach the outside. It was a matter of stamina.

The sky grew dark and the sun went away; a cooling wind came and the sluggish feeling left him. For two days he had eaten and slept like a native, bloated himself upon the fresh meat, and now it felt good to walk again, to move. His water tins were full.

Evening came and he walked on until it was too dark to walk safely. He found a sandy spot close to the cliff wall and fell asleep almost instantly.

Before dawn, O'Brien was quietly scaling the cliffs, heading toward the baboons' den. It was cold and dark and the rocks were clammy on his bare feet.

He climbed steadily and at last reached the top of the ridge. He sat on a tilted rock slab and rested. The world brooded in primeval blackness but far away the horizon was shattered with the diffuse light of approaching dawn. He got up, still breathing heavily, and moved along the canyon edge toward the peak. Twenty minutes later he crossed the cliff top, moving from slab to depression, sometimes crawling. He found the broken cliff face and started down, step by step now, afraid of dislodging a stone, fearful of slipping and going off into the black void below.

It grew lighter but he could not hurry. He cursed himself for not starting sooner but then suddenly he found the niche and lowered himself into it. He thought of a foxhole he'd had in Okinawa. . . .

Some time later a baboon roared and he came out of his sleep-stupor. It was fully light now and the bend in the cliff wall seemed even closer than the day he'd been here and decided on the ambush. He raised his rifle, smiled to himself in the knowledge that even the sharpest-eyed animal couldn't pick him out of the darkness.

The baboons loitered around the den, sullen and sleepy. Only the young were frisky but they were careful to stay out of reach of their elders, wary of cuffs, trying not to be noisy. O'Brien studied them, realizing that his time was limited. Any moment they might break away and go off foraging.

It was easy to spot the leader. He sat alone on a round pillar of stone to the left of the den entrance. Other big males were close but apart from him; in time he would decide which way to go, the scouts would go out and the troop would move off.

O'Brien's rifle cracked. The baboon leaned sideways and fell off into space, smashing on the house-sized boulders hundreds of feet down. In the moment of shock and paralysis the rifle cracked again and one of the males bounded sideways and rolled off into space with a torrent of loose shale. Then the cliff was alive with animals trying to escape.

O'Brien concentrated on the big males. One of them simply stood and looked toward him, teeth bared, challenging. Then he pitched into space. O'Brien was elated. He swung his rifle toward the mouth of the den, knowing that some of them would head back into it from instinct. A female with a baby was in the opening and he shot it through the body.

And one last shot—a long one. Another big male was climbing as fast as he could up the sheer rock wall. The rifle cracked and he fell backwards, plummeting down.

Silence came. Nothing moved on the cliff. He got up, crawled down to the ledge and began the careful climb upward. He was more than satisfied. The leader alone would have been enough; as it was he'd killed three more males plus the female and the baby. They'd never come back to the den now, they'd find another place, but he'd find it and plan something else. In time they'd all be dead. First of all the males, the big ones who were dangerous, who might kill him if they cornered him somewhere—the fighters and the scouts. The rest would be wiped out once these were gone; the young would grow up without the benefit of their teaching, timid and afraid of him, thinking him invincible.

The next day he headed for the peak and descended into the third canyon, the one most distant from the cave. The baboons were there. The sentinels watched him from high vantage points and melted away when he came within range. He spent the day stalking them and fired his rifle once at one which he surprised by an arduous backtracking stratagem. The animal screamed, leaped into the air and then somehow managed to bound up an almost perpendicular cliff.

The day was not entirely wasted. He came home with more tsamma melons and two yellow lizards that he had killed with a gnarled club. He found himself thinking of baboons constantly. A dead baboon was better than a live one. It was one less belly to fill. If all of them were dead there would be no competition for the meager food resources of the mountain. There was nothing he could do that was as important as killing baboons. The others could look for honey and lizards and melons. He would kill.

CHAPTER V

SMITH was dying of thirst.

There was no place to hide from the sun; the world was flat and hard and dry and there was no water, no shade. He walked across the terrible land looking for a place where he could lie and rest out of the sun. He would be dead soon and he did not care; he understood now the strange apathy that precedes death and makes it tolerable. He was about to sit down, lie down, when he saw something ahead on the flat shimmering horizon. A *tree* . . .

His tongue was something strange, sausage-thick, hot. It was early morning; he had drained the last shell sometime in the night; he would die today, before the sun set. He staggered on, finding it difficult to keep the tree in front of him. Something was wrong with his heart. His forehead was suddenly cool and he retched.

He sat down. He'd rest awhile and wait until the dry heaves went away . . . his heart fluttering now like a frightened bird trapped in his chest. After a while he remembered the tree and got to his feet and walked toward it. It seemed far away.

He realized he was naked.

During the night an unbearable hotness had come over him and he had stood up to catch more of the cool air blowing from the east. He began walking into it, forgetting his empty ostrich shells, his shoes and hat. He took off his pants and shirt, carried them for a while until there no longer seemed a reason. He held his burning throat and went on through the night until he fell exhausted in the sand. And then the sun came again.

The tree was gone. He stopped, discovered he was walking away from it. As he watched, the tree became two, then four, then one again. . . .

He walked to it. The ground under him suddenly was very far away. He felt as if he were walking on stilts. He came toward a large stone, tried desperately not to step on it but somehow he couldn't avoid it. He tripped and fell, swore.

He began to crawl. The dust entered his eyes and he closed them and crawled on over the baked earth and the stones. The pain did not matter; he had to get to the tree so that he could die in the shade.

He slumped down and rested for a long time as the sun rose higher. A naked man lying in a vast flat plain where nothing lived. A vulture came from far away and circled. Then another.

Smith opened his eyes and looked ahead and after a long time he saw that his tree was not a tree but a tiny bush less than a foot high, a strange growth with thick, rubbery leaves. He was ten feet from it.

He gathered his strength and crawled toward it, put his head under its tiny branches, its few dozen leaves. He brushed the pebbles away until the ground was soft for his cheek. He would not move from here; it was pointless; the country all around him was the same, parched and desolate.

The sun rose higher and higher, cruel, pitiless.

Hours later he opened his eyes.

Why didn't he die?

He saw himself objectively for an instant, as if from above. He was lying on the sand under the tiny bush. Then the picture slowly changed as if one viewed it through a camera that was moving away. He lay in the middle of an acre of sand, then ten acres, then a hundred acres. A square mile now and he lay huddled in its center, cowering under the tiny bush for protection. Then it became ten square miles and there was no change in the topography of the country. No trees, no water—sand and stones and nothing more, as bare and desolate as anything he had ever flown over, as terrible as some stark and sterile moon. Now a hundred square miles.

He drifted off again. The whole world was pain.

When he opened his eyes he saw a foot, a dusty, withered, yellow-black foot, very small. He watched it for a while and then it moved, came at him, prodded his shoulder. He turned his head, looking upward, but the sun hit his eyes and he turned away, shielding his eyes with one hand. He sat up slowly with great effort.

A tiny wizened man stood in front of him. An ugly gnome with a face that looked a thousand years old. A pygmy with yellowish skin.

There were others, ten or twelve, women and children waiting in the background.

Smith tried to smile. Bushmen . . .

The wizened gnome watched him, pug-nosed, bulbous-browed. He was perhaps five feet tall and carried a bow smaller than a yardstick. Five or six arrows protruded from a quiver that hung from his hip, a quiver that seemed to be made from some kind of bark. And two garments: a triangular-shaped loincloth and a loose animal hide over one shoulder. A skin bag, half-filled, hung from his waist.

The Bushman began to talk. It was as Smith had read about and heard Grimmelmann describe: weird sounds, not quite human, clicks and smacks, tongue noises, croaking sounds, sudden kisslike sounds, all of it unlike anything he'd ever heard, primeval and frightening. What was the little animal-man saying? What would they do with him? Suddenly he wished he were alone; it was better to die alone than at the hands of paleolithic men. They would torture him, cut him up, eat him. He searched the ground around him, found a rock the size of a brick.

One of the others broke away and came toward them. A tiny wizened woman with a face more Mongoloid, ferretlike. She wore a loose, shapeless hide and carried a stick to which were tied three ostrich eggs. She undid one as she came toward him and handed it to the man. Smith reached for it. Water. They carried it that way. The man removed a plug from it and gave it to him and he drank. The liquid was hot and smelly and salty but it was water and he was going to live for a while longer. He forced himself to hand the shell to the man. If he took too much they might decide he was too much trouble and shoot him with a poisoned arrow.

The little man walked away from him with the ostrich egg and joined the others. And he began the noises again, the talk; some of the others spoke but most of them stood and listened. This one was obviously the leader and the group was his family or blood group, a tiny clan perhaps.

Smith got to his feet. They could save him, they could take him out of the desert. The dizziness hit him again and he staggered sideways, trying desperately to straighten up. He must not be a burden; they were going somewhere and he wanted to go with them. They wouldn't hurt him but they might abandon him.

He stood still and the earth stopped moving; the dizziness left him. The Bushmen looked at him and began to laugh, pointing at him.

They began to walk away. One of them pretended to be dizzy and the others joined in the fun. Smith watched them, half-smiling, then realized that they were leaving him.

"Hey, wait a second, will you?" It was his voice, but cracked and hysterical; his mouth hurt, his tongue sausage-like, unwieldy. The Bushmen stopped and looked back. He walked toward them trying to talk to them in sign language, pointing to himself and to them and making little walking movements with two fingers, the kind children make on table tops.

They understood. Some scowled. Some laughed. They all looked to the Boss. He rubbed his wrinkled jaw and rubbed his peppercorn hair and pulled an ear lobe. He made a motion to Smith, a motion that said he might join them. Then he turned his back and walked off and they all followed; a dozen tiny men and women and children and one tall black man making their way across the lunar landscape.

He realized he was naked. Stark naked. And slowly through the haze of time and pain and shattered memory it came back. He remembered the cool night, taking off all his clothes and walking through the night with the wind on him; the cold rushing across the desert. The heat had driven him insane for a time.

He walked on trying not to step on the big stones; his feet hurt but his head was clear; his stomach made strange gurgling sounds from the water. He decided to stay a little behind the Bushmen but it was not easy; the little people walked at a brisk pace.

Then it came to him. He had spoken to them in English and they hadn't responded; to them it was a foreign sound, meaningless. It could be that none of them had ever heard English or German or Afrikaans. They were true Bushmen living in the most remote parts of the desert and shunning white men. And that was the terrible wonderful crazy joke about the whole thing. *He was a Negro.*

If he'd been white he'd be dead now. They would have stayed away from him, let him die of thirst. Or they might have murdered him. Strange black men were bad enough, but white men alone and unarmed and helpless . . .

They thought he was a native African.

He might still be in trouble, for there was little love between the Bushmen and their Negroid neighbors. They were hunters and the others were cattle grazers and villagers and the rift was as old as time. But there was nothing else he could do. He had to stay with them or die.

They went on and he followed, almost trotting to keep up with them.

The ground became firmer again, reddish with dry tufts of grass and dry trees standing alone in the barrenness. Smoke ahead. The Bushmen began talking and the pace picked up until it was a true trot. Smith fell behind, his legs trembling, half-running to keep up. But he knew that they would stop and rest, eat perhaps.

Some of the older children shrieked and ran ahead of the main group. There were three men at the fire, one standing and the others bending over the fire. Three gazelles, two of them cut open and half butchered, lay close to the fire. The children examined each animal and one of them began to act out the hunt. The hunters looked at Smith for a long minute and asked the old leader questions and then forgot him.

Now all of them fell upon the gazelles. They began to cut pieces of meat from the carcass with sharp flints. One of them had a steel blade, another a square piece of copper with a bright, honed edge. Some of them cut pieces of meat, dropped them into the fire and turned back to work on the entrails with the others. They clicked and clacked and the noises were happy now; they cut and tore at the raw meat with bloody hands; they pulled the roasted meat from the fire and tore at it like starved dogs, grunting and calling to one another. The hunters had obviously gone off ahead of the main group, before dawn perhaps, to stalk game with their tiny bows. And they had been successful and carried the game to this prearranged spot. It baffled Jefferson Smith. It had not appeared that the group followed a trail. Yet somehow they had gone straight to where the hunters waited.

And Smith found himself tearing at one of the carcasses with his bare hands trying to rip a piece of bloody flesh from it. He had not planned to touch the meat but the sight of it and the smell of the slices roasting in the fire made him lose all reason. They might kill him for touching their kill, there might be taboos and rituals, but he did not care. He was crazed with hunger and he could not stand and wait to be offered some of the kill.

Next to him one of the older children worked with a thin flint, a tiny boy cutting with skill and precision. The boy looked up, saw him, grinned and finished cutting. He handed the meat to Smith and began laughing. The others near him looked up and it became a joke.

But Smith was gone. He found a solid thorn branch and snapped it over his knee. He pushed the sharp end through the meat and crouched next to the fire. His stomach was convulsive with the anticipation of meat: rich, red, dripping and now cooking over the fire.

He ate it. A pound of roasted gazelle torn apart by his own teeth and fingers gritty with sand, part raw, part burned. He went back and got another piece now, cut it himself with a paleolithic flint he found near the carcass. He squatted next to the others and roasted it, watched the juices bubble and dry up, watched the meat char. He got too hungry to finish it so he stopped like the others and ate that which was cooked. He felt the strength return to his body, felt the glow of hot meat in his stomach. He was alive.

Bain told the others about the hive while they ate their breakfast outside in the early warmth of the morning sun—a breakfast of melon and gemsbok soup and roasted lizard. They stared at him for a while in open disbelief. He told them of the coffee can and the sugar and of tracking the bees to their hive.

"Why the big secret?" O'Brien asked. "Why didn't you tell us about it before?"

"I wanted to think about it for a while," Bain said. "I had to figure out a way to get rid of the bees and get to the honey. It won't be easy."

O'Brien was visibly angry. "It's easy enough to get rid of the bees."

Bain looked at him. "I will not permit them to be killed."

It was an ultimatum. The others looked at him. It was a new side of the man they hadn't seen, tough and challenging.

"Aw, don't be silly," O'Brien said. He sensed that Grimmelmann and even Grace were with Bain.

"I'll be in charge of this operation," Bain told him. He looked around at the others. "I found the hive. I know how to get into the cliffside. The bees will not be killed."

"I agree with you," Grimmelmann said. "There is no sense in killing, killing, killing. . . ."

"What's the difference?" O'Brien said.

"Why kill them when it's not necessary?" Grace said.

"We might have to," Bain put in. "But I'm going to try to drive them out."

"How?" O'Brien asked.

"I'll show you when we get there," Bain told them. He got up and went back into the cave to collect what he would need.

Bain led them toward the hive. He carried the long wrench; the big coil of rope hung from his right shoulder. O'Brien carried a suitcase, which he changed from hand to hand as they went along. There was a hatchet in it, some of the nails and some melons. Grace carried the battered canteen cup that they'd wired to a long stick. It was almost full of hot coals from the permanent fire. Grimmelmann carried a small airline bag containing the canteen, the whiskey bottles and a small tin, all filled with drinking water.

They did not hurry but stayed close to the cliff, in the shadows, walking along the way that was now becoming a recognizable path.

They reached the cairn that Bain had built and saw the black bees buzzing above them. They put down their burdens and rested, drank some of the water and ate some of the melons.

Bain studied the hive opening and the area around it and was happy with himself for remembering it in such detail. The cliff here was not smooth; great overhanging slabs, fissured and cracked, hung to the perpendicular sides. The hive opening was at the side of one of these slabs, close to the cliff, protected from above and on one side by outward-jutting rock. It appeared that the opening led to some cavity behind the big slab, a cavity filled with wax and honey and pollen and bees. The slab was eight feet long and five feet wide; it hung on the cliff wall like a giant shingle.

Grimmelmann joined him, shielded his eyes from the glare and studied the cliff.

"I do not think you will get this honey," the old man said.

"I'm going to knock off the whole slab," Bain told him. He walked to the cliff, stood under the slab and studied the rock wall. It was climbable. He could reach the top of the slab and examine it. O'Brien joined him. Bain took off his ragged shoes.

"Boost me up," he said. The big man cupped his hands and Bain stepped into them, grabbed a lip of stone and began climbing. Three minutes later he was twenty feet above the others, studying the top of the slab. On the far end, over the hive opening, it was a foot wide and it maintained this width almost to the end he clutched. He pulled himself higher, ran his hand along the back. He had hoped for a wide, deep crack but there was none. The slab was part of the cliff it clung to; the narrow ledge had been made by the falling away of some chunk above, the remains of which had long ago been turned into shale and sand by time and the elements and was now part of the canyon floor.

But there was one spot close to the cliffside where the rock was crumbly. Bain picked at it with his finger, dislodged a fragment of black stone. He put his forefinger into the hole and strained at another piece. It moved but did not give. He reached back carefully, pulled the wrench from his belt, put it on the rock shelf and found a more secure foothold for his left foot. Below the others watched him, wordless, apprehensive.

He took the long wrench and hammered at the thimble-sized hole; the loose bit broke free. He cleaned out the hole again, inserted the end of the wrench and began smashing it up and down. The stone was resistant but it was stone and it gave way before the cold steel. He withdrew the end and smashed again at the edge of the hole. Sweat poured from every pore; his arms ached. After five long minutes he had a hole the size of a pack of cigarettes, a hole that had been filled with shattered and weakened stone, a hole that could be enlarged only with tremendous effort, for the stone surrounding it was solid and almost impervious to the smashing wrench. But Bain was satisfied. He rested for a time and then crawled down to rest in the shade.

"We can do it," he panted to the others, "I know we can do it now."

"Knock off that slab?" O'Brien said. Grimmelmann had talked to him, filled him with doubt.

"Yes," Bain said. "Just a matter of time. Now listen to me, all of you. O'Brien, go find a dead tree and make a ladder up to the top of that ledge. It'll be easier, going up and down. When you get up there make a fire in the little hole and keep it going. Grace can collect stuff to burn, good hardwood if you can find it. Here's the idea: we get a good fire going in that hole, the rock all around it heats up, hotter and hotter. Then we dash cold water on it. What happens?"

"It cracks!" O'Brien said.

"It cracks," Bain said. "And splinters and crumbles. Then I go up again and dig it out with the wrench and smash some more loose. The hole gets deeper and broader. We start the process over again. That's how all the ancient people used to work rock. All you need is fire, fuel and time."

"Very good," Grimmelmann said. He nodded his head. "Very good, very good."

Bain turned to the old German. "While they get busy on that I'd like you to help me on something else. Getting rid of the bees." He stood up and walked away from the other. Grimmelmann followed him.

"Let's annoy them," Bain said. "Isn't it true that if you really upset them they'll swarm?"

"*Ja*," Grimmelmann said. "We might force them to swarm, to leave the hive. We have to make it unbearable for them. Smoke is no good. It only quiets them, makes them easy to handle."

"I wasn't thinking of smoke," Bain said. "What do you think of this? I'm going to climb around the cliff until I find a spot where I can drive in a heavy piece of wood or maybe my wrench; a place maybe fifty or a hundred feet up, easy to get to. We find a big solid rock and wire it to the end of the rope. I take the other end up and make a turn around the protruding stick. We haul up the rock until it's level with the hive opening. Then we use it as a battering ram, smash it against their home."

The old man nodded. He saw Bain's scheme in his mind: a pendulum made from a rope and a stone. The rock would be twenty feet in the air but they could control its movement with another piece of rope. The boulder would smash against the cliff. Inside the secret hive, heavy combs of honey would fall, eggs would break loose from their octagonal homes, workers would be killed, squirming pupae would die as their liquid food drained away. An earthquake in the insect world.

And it would not stop. The workers would start on the damaged comb, the escaping wealth of honey and pollen and grub and food. The queen would stop laying eggs. The hive order would be destroyed. The hammering would go on and on, hour after hour, until the hive was no longer an orderly totalitarian world of precision and ritual but an anarchistic state on the verge of insanity.

The hive would swarm. The queen would communicate to the workers and the general movement would begin, toward the strange outside world which the queen had seen but once. A great formless mass of bees would pour out of the opening and whirl away across the canyon. It would find a resting spot and cluster on some high pinnacle; scouts by the hundreds would search for empty crevices. One of them would find the next home and the queen would go there, half smothered by attendants and protectors. She would survive and when new white comb was ready she would begin to lay her eggs. The life of the swarm would continue.

"*Ja*, it is a good plan, I think," Grimmelmann said, nodding his head. "Let us get busy."

[124]

Sturdevant walked on.

He was in the Namib Desert. There was no doubt about it now: the hot wind at his back heading for the cooler ocean; the dreadful sand desert, the land sloping downward, the river which ran for a time and then frittered itself away in the heavy sand. At times the wind was so strong that it picked up the sand, swirled it along, creating sandstorms.

He might make it to the sea, to the Skeleton Coast. His rifle was gone. He had used up the ammunition and left the weapon back in the gorge.

He drank again and then stumbled on, found a place to hide from the sun. The pools were running out; he could not risk any more daytime walking. The water tins were empty.

The Namib. A thousand miles of sand running along the sea and drifting back in some places a hundred miles. He was somewhere in it; every step forward was a step closer to the sea. But how far? Would it be wiser to stay in the river bed? There were permanent pools farther back up the watercourse in the narrow gorge. Ahead of him was sand and the sea. . . .

And the sea would be salt. Cold. The icy-cold Benguella Current swept up from the Antarctic. If he reached the sea he could somehow survive or he would die happily in the cold water.

Night came and he walked on. He was barefooted, for his shoes had fallen apart long ago. He was beyond fatigue. He walked and slept but it was more from habit than necessity. His body was now nothing more than bone and corded muscle, gaunt and almost weightless.

The moon came and the landscape turned bluish white; the cliffs were gone, replaced by sloping sandbanks. After a time he left the river course and walked along the banks, looked for lights, roads, listened.

He grew very tired, sat down in the sand.

Keep moving!

He obeyed. He got up and walked on. There would be no more pools, for the river bed ran through pure sand. He thought of the people he had known and arranged them alphabetically: Allen, Bentley, Collins, Dobbs. . . . Then he would recall poems he liked and try to recite the first line of each. He tried to remember all the places he had ever slept, all the books he had ever read.

And then in the dead of night a strange sound that he heard but did not understand for a long time, a familiar noise that reached his drugged brain. The sound of ocean surf.

He started to run and saw the moonlight shimmering on the ocean, ran toward the dark waves that rolled in and curled violently as they died on the hard beach. He fought loose from his pack, threw the water tins to one side.

He stood and let the sea slosh over his bare feet. He had been allowed to live and complete the incredible walk. He'd save the others now.

He sat down and let the sea run around him. It was cold. He took a mouthful and then spit it out, the dryness gone from his throat. He walked along the beach and found tire tracks. He began to follow them.

He saw a building in the distance, a small white building on the dunes safe from the heavy Atlantic surf. He hurried toward it, walking between the tracks he'd followed, the wide tracks of a truck or Land-Rover.

The door was locked. There was a sign: the building was the property of an international diamond monopoly. He had made contact with the civilized world.

He broke a pane of glass and forced the single window up, crawled in. The small building was a combination storehouse and living quarters, separated by chicken wire. He stood barefooted on the cement floor and looked around: cot with blankets, a kerosene stove, shelves of canned goods, mirror and basin, small bookcase filled with paperbacks and old magazines. He walked to the storeroom. Drums of oil here, gasoline, cases of tinned food, a box of work clothes. Crates and boxes from England and America and the Union.

He was somewhere along the coast of South-West Africa.

He found a can opener and ate tinned beef and peach halves and whole corn. He made a pot of coffee, found the aroma strange and almost sickening and decided not to have any. He had to let his system get used to civilized food, rich food, sweet food.

He heated more water and began shaving.

He was going to stay here for a time. He was too tired to move on, walk down the beach. The razor worked along the edges of the tough beard and the long reddish hairs fell away. He lathered his face again; it felt good to shave again, to be clean, civilized. He would have to give himself a haircut too and put on some fresh clothes.

It was not always called the Gem Coast.

The Portuguese saw it first in their search for Prester John and the mythical golden cities of the medieval imagination. They found a few Bushmen along its desert shore, naked mollusk eaters, fishermen, small tribes who waited for the greatest of all gifts from the salt ocean: an occasional great whale dead on the cold sand.

There were few harbors but the sea rovers found them and sent armed conquistadores into the desert beyond; they struggled through the deep sand and fought the insects and the Bushmen of the interior and staggered back to their ships. It was the most terrible world they had ever seen, worse than the ice world of the far north, worse than the Congo jungles. They cursed it and sailed away. One of them, bolder than the rest, or perhaps more foolish, sailed on southward and came at last to a gentle cape. Diaz.

The world shunned the coast until the eighteen eighties. A German named Luderitz wrangled twenty miles of barren coast from a Hottentot chief. He petitioned his government to protect his trading interests but was for a time ignored. Then the colonial fever gripped Germany and she took not only the twenty miles but the vast area around it, larger than herself. It was her first colony.

It was a glory that was soon to die. The Great War came and a South African army ended the German rule. The area became a League mandate but its real ruler was Capetown.

Then someone found diamonds in the sand near the Orange River. A great rush for easy wealth started. Now it was the Gem Coast.

Later, he made himself a cup of tea and opened a can of pears. Then he curled up on the cot and tried to sleep, listening to the surf pound on the desolate beach. The door was open now and the stuffiness was gone from the small building. It was midday.

This was the Gem Beach and the building was some sort of a way station, a supply depot, one of several probably along the tremendous stretches of the coast owned by the company. They did not mine diamonds here; they simply picked them out of the heavy sand. Alluvial stuff. A pocket was discovered and bulldozers and scores of men moved and shifted the sand, picking out the rare stones—each year millions of dollars' worth of diamonds for New York and London and Paris, from the remote beach to the luxury shops of the outside world.

He shifted his body on the narrow cot, rubbed his head. The long hair was gone; he had found scissors and a comb and sitting outside in the sand, the mirror propped before him, he had cut away the snarled mass of reddish hair, let the wind take it and blow it away. And he had clean clothes on now, plain white underwear and a one-piece, zippered work suit, heavy wool socks and high work shoes, all from boxes in the storeroom. Work clothes for the company's native labor force.

He was filled with good food and he was clean and shaven and comfortable. He would stay here and grow fat until someone came.

Three hours passed and he awoke and got up.

It was difficult to sleep. He saw them in his dreams: Mike Bain and Grace Monckton and O'Brien and Grimmelmann and Smith. They were waiting for him, starving, sick, desperate, waiting for him to come back in a plane and save them. It was his duty to save them, his duty. . . .

He walked out of the door and smelled the strange salt air. There was no boat to take him down the coast, no vehicle. The beach south of him stretched away and away. How far to some place where there were people, telephones, a radio transmitter?

He turned back and went into the storeroom, took one of the rubber tires and rolled it out of the door, down the dunes to a level spot on the wide beach. He went back for matches and a can of motor oil. The beach was strewn with bleached driftwood, and for half an hour he worked, carrying wood, piling it on the rubber tire. He poured the oil over the pyre and set it on fire.

Black smoke snaked its way into the clear sky. If anyone saw it they would certainly come and investigate. He sat in the sand and rested, watched the flames attack the dry wood.

He went to bed soon after darkness came, after a meal of canned ham, whole corn and pineapple slices. And he drank coffee this time, good rich coffee with cream and sugar. The fire had died down. In the morning he would make another farther down the beach where there was a new supply of driftwood.

Then he came awake, suddenly. A strong light blinded and something was prodding into his leg, hurting him. Voices.

He sat up and the blinding light moved to one side and he saw that it was a flashlight. A big man was standing in the doorway, a white man with a flashlight in one hand and a pistol in the other. He wore a white-brimmed hat, a light windbreaker and heavy work pants. Behind him another man, younger with a shock of blond hair and a thin mustache.

"Don't try anything, now," said the big man. "Just hold steady."

"Jesus," Sturdevant said. "I can't believe it, I can't believe it."

The two men came into the building. The blond-haired man carried a shotgun. A Negro appeared and stood in the doorway. The big man carried a kerosene lamp to the table, touched a match to the wick and adjusted the flame. Sturdevant rubbed his eyes and yawned slowly.

"You were silly to try it this way," the big man said.

"Better give us the stones now," the other man said. He waved the shotgun.

"Stones?" Sturdevant asked.

"We mean it," the big man said. "Give us the diamonds now and it'll go easier with you later."

"Diamonds?" Sturdevant said. He began to laugh. They had come with guns, not to rescue him but to arrest him. They thought he was a thief, a diamond poacher.

He cleared his throat.

"My name is Sturdevant. I'm a pilot. My plane went down inland from here, hundreds of miles I guess, a hell of a walk anyway. Somewhere deep in the Namib. My plane went down. Crashed. There are five people trapped back in there, on a black mountain sitting all alone in a desert of pure sand. They're starving to death. I made it here, all the way across the sand, down a dry river bed."

"You *walked* here," said the one with the blond hair. "You say you walked here from the interior?"

"Yes."

"Impossible. You should have made up a better story."

Sturdevant scowled at him. "Who the hell are you?"

"Give us the stones," the big man said. "We need the stones first of all."

Sturdevant shook his head back and forth. "If I came here to steal diamonds why the hell would I make a fire?"

"What fire?"

"Go look outside on the beach. I burned up one of your company's tires too. You can bill me for it."

The big man nodded to the Negro and he vanished into the night.

"If you did make a fire it was to signal the plane you're waiting for, or the boat. What was it anyway?" It was the blond-haired one again.

"What's your name?" Sturdevant asked.

"Bauer," said the young man.

"Why don't you believe me? Why this ridiculous idea that I'm a gem thief? It's fantastic."

"We *know* you're here for the diamonds," Bauer said. "This is all company property. There's no way in or out except through us. You found out somehow about the pocket nearby, probably from some worker you bribed. It happens more often than you think. A small plane dropped you here and the plans were to come back and get you. If you made a fire it was to signal the plane in the night, not to attract attention. And something went wrong. Your friends pulled out and left you here. Bad piece of luck all around."

"And you couldn't have walked here from the interior," said the big man. "We know the desert. Absolutely no water. You couldn't possibly have come that way."

"I had two tins of water," Sturdevant said. "I carried them on my back for days and days until they were almost empty. Then I found a low spot and dug and found water. I had the pools in the gorge."

"Where are the tins?" Bauer asked.

"Back in the sand somewhere," Sturdevant said. "I had a rifle too but I ran out of ammo and left it behind. I lived on lizards and a big turtle and carp in the pools."

"You can sure tell a story," Bauer said.

"There have been no plane crashes either," the big man said. "It's been almost three years since a plane went down within a thousand miles of here. We know that for a fact because we keep a sharp eye on airplane information."

"What airline?" Bauer asked. "What outfit?"

"My own," Sturdevant said. "My own plane. Why don't we go somewhere and check on all this? I'll give you people to contact to verify all this. I'm known all over hell."

The Negro came back and nodded to the big man.

"We got a little settlement up the coast fifty miles. With a jail. Next month sometime a truck will take you down to Oranjemund to the regular police. We're C.D.M. people. I'm Patterson. We better go now."

"Take me there now," Sturdevant said.

"Next month," Patterson said. "It's a hell of a drive. A special truck comes around with the mail and all. You'll have to wait. You're going to jail for a few years anyway so what's the hurry?"

"I'm not going," Sturdevant said. "I've got to reach somebody and tell them about my passengers. They're dying back there on the black mountain, a place that from the air would look like a black hand. I've got to go on. I'm responsible."

"Don't be foolish," Bauer said. "We told you before. The story's no good. No plane's been reported down and you couldn't have walked out anyway."

"And you don't look like a guy that has been through anything rough. You've been here four or five days maybe, down at the diggings, raking up stones. And your friends got cold feet and didn't come back for you."

"I shaved and cut my hair and the clothes are from the back room," Sturdevant said. "I came here yesterday morning wearing a ragged pair of pants. Nothing else."

"Let's see the pants," Bauer said.

"I threw them into the fire," Sturdevant said.

Bauer laughed. "You burned your own clothes all right and put on company clothes in case somebody found you at the diggings. You better give us the stones now or we'll get mad."

"Do that," Patterson said.

"What a pair of idiots," Sturdevant said. "Jesus . . ."

"Don't get sassy," Bauer said, "or we'll put handcuffs on you."

The big man turned to Bauer. "Let's go. We'll take him back now." He motioned to Sturdevant to get off the cot and go outside. Sturdevant did and felt Bauer in back of him with the shotgun. A pair of idiots.

The big man snapped on the flashlight, blew out the lamp and closed the window. He took out a ring of keys, selected one and locked the door.

They walked down to the beach. It was cold and Sturdevant wished he'd thought to bring a jacket. They came to a Land-Rover and Patterson put him in the front seat next to Bauer who got behind the wheel. Patterson and the Negro got in back. The lights came on and the motor roared and the truck rolled forward down the hard-packed sand with the surf roaring on one side and the gloomy dunes on the other. Sometime later the headlights hit a sun-bleached sign:

Hours later they came to a group of dark buildings. Two elderly men came and stared at Sturdevant as they took him to a small cement annex with narrow slits for a window and a heavy oak door with rusty iron hinges.

Patterson's flashlight explored the tiny room. There was a narrow cot. And a pail. Nothing more.

Sturdevant stiffened. Bauer pushed him inside and began to close the door, shutting out the night and the air.

"No . . . please . . . no . . ." He was fighting the door, trying to hold it, feeling the clamminess close around him. And then the door closed; he heard the raw scraping metallic sounds as they locked it. He was in almost total darkness. He turned, felt his way carefully across the space to the cot.

Suddenly all the fatigue and worry and despair broke within him. He began to cry uncontrollably.

He woke up. Somewhere a dog was barking. It was close to dawn. He lay for a long time without moving. He was alive and it didn't seem possible; he was alive and safe from the sun, he was cool and there was food and rest. He closed his eyes, turned slowly on the cot, yawned. He could spend a month here and it would not bother him, six months. He could sleep and drink and eat and make up for the impossible trip through the desert. They'd said he'd be here a month. A week back at the black mountain was an eternity. Maybe some of them were already sick, dying. He had to get out of here and get help. They were waiting for him back at the canyon: Mike Bain and Smith and old Grimmelmann and Grace and O'Brien. They could not endure an added month.

He sat up and looked at the barred window. The shock of last night had worn off; the disbelief was gone. He was no longer numbed by the fact that they didn't believe him. He had to start fighting again, make them believe him.

He stood up and walked to the window. The dog had stopped barking. He shouted and the barking commenced, furious now. A door banged somewhere. He grasped the iron bars, took a deep breath and shouted as loud as he could.

Let me out of here!

The settlement came awake. Shouts, orders, the insane barking of dogs, doors banging, curses. Sturdevant smiled. It was going to get rough again, very rough, but it had to be.

Let me out of here!

Footsteps coming closer, angry voices swearing, flashlights cutting the gray-black dawn.

"Bastard's askin' for trouble."

"Maybe he's crazy."

And then the fumbling at the door, the screech of the bolt and the rusty hinges. Lights in his face, blinding him. Patterson and Bauer and others, angry faces puffy with sleep. They were silent for a moment, watching him.

"There has been a plane crash," he told them as if for the first time. "You've got to take me out of here. We've got to search for the survivors."

He watched Bauer's body turn, saw the fist coming and did not try to move away. The blow caught him full in the stomach and he went down gasping, hurt. Hands found him, pulled him up.

"You gonna keep on with that?"

"My name is Sturdevant. Check it out. I got a pilot's license."

"You gonna stop it?"

"From the air the place might look like a great black hand with sand all around. . . ."

Bauer hit him again. His jaw exploded in pain; he reeled away and scraped the rough cement wall.

"Maybe he's telling the truth," said a new voice.

"Break his goddamn neck that's what we should do."

"The law's too easy on these birds."

Sturdevant found his balance. "I walked across the desert with two tins of water. Once I killed a big turtle. And lizards. I had a rifle too . . ."

"Get him out of here, outside."

They pulled him through the narrow door, tearing his shirt. A glancing blow sent him reeling into one of the figures. Patterson.

"Better cut it out, feller. Get smart."

He stood alone again, the sky milky blue, some of the stars still strong. A strange hour between dawn and day. There were more men standing around him now and others coming, their flashlights bobbing. Dogs, restrained by leashes, raged and snarled at him.

"Son-of-a-bitch woke up the whole camp."

[133]

"They caught him waitin' for a plane. Down Number 4 shack."

"You must listen to me," Sturdevant said. "A plane crashed back in the desert. They're waiting to be rescued. They can't wait . . ."

Somebody hit him and he went down hard. He spat blood on his hands and knees.

"You have a radio," he told them. "Check with outfits that know me. I can give you names. I have responsibilities . . ."

"Dressed up jus' like a company man."

"Teach him some manners, Gert."

They pulled him up, held his arms, twisted his head around.

"You gonna quit!"

"I'm telling the truth, you stupid bastards."

He tried to escape the blow. The wind went out of him and he crumpled back on the hard ground fighting for air, finding it while they kicked him. He vomited and began to cry. Some of them would believe him eventually, one of them. He'd convince one of them by standing up, fighting, suffering.

"You had enough now?" They shook him.

"Plane crash . . . help them . . . radio . . ."

"He's fainted."

They dragged him across the hard ground and pushed him through the door of the tiny jail and locked the door. They walked back to low buildings talking and laughing and smoking cigarettes.

The bees fled from the cliff, deserted the stone hive, swarmed to some lost rock hole in the black mountain. On the third morning Bain and the others found them gone except for a few dazed workers who crawled and buzzed aimlessly before the narrow opening. The pounding of the big rock had driven them away as Bain had predicted. Now they could concentrate on the job of cracking open the cliff and extracting the precious honey.

They had built a fire in the tiny hole Bain had found on the top of the big slab that seemed to cover the hive. O'Brien had started it with grass and twigs and bark, then adding wood. The fire burned, building up a bed of coals, and the surrounding rock grew warm, then too hot to touch. Bain had left his work on the swinging rock and climbed the rickety ladder that O'Brien had started; he carried the canteen cup filled with water and he sloshed it over the fire and the hot rock nearby. The fire died, hissing and smoking; the water spilled off the ledge, dripped in on sand and shale below.

Bain worked into position and pulled the wrench from his belt. He smashed it down around the hole filled with sodden ash and something gave; the weakened rock gave way under the steel. The cold water had caused an uneven cooling of the rock and it had cracked and splintered. Bain picked out a piece the size of the original hole and dropped it down for the others to see. He dug out the wet trash and then started smashing the rock again.

They did not start another fire in the enlarged crevice. Bain decided that they would drive the bees away first. Grace and Grimmelmann went back to the cave and O'Brien stayed to help with the hanging rock.

It was ready within two hours; a fifty-pound boulder hanging in a cage of wire which was fastened to the rope. They fixed a lead rope to it and began smashing it against the hive opening.

The rock and the cliff met with a heavy impact, chips of rock sprayed the area; a sudden flow of black angry bees emerged from the slit and they backed away. The big rock bumped and thumped and grew quiet. Bain found the lead rope and brought it back as far as he could, aimed the rock at the hive and let go. It crushed against the cliff and bounced away.

"I don't like it," Bain said. "We're bastards to do this."

O'Brien wiped sweat from his face. "Will it really work?" He didn't care about the bees.

"Yes," Bain said. "It'll work. They can only take so much. Then they'll take off for a quiet place."

An hour later they went back to the cave.

And now the honeybees were gone.

They filled the enlarged crack with the hot coals they had brought from the cave, added hard, dry sticks, waited for the stone to grow hot. When it was ready O'Brien threw the water on it and then hammered away the shattered crumbs of stone with the battered wrench. The crack had grown deeper. Bain sharpened some of the dry sticks and hammered them deep into the new fissures. The fire was started again.

"Only one trouble," O'Brien said.

"What's that?" Bain asked.

"When the slab goes it will bury us under it."

"We'll start doing it by remote control soon," Bain told him. "We'll find a crack somewhere above the ledge, drive a stick into it and fix a

[135]

bottle or the canteen to it on a string. We pull the string, tip the bottle and spill the water. All from a good distance."

The big man nodded. He walked to where the big rock hung motionless from the long rope. He took the lead rope and backed off with it until it was as high as he could get it. When he let go the heavy rock swung through the air and smashed against the lip of the ledge.

"It's a little early for that," Bain said.

"Just practicing," O'Brien said. "And it might have jarred the damn thing a little."

They worked all day on the ledge. Grace came with more hot coals. They sweated on the hot ledge, smashing weakened rock, driving heavier pegs deep into the growing cavity, drying it out with rags and grass and starting a new fire.

Bain fixed a device to pour the water into the crack by remote control. O'Brien began to batter the ledge with the hanging boulder.

"Very soon now," Bain said as they watched the smoke rise from a new fire. "Maybe this is it."

They sat in the shade. After a while O'Brien got up and carefully climbed the ladder with a handful of dry sticks and fed them to the fire.

"Let's try it," Bain said. They all got up. Bain walked to the cliff and found the string that would trip the bottle of water. He backed away with it carefully under the string which was taut. They looked to the bottle and saw it was tilted almost sideways. Then Bain pulled and it turned upside down and the water flooded from it, hissing on the hot fire, running into the deep crack filled with heated ash.

O'Brien grabbed the lead rope and pulled the big boulder back, aimed it and then ran halfway to the cliff with it, flinging it away at the final moment.

There was a violent snap almost like a rifle firing and the great slab of rock fell outward as the big rock smashed against it, hitting the ground with such force that all of them were shaken.

They did not move. They did not believe that they had done it. The slab was gone from the cliff face and in its place a great hole was filled with layers of discolored comb. Some of it fell away and plunged to the ground. They walked to it, picked it up, licked the amber honey that oozed from the breaks.

"Fantastic," O'Brien said. "I've never seen anything like it." He bit into a clean piece of comb. They were all eating the honey now, feeling its strength, its natural sweetness.

Bain walked over and studied the great slab, saw the successive discolorations which marked the reach of each fire and each split. They had broken off a great piece of rock with patience and a simple process as the ancient Egyptians had. They had honey now, hundreds of pounds of it perhaps.

"Now to get this stuff safe in the cave," O'Brien said. He picked up the ladder which had fallen sideways, away from the slab, placed it against the cliff and made his way up to the hive. "It'll be a hell of a job, I can tell you that," he told them. He broke off a big chunk of comb and dropped it down to Bain. They had no containers, no place to keep the liquid food except in its own wax. They would have to carry it back to the cave in bags, in suitcases, and pile it in the cool cave.

Bain and Grace carried the first load back the long miles to the cave. Then Bain took a torch and with Grace and the old man walked as far back into the cave as he could, and piled the dripping combs on the cool floor under the *kloof*. They hurried back to O'Brien.

It took them the rest of the day to clean out the deep hive; they staggered along in the canyon under the great loads of honey. O'Brien made the most trips, carrying hundred-pound loads in the sleeping bag, magnificent in his strength, his corded body covered with sweat and honey and sand. Grimmelmann carried small amounts and he did not hurry; Bain and Grace worked feverishly.

It was imperative to hurry. To leave the honey unprotected would have been disastrous. Even as they worked the swarm of looting bees and other insects came to feed upon the treasure. And small birds grew bold and hovered annoyingly close. Ants learned of the sacking and they came, militant and determined to share. A baboon came close and watched them cautiously.

And then it was over. There was no more comb worth bothering with. They were bone-tired as they had never been, covered with honey, gritty and filthy from cutting and carrying the comb. They went to the water hole and washed, walked wearily to the cave and collapsed in the sand. They were heavy with the rich honey; they had the strange sensation of being overfed.

Night came. Grimmelmann brought in the fire and built it up. The others did not stir.

Jefferson Smith had been with the Bushmen for three days. They were heading somewhere, moving across the arid plains and through the sparse grasslands. The country improved; the sand desert fell behind as they moved north and there were more signs of animal life, more tracks and birds and cover. Smith remembered what Grimmelmann and Sturdevant had talked about: the Kalahari wasn't a true desert, it was just lacking in surface water. It was the Great Thirstland.

The day after they found him, the day after the feast of gazelle meat, he had gone with them and observed a strange practice. He saw them make sip wells in the dry sand of an old watercourse and suck water from it. An old woman dug a hole in the sand deep as her arm would allow. She collected grass and rolled it into a tight ball the size of a grapefruit and put it in the bottom of the hole. Now a long reed was inserted into the ball of grass and all the sand pushed back into the hole.

The old woman took an empty ostrich shell and sat it upright in the sand near the protruding reed. From her bag of belongings she took a small stick. She sat down and made herself comfortable. Then she put the short stick in the side of her mouth and placed the other end in the opening of the eggshell. She grasped the hollow reed, put it in her mouth and began to suck. For several minutes nothing happened. The old woman strained and Smith could see that her body was directed to the one effort; her shoulders bent and her old back strained. Sweat ran from her wrinkled face.

And all at once a trickle of water began to run down the short stick, from her mouth to the ostrich shell. There had been no water in the hole but the sucking had created a vacuum and from the moist sand around had come the water, seeking the ball of grass and penetrating it, leaving the sand behind, following the vacuum up the hollow reed. Fantastic—the reason why the Bushman could live where others perished.

Now they walked along and came to the beginnings of a vast grassland; sparse clumps of brown grass dotted the red sandy soil and scraggly trees became more common. Two hunters broke away from the group and trotted away to the west.

The afternoon died and they walked on until they saw ahead a trailing line of smoke in the sky and hurried to the hunters and their kill. They fell upon a big springbok and dropped the dripping meat into the big fire. Smith ate two chunks of it before he stopped to rest. He was like the Bushmen now, gorging himself with meat when it was available, eating all he could hold. Life was the process of living, of eating and drinking, of surviving. He was naked but he was not alone. The wild Bushmen were his friends now, they tried to talk to him, smiling when he did not understand. And he had names for some of them. The woman who first gave him water was Maggie. The leader was Plato because he looked amazingly like the textbook bust of the Greek. Then there were Fu Manchu and Wrinklebelly, the two hunters. He had even named some of the children: Beetle and Number One Son and Nasty.

He felt sure that they would not kill him now. They were wild but they were not brutal. They might hand him over to some white man, some district commissioner or police patrol. They would bring him somewhere, for they must know that he could not survive alone, without their meat and water.

He found a place to sleep and lay looking up at the great sky. How far was this from a city with electric lights and automobiles? How many miles, how many years, how many centuries?

When dawn came they moved on.

The desert was left behind. They moved through grassland now, flat and dry except for an occasional *vley*, green and noisy with birds and ringed with the spoor of kudu and gemsbok. Smith sensed a new element in the clicking talk, an excitement. They no longer spared their water. The children ran and leaped and played with more abandon. Fu Manchu went off alone and they caught up with him a few hours later. He carried a young gazelle across his shoulders. They did not stop to eat it, but hurried on across the featureless grassland.

They came to other Bushmen, to a tiny village of perhaps twenty little people. The villagers rushed to them and there was the age-old exchange of greeting and gossip and acclaim. They gathered around Jefferson Smith, eyed him with wonder and disbelief, the women embarrassed, a few of the men truculent. The leader of the village talked with Plato, clicking and gesticulating and pointing. Smith grew afraid. He was completely helpless in the hands of Stone Age people. It was quite possible that most of them had never seen a stranger at such close range, a Negro, an enemy; it was possible that none of them had ever seen a white man. They were the last few wild humans left in the world and he was among them, in their power.

But they did not harm him. Some sort of a deal had been made between the two leaders. They all walked slowly to the cluster of trees where others waited.

There were several huts that looked like messy beehives, made of grass and thorn branches, each hut built close to one of the low, wind-twisted trees which seemed to hold it upright. A few old people sat around in front of the huts, almost unconcerned over the arrival of the new group; they sat warming themselves in the sun, close to smoke-less fires like ancient mummies, their yellowish bodies incredibly wrinkled. They looked older than anyone Smith had ever seen.

Thin dry strips of meat hung from some of the branches of the trees and next to most of the shelters there were neat rows of ostrich shells half buried in the soil. The water supply. The villagers melted away from the newcomers and some of them returned to their tasks. They took Smith to an empty hut and made it clear that it was his; he smiled and sat down before it and nodded. A child came to him with an ostrich shell; another ran off and came back with a tsamma melon. He was hungry and he chopped it open with a short stick and ate it and the children gathered and watched him. He made faces at them and offered them bits of it but they backed away, tiny pygmylike creatures with quick eyes, frightened and fascinated at the black giant the strangers had brought from the far desert.

Smith watched the villagers too. The apricot-skinned women pounding with mortar and pestle, scraping skins, coming in from the far veldt carrying their digging sticks and animal skins lumpy with roots and tubers. Some of them cooked in clay pots, others carried tiny infants slung on their hips. They pretended not to watch him but their interest was impossible to hide.

He stayed at the Bushman village for three days.

The fear left him. They were not going to eat him or sacrifice him in some gruesome fashion; they fed him and did not bother him and in the end Fu Manchu and Wrinklebelly, the two hunters, took him with them on another trip over the grassland.

He was almost sad to leave the little group of villagers but he sensed that the group was about to break up and scatter to find the ever-moving and quickly depleted food supply. They were hunters, foragers; the huts might be used only a few weeks a year; the group might move in a great circle with the seasons. No civilized men had ever really lived with true wild Bushmen, knew the cadence of their dreams, their soul.

Perhaps the meeting of the two groups was some annual affair for the young to seek mates outside of their blood group, their clan. Smith studied them and saw timid love play between some of them, sensed in some of the talk among the older boys an excitement when one of the supple girls passed.

There was much dancing. Every night. One dance was quite obvious, a sort of mimic war between two rows of men who faced each other on their knees, each line shouting at the other, shaking their arms in mock anger, writhing in fury, groaning with effort. It was followed sometimes by another game more familiar to Smith. The two rows faced each other, clapping and humming, and then suddenly they would all hold up their hands with a certain number of fingers raised. If the opposite man had not matched the first man the latter advanced toward him with a short hop, toward a line drawn between the opposing teams. It reminded Smith of matching coins, of tug of war.

And other dances that sometimes went on into the night, dances that Smith watched from the door of his hut until he fell asleep. A group of the men dancing around a big fire of thorn, hardly moving, their bodies in great turmoil as they tried to move by taking the shortest step possible. The women circling them, clapping and stomping too in rhythm. And once a dance which portrayed a hunt: a graceful Bushman leaping around the fire and over it with his hands close to his head, two fingers raised like horns.

They played a curious game once too, a game that Smith watched, found himself enjoying, wondering if he should try to play and then deciding against it, afraid that it might break some taboo. The men gathered in a flat space to one side of the huts and they each held a long willowy rod, a thin supple stick. One of them took a peculiar object and hung it on the end of his stick, a hard bulb of some sort hanging on the end of a leather thong. On the other end of the thong was a heavy feather. Suddenly the man whipped the object into the air; it rose high and then plummeted downward, the feather fluttering behind the thong. The men raced for it and the fastest leaped high, caught it with his stick and flung it back into the sky. The men moved with incredible speed and agility. The game reminded Smith of badminton and lacrosse—fantastic to watch. He wondered how old it was, how long it had been played by the little men.

Civilization was a thin crust. He had broken through and was himself a Bushman in all but outlook. And if he stayed here or in any uncivilized group he would in time think as they thought; his offspring would be wild men.

The thought terrified him; the delicate arrangements and systems that made life on the outside so easy; the massive industries balanced on knife-edge adjustments; the handful of men who kept it all running and the fewer who were able to improve it, add to it. Modern man was a parasite living off the fat of the past, living on the dividends of a few great brains. He did not gather his food or build his home or rear his children; his hands and his brain were soft; he consumed and manipulated and lived isolated and aloof from the natural world about him. It was comfortable, it was good, it was civilization; but it could vanish overnight if the mechanisms which fed it were destroyed.

He awoke. Fu Manchu was grinning at him, shaking him. Smith crawled behind him out of the hut, stood up and stretched, saw that it was the moment before dawn. Wrinklebelly came and spoke with the other hunter. Smith found one of the eggshells next to his hut and drank from it. An old woman came with a big earthen bowl and the three of them ate from it. Smith wondered what it was . . . chopped-up tubers and roots maybe with ground-up grasshoppers and ant eggs, or tough meat pounded and made edible by the mortar and pestle method. He did not really care. He was hungry and it would keep him alive and nothing else mattered.

And then they left. The two hunters took him gently by the elbow and pointed far away, then to him, then to themselves. He nodded and followed them, smiling and waving good-by to the tiny children and the old people sitting near their huts. Most of them waved back.

He hurried after the little hunters. There was excitement in him; he felt, for some reason, that they were taking him to some place closer to civilization. He was a liability and they were going to get rid of him. They would not murder him, not now. They knew he was from the outside world and they feared that world, feared it and over-estimated its power over them. They would return him to it and not offend the black men who lived around them. The wars were over; a peaceful act would save one of their own someday.

The country improved. The trees grew thicker until they were al-most parklike but then they ended and the men came to a dry area with a few palm trees growing in the sand. And later the sand went away and they came to a vast reddish plain filled with scrub. The

Bushmen moved in a straight line and Smith followed ten feet behind.

They came, sometime in the early afternoon, to a settlement. They climbed a low ridge and far away there was a group of low buildings and a few lines of smoke trailing into the windless sky. The Bushmen talked excitedly, grinning, and began walking toward the village.

Smith was excited. It wasn't another Bushman village; there were mud buildings and the glint of corrugated iron. There was the look of civilization about it. The Bushmen were bringing him to safety. He hurried after them.

And from the village came a group of people, men and women and children, some of them gaily dressed, all of them noisy. They came closer and closer across the dusty plain and then suddenly stopped. And the Bushmen stopped. The noise died now and Smith realized that the Bushmen had their little bows in their hands, that some of the Negroes in the opposing group carried spears and clubs. They did not trust one another completely.

A man broke away from the large group and came toward him, a little man, gnarled and grotesque, wearing a castoff suit coat and filthy trousers. He was obviously part Bushman or Hottentot and part Negro. He came to within twenty feet of Smith and began talking to the Bushmen in their hissing-clicking-sucking language. They talked for several minutes. The man grew restless and angry, happy; he laughed, scowled, scorned. The crowd behind him began to edge closer. Fu Manchu began an excited speech and motioned with his bow and tiny arrow. The interpreter screamed to the mob in another language and they backed away. They knew of Bushman poison.

And then the talk was over. The ragged leader returned to his people and talked for a time with some of the other shabby men. Then two older boys raced away to the settlement.

Through it all Smith had stood wordless, half afraid that something would go wrong at the last moment, that the Bushman would grow angry with the others and take him away. It was obvious now that they were selling him, trading him to the others. He stood in the sun and waited and saw the women pointing at him, snickering at his nakedness. Soon now it would be over.

He studied the strangers. There was something wrong about all of them. They were not as tall as they should be and they were weak-looking, dirty. They were something between the Bushmen and civilized natives; they lacked the wild nobility of Fu Manchu and yet they were not westernized. They wore the castoff rags of the white man and had none of their own. There was no uniformity of color among them. A few had the apricot color of the Bushman and others were obviously pure Hottentot. And some of them were black and others almost white. One had a Malay's face but it was twisted and degenerate; another had peppercorn hair and mottled skin.

He had heard of groups like this in the Kalahari; Sturdevant had talked about them once in the cave. They were in-between people, the refuse of two worlds, hopelessly inbred and isolated in remote settlements, strange half-castes shunned by the white, the black, and the Bushmen.

The two boys came back from the settlement, leading a fat heifer. The leader took the rein and led it toward the two Bushmen. Fu Manchu went forward and took the animal. Wrinklebelly stood and faced the crowd and it broke up and turned its back on him and began to drift back toward the settlement. Wrinklebelly began edging away, walking backwards a few steps at a time. Beyond him Fu Manchu led the fat cow.

Four of the men came toward Smith. He was suddenly afraid and turned instinctively to watch the two little Bushmen fade away. The men began talking to him. He shook his head in misunderstanding. He knew that he must not speak English, not until he saw a white man. He did not trust the ragged, dirty men before him. He felt that if he spoke English they would shrink away from him and then fawn over him and then, when they reasoned it all out, they would kill him. He felt these things and he did not speak to them. He grinned and grimaced and shook his head and after a while they grew tired and led him back to the settlement.

He could smell it long before they came to the first mud house, the smell of a village without plumbing, lying in the sun, inhabited by barbarous, listless people. The smell made him sick.

He walked with them not as an equal but as a prisoner. They had tried to question him and he recalled now that they had been sharp and curt with him. They had bought him from the Bushmen. *He was a slave.*

They took him through the stinking village. The people no longer stared at him. A ratlike dog snarled from the narrow off-center door of one of the mud hovels. Refuse was strewn all over the rutted street and in the festering alleys. They walked on and came to the end of the street to a partially built mud house. Three men stopped working for a moment and looked up listlessly. They wore assorted rags covered with wet clay. One was an old man, black-skinned with white hair. Another was a boy with a Hottentot face and a big-boned whitish body. The third was almost all Bushman but there was the look of the feeble-minded in the slack face and strange eyes.

And there was another man who sat in the shade of a half-finished wall. He got up and came to the others. He was relatively tall and carried a heavy club. He shouted something at the three workers and they returned to their tasks.

He came to Smith and studied him while the other men talked. Suddenly he reached forward and took Smith's arm and pushed him into the half-finished hut, shouting at him. Smith stood and wondered if he should speak, tell them who he was, an American. They would understand some English, enough.

The boss was shouting at him, waving his club. The other men joined in the shouting, their animal-like faces twisted, dangerous. Smith fumbled backwards, bumped into the old man. He nodded to the advancing men. He would work, he would obey.

He found that the men were making mud in a pit and then carrying it to the walls, a handful at a time, smearing on a spot which the sun had already dried. A tedious, primitive task. He joined them, still naked, still frightened by the heavy club and the abject people.

The four men went away and the guard came back and stood watching them for a while. No one spoke. They threw dry clay into the pit and sometimes added water; they stirred it with their feet, carried it dripping to the lumpy walls. Smith worked harder than the others; he knew that he was being appraised. He sensed that the guard wanted to beat him, to make him realize that he was a slave, that he must obey instantly.

The day wore on, and Smith began to relax. He had survived the desert; he was alive. He would be alive tomorrow and the day after that. And someday it would happen: a white policeman would come to the settlement, or a cattle inspector or some wandering busybody, someone who would save him, take him away, free him. Until then, he was a slave.

CHAPTER VI

GRACE MONCKTON and Mike Bain got up and ate some honey and a melon. Then they walked down the valley to forage. Grimmelmann was still resting in his bed. O'Brien had left while it was still dark.

They wandered for two hours along the cliff edge, finding lizards and chasing them, resting in the shade of great boulders, going on. As they got farther away from the cave the cliff grew lower and easier to climb.

Grace cornered a brown lizard and clubbed it to death. Mike cleaned it with a penknife and they wrapped it in a cloth.

"I think we could climb to the top here," Grace said.

Bain looked up, studied the faults, the long inclines.

"Let's try it," he said. He had never been this far down on the cliff top. They might find a new colony of lizards.

They started up, not hurrying, picking their way along. They came to a sheer wall and stopped.

"There's only one way," Bain said. "I can reach the top if you can hold part of my weight in your cupped hands."

"Let's try," Grace said. "I don't want to go back the same way." She cupped her hands, braced her feet against the stone, waited. Bain studied her and the rock wall. He backed away and then ran toward her, put his bare foot in her locked hands and flung himself upward. He felt her strain and push and then her hands parted. But he had a grip on the edge of stone above and he pulled himself up.

He lay flat on the hot stone, reached down for the girl and found her wrists. He pulled her up slowly and surely and she helped him, finding purchase on the rock with her bare toes.

They lay exhausted on the stone. The rest of the climb would be easy.

[146]

Bain became aware of her. He could smell her hair, her warm body; her breasts strained against the tattered, half-buttoned blouse; her golden thighs were only half covered by her ragged skirt.

She turned, saw that he watched her and smiled. She wondered about Bain; he was handsome in a haggard way.

They got up and continued the climb, wordless.

They killed two more sleepy lizards. Bain threw a stone at a small hawklike bird but he missed and they watched it fly away over the vast desert. He realized that he hated O'Brien. When night came Grace would go to him as she now did every night.

They walked on along the top of the escarpment and the rock was hot on their bare feet. They came upon a deep, well-like hole in the solid rock, a circular pit that was twelve or fifteen feet deep and the same distance across. They stood and looked down into it.

"What caused this?" Grace wondered.

"I don't know," Mike said. The sides were too smooth to allow anyone to climb down; he had an urge to descend into the pit but it would be impossible without a rope. "Maybe long ago the hole was a chunk of softer stone that got mixed up with the granite. Time and the elements might have worn it away."

"It's strange," Grace said.

Bain reached for her, found her wrist, held her. "Be careful, the rock's slippery." He pulled her back from the edge of the pit. She was close to him again, warm, sweaty, golden-haired, beautiful.

He let go of her wrist and walked on. She was O'Brien's.

Jefferson Smith worked and slept and ate. He grew accustomed to the monotony of his new life. He waited for his rescuers to come.

He wondered about the others, about Grimmelmann and Mike Bain and Grace. What would O'Brien do with them? He did not like to think about it, for there was nothing he could do. He could not run off and cross the desert, he could not assert himself or identify himself without running the risk of being murdered. He was trapped. There was nothing to do but wait and hope, live from day to day.

He studied the people, the pattern of life in the small community, and was appalled by their ignorance and filth, their weary existence. They had forgotten their old ways and had not learned the new. There was a lethargy in them, an emptiness; they tended their scrub cattle and their dusty gardens and existed, but their life was without hope and art and music. They seemed to have no traditions and no future. They were uncomfortable and dirty and sad.

The building, the shapeless hovel that he and the other slaves had made with mud and sticks, was at last finished and they were put to new tasks. They carried heavy skins of water from the well to the powdery dry fields, watering each individual plant and vine. They ranged from the village and collected bundles of sticks. They repaired cattle pens and collected sun-dried cakes of dung.

He had been given a tattered pair of pants and a squashed straw hat and he looked now like the others, for they had lost the skill of making their own clothes and wore castoff Western clothes and rags, except for some of the ancient women who covered themselves with crude leather aprons. He withdrew into himself. He did his work and waited for the day to end. They were not guarded at night but he no longer thought of fleeing. He was glad to be alive.

He slept in one of the hovels with the old man and the light-skinned boy and the feeble-minded Bushman. Supper was brought to them by one of the village boys, a soup usually or porridge with scraps of meat in it and some kind of bread. It was enough. It filled his stomach and allowed him to sleep and think. He wished for paper and a pen, for the urge to write was still strong in him. He longed for his diary. Sometimes in the night he would visualize a white sheet of paper and he would write neat black words on it, fill an imaginary page with recorded thoughts.

Could I find the mountain again? Was there really such a place? We relived the whole drama of existence there. Would I kill O'Brien now? Think not. Don't believe any of us would have lasted long without him and his hunter's instincts and his gun. Yet he might destroy us all in the long run. I think now that I shall be here for a long time. Perhaps I can discover something here, learn something. There are no ideas in the village, no books. Only people and work.

Then he would fall into a dreamless sleep knowing that soon another dawn would come and another endless day of toil.

One evening, when there was yet another hour of light left, he walked through the village. No one bothered him; the people knew him as a speechless slave and did no more than glance at him. He came to the outskirts of the settlement, to the last house, and stood for a time looking off toward the flat horizon. Should he try to escape, run, find someone and tell them of the plane crash? No. He would not run. He couldn't expect any more luck. He'd survived the crash itself, the black mountain, the desert, the Bushmen and now these people.

The sound of a crying child came to him as he turned and walked back past the mud house. A young woman sat outside it holding a child in her arms and the child cried and held forth a thin arm. There was a dirty rag wrapped around the end of the thumb; the arm thrashed and the rag fell to the dust and Smith saw that the child's thumb was swollen and inflamed, infected. He came closer, interested.

The woman looked up at him, a soiled bandanna wrapped around her head. She rocked the child, hummed to it.

He knelt before her and took the child's tiny hand and studied it. The thumb should be lanced and drained and cleaned. The woman was frightened. She turned her head toward the low door and shouted. A man appeared, angry and sleepy. Smith quickly pointed to the child's hand, then to his forehead, then to his chest, nodding and smiling. *I can make the child well.*

The man looked at his wife. Hesitation. Wonder. Agreement. Smith got up and pushed past the man, through the door, into the mud house. He began to search for things: a bowl for boiling water, a pin or knife or needle, clean rags.

By the time he had finished, a crowd had gathered. The little girl had stopped crying and clung to her mother. The infected thumb had been cleaned and drained and wrapped in a clean strip of cloth that he had boiled and wrung dry in his hands. He would come back in the morning and look at it.

No one had bothered him or tried to stop him. They had seen that he was trying to help, that he was adept. He stood up to go but a young boy touched his arm gently, pointed to his foot and then raised it carefully. It too was swollen. Smith motioned for the boy to sit down. He washed off the dark-skinned foot. It had been punctured by a sharp thorn.

He began to work on it, motioned for more hot water. Was it possible that these people were without the knowledge of rudimentary medicine? Perhaps their village doctor was away or dead. He looked up at the faces around him. They seemed less abject, less cruel; he did not hate them now. They were backward and primitive. They were, in a sense, prisoners themselves, trapped in the desert like Grimmelmann and Bain and the girl. If he would help anyone he should help these people. The fact that he was their slave did not matter.

[149]

A woman brought him a new bowl of hot water. A man came with a torch and stood close to him.

He began to wash the boy's swollen foot.

Grimmelmann remembered the big lizard he had seen and one morning he took O'Brien to the place. It was across the canyon and closer to the peak than the cave was. They searched among the rock slabs in the shadow of the cliff for the reptile's lair. Grimmelmann found it and O'Brien nodded.

"I'll get him," he told the old man.

"Can I help?"

O'Brien considered it, then shook his head. "You might do better at something else. It may be a long wait."

The German nodded. He'd go farther up the canyon and hunt smaller lizards and then maybe he would cross over to the other cliff and work his way down to the pool. He could stay out of the sun that way.

O'Brien watched him go, then turned and studied the crevice where the big lizard was supposed to live. There was nothing to do but wait. He hefted the rifle and walked back until he found a vantage spot. He made himself comfortable, drank from his water bottle and set it carefully in the shade. Using a bullet to kill a lizard, even a big one, did not appeal to him but if it was as big as Grimmelmann said it was, it might be worth it. He would see.

He watched the crevice.

An hour passed. Something moved. The lizard came halfway out of the hole and turned its reptilian head from one side to the other. O'Brien raised his rifle very slowly. The lizard was huge as Grimmelmann had said—a yard long, heavy and dragonlike. It would provide them with many meals.

He waited until it crawled ten feet from its hole and then squeezed the trigger. The lizard jumped and then flipped over on its back, its short legs clawing the air, its long tail whipping the sand.

He put the rifle down and walked toward it, hunting knife in hand. Then suddenly the lizard rolled over and began moving toward the hole in erratic strides. It was hurt and bleeding but it was moving too fast for him. He cursed and leapt for it, tried to turn it, flip it over, slow it down so he could stab it. But it was incredibly strong and he could not halt it. He felt the slippery tail slipping from his grasp. He dropped the knife and touched his sweaty hand to the sand and

[150]

grabbed just in time. The lizard's head vanished into the hole, its front legs found purchase on the hard rock, the heavy, meaty body began to move deeper into the crevice. O'Brien grunted and heaved; felt victory for one brief instant and then defeat as his pull slackened. In a moment only its long tail was visible. O'Brien let himself fall backwards in the sand and braced both feet against the cliff. He straightened his arms and leaned back, resting his muscles, letting the lizard fight his weight. The reptile fought and squirmed for a moment and then it too rested. They had reached a stalemate.

O'Brien) studied the heavy tail that he grasped. It was tough and covered with a scaly armor. He gave it a sudden jerk but nothing gave. He knew now that the lizard had inflated its body with air, that it was bigger than the opening, wedged into its narrow home. Getting it loose now would be difficult, a matter of stamina. He would have to wait until it bled to death or weakened from the strain of his constant pull.

The sun grew hot on his almost naked body. Insects, drawn by the blood, came and annoyed him. Ten minutes passed, half an hour. His arms ached. Sweat ran into his eyes. A fly stung his arched back.

Die, he told the lizard. Get it over with. Hurry.

His bullet must have missed the head entirely and passed through a less important place, the heavy folds of flesh under the neck perhaps. He had not checked the sights on the rifle. But he had spent a precious bullet on it nevertheless and he could not let it slither away into a hole to die and rot. He needed the meat.

The sun rose higher and burned down on his motionless body, on his bare head. He relaxed once and felt the lizard pulling away but he fought it and gained the lost inch. He could not relax. Never. He thought of the rifle and the knife six feet behind him on the sand. He had been careless.

And he was thirsty and thought of his water bottle sitting in the shade. He closed his eyes, shielding them from the glare. Let go, you son-of-a-bitch, he whispered. Bleed and go weak and quit. I'll never let you go, never.

More insects came and swirled around his sweaty face, gnats and heavy flies. They tortured him, crawling close to his eyes and into his nostrils, stinging him. He shook his head, tossing his long hair. He found himself shouting at them, trying to blow them away, cursing them. Once the torment was such that he used one hand to slap and squash them but the lizard began to pull against the one arm and he almost lost it.

[151]

He hung on, trying to rest one arm and then the other by letting each one bear the most pull in turn. He shifted his feet and his cramped legs. He kept his eyes shut all the time now, for he had no need of them and they were safe from the salty sweat and the tiny bugs. He began to tug and fight with the lizard and saw it in his mind: scaly and puffed with air, snake-eyes glinting with an ancient fire. Grimmelmann had said they were old creatures. The old man had talked to Smith about how perfect these big lizards were after eons of adaptation and selection.

He had never been so hot. He felt himself reeling, saw a thousand colored lights, felt nausea rise in his throat. The soles of his bare feet became raw from pushing against the hot stone. His whole body began to tremble.

Die, you son-of-a-bitch, die.

I'll never let you go, never.

Grimmelmann found him two hours later muttering and groaning, crouched against the scorching black cliff with a host of insects swirling around his great black-maned head. For a moment the old man could not move. O'Brien appeared to be dying. His drawn sweaty face, swollen from insect bites and bloody with their mashed pulp, was almost unrecognizable.

Grimmelmann picked up the knife and spoke quietly to him, half afraid that the shock of his presence would cause the big man to let go of the lizard. And then something happened which the old man never forgot. O'Brien opened his eyes, looked at him for a few seconds and *smiled*.

Grimmelmann held the knife in his teeth and bending down grabbed the tail ahead of O'Brien's white-knuckled fists. It came out of the crevice. Grimmelmann stabbed its underside, cut into its stomach, and the air went out of it and blood came and covered them, spurted in their faces. He stabbed again and again and O'Brien fell backwards as the reptile came free from the hole. Grimmelmann cut its throat and after a time O'Brien let go of it and staggered away toward his water bottle.

The old man carefully butchered the big lizard. He had changed his mind and come back rather than cross the canyon floor farther up and go to the pool. It was a good thing. O'Brien might have died soon from the sun and the great effort.

He wrapped the meat in his shirt and joined O'Brien in the shade of a rock slab. They stayed there the rest of the day resting and sipping their water. When the sun went down they walked slowly back to the cave.

A week passed. There were four of them now and the food that they found lasted longer. O'Brien shot a heronlike bird that he found roosting high on the cliff. And there were still plenty of melons and honey and lizards and good water. One night around the fire Bain suggested a hunting trip to O'Brien.

"I'm willing," said the big man. "We might get lucky and get a zebra or gemsbok."

"Anything would satisfy me," Bain said.

"We need more meat," Grimmelmann said. "Raw, red meat."

"You want to go tomorrow night?" O'Brien asked.

"Sure," Bain said. "I think I'm strong enough now to stick with you. You hunt and I'll lug the water. I'd like to see a nice sizzling chunk of meat again."

"We'll get something," O'Brien said. "And we might as well be out there hunting. All I can do here is stalk baboons and they're too smart for me now."

"I wonder where Smith is?" Bain said.

The others were silent for a time. They watched the fire leap against the blackened rock.

"He's dead," Grimmelmann said.

"There's always a chance that he might be holed up somewhere," O'Brien said. "After he left me he might have gone on for a few days and then stumbled upon a water hole somewhere. He might be there now."

"Dead," Grimmelmann said. "Both of them dead in the sand. I hope you two don't get such ideas. I tell you there is no way in or out of this place except for Bushmen who know where to suck in the sand for water. For them it is nothing. A hundred years ago this was a busy place. Coming and going. But Bantu and Boers were kept out by the great distances and the lack of surface water. It might well have been one of the last strongholds of the wild Bushmen. Then perhaps some refugees fell sick with smallpox and there was a great dying here, a great dying . . ."

The others listened and the old man grew suddenly self-conscious. He looked at Bain and O'Brien. "Do not try to get out of here, do not get the idea that Sturdevant got, and Smith. They were brave men but

[153]

foolish. We are a tiny speck in an ocean of desert and semidesert. If there was a way in, there would be signs of man here. White men would have carved their names on the soft stone near the water; there would be signs. No one between a Bushman and a modern man with an airplane can come here. You must know that by now. No others can cross the sand with wagons and oxen as they did in the old days and no man can carry enough water."

"They'll come back," Grace said.

"We will," O'Brien said. "This is a hunting trip. I've reached about the same idea as you," he said to Grimmelmann. "I'm going out after meat. When we get some we'll hurry back. If we have the water we'll camp and make biltong."

Grimmelmann nodded.

Bain and O'Brien slept late into the next day and when the sun grew weak they set off, each carrying makeshift packboards filled with ostrich eggs. And O'Brien carried his rifle. They walked in a new direction, resting each hour. When the sun came up they dug a wide trench in the sand, covered it with a few scarce lengths of thornbush and draped their clothes over it. They drank as much water as they wanted and lay naked in the relative coolness of the scant shade.

"How do you feel?" O'Brien asked.

"I'm tired but so are you," Bain said. "I think I can stay with you if you don't push it."

"This life agrees with you," O'Brien said. "You look better every day. You've lost the fat and you seem stronger, have better wind."

"Except for the constant hunger I do feel better," Bain said. "If we only had more to eat . . ."

"We can't last long back there," O'Brien said. "Too many of us still, even with Sturdevant and Smith gone."

"Overpopulation," Bain said.

"I may try to make a break for it soon," O'Brien said.

"Don't be nuts," Bain said. He yawned.

"I might do it," O'Brien said. "We can't go on too much longer. Not four people."

"Maybe a plane will spot us," Bain said.

"Ten years from now," said O'Brien.

Bain closed his eyes and felt the weariness in him. He wiggled in the sand and made himself comfortable. He fell asleep with O'Brien talking to him.

Evening.

They got up and began walking across the sand that was still hot. Streaks of orange in the sky and then the sand became purple and a breeze came. They stopped for ten minutes and sipped some water.

"Smith must have been nuts to try it," Bain said.

"I told him that," said O'Brien. He squatted in the sand squinting, always alert for movement. For an instant he reminded Bain of the soldiers on Saipan, bearded and filthy and very dangerous in their holes. One of them had almost shot him by mistake.

"He was a good Joe," Bain said.

O'Brien nodded. He got up and Bain followed and they walked on. It became dark. The moon turned the landscape a grayish white.

Bain thought the night would never end. He fell behind O'Brien and then, when the hunter rested and waited for him, they decided it was best to walk apart. O'Brien first, ready with the rifle, and Bain behind.

Just before dawn a miracle happened. O'Brien walked up a rise, peered over it and saw a great herd of gemsbok, hundreds of them standing silently and motionless in the moonlight. He blinked and unslung his rifle just as they began to race away. He fired three shots.

Bain came up and they searched the area as the light came. They found a big animal lying in the sand still alive. They moved away from it; the wound was mortal and the animal would not get away. They could not spare another bullet to put it out of its misery.

Mike Bain wandered off and began to collect thorn branches and O'Brien started to butcher the gemsbok. Flies came from nowhere and gathered on the raw, bloody meat.

They made a small fire and roasted strips of choice meat, bolted them down half-cooked. They drank deeply from the eggshells.

"Two days from the mountain," O'Brien said.

"How much can we carry?" Bain asked.

"I don't know," the big man said, wiping his beard. "Two days' walk is rough with a heavy load. We'll have to see."

"You hit the jackpot," Bain told him. The hunger pain was going, he could feel strength returning.

"If I'd missed one of them I think I'd have shot myself," O'Brien said. "All that meat . . . it's fantastic that they can live in such large herds. Grimmelmann told me once of seeing great herds of zebra, hundreds, thousands. I believe him now."

"I keep thinking about Sturdevant," Bain said. "He had the other rifle. Maybe he's still going."

"I'd like to think so," O'Brien said. "I liked that Dutchman but I think he's been gone too long. They'd be able to find this mountain of ours if anybody could get to the outside. But nobody knows we're lost."

Bain cut another piece of meat with the sharp hunting knife, dropped it in the fire. "You think he's dead then?"

O'Brien nodded. "We might be twenty miles from help right this moment. Or five hundred and twenty. Sturdevant was just unlucky. The next guy may not be. Maybe Smith made it. He had a lot of water and maybe he'll get lucky."

The sun grew hotter; swarms of black flies gathered on the meat.

"Let's bury it and find some shelter," O'Brien said. "I can't eat any more for a while anyway."

They got up and groaned. They had stuffed themselves with the meat and now they had to bury it before the sun and the flies spoiled it completely. They scraped a shallow hole in the sand, pulled the carcass into it and covered it. The flies fought for it until the last, dying with the meat they sought, suffocating under the sand. O'Brien cursed them.

"I saw something when I was getting wood," Bain said.

They picked up their packboards and walked on. A rock angled up from the stony soil creating a pocket of shade, enough for their bodies and the precious water. They crawled under it and fell asleep almost instantly.

The sun ruled the land and nothing moved. The ants fled underground to their cool caverns, to their cisterns of water. The heat shimmered across the baked land. The sun descended, grew weak, made long shadows. Evening came. A slight breeze.

In the shadow of the rock the two men slept.

CHAPTER VII

G RACE MONCKTON and Grimmelmann were eating breakfast when they looked up and saw O'Brien. He came up the
canyon with a great burden on his back. For an instant they thought
it was Bain but as he came closer they saw that it was a heavy load
of raw meat. The big man's shoulders and arms were caked with
blood, sticky with sand. A swarm of small gnats and flies worried him.

He was too tired to speak. He went past them into the cave and
they followed, helped him cover up the precious meat to protect it
from the sun and the egg-laying flies.

He stretched out on a torn blanket, groaned. They brought him
water, honeycomb.

"Bain left me," he said. "Left. Gone. Just like that crazy Smith . . ."

"You came back *alone?*" Grimmelmann asked. "You permitted him
to leave you?"

O'Brien closed his eyes. "He left while I was sleeping. Took all the
eggshells but one. I just made it back to the last station. I followed
his tracks for two, three hours. Had no water for much more. Lucky
he left me the rifle."

Grace Monckton began to cry. She walked away and went to her
bed. She wanted to lie in the darkness. Think. Mike Bain now. One
of them. Throwing his life away on a slim gamble of finding the
outside. She could hear Grimmelmann talking with O'Brien and then
the talking stopped and the old man went outside.

Now there were three of them.

They gorged themselves on the gemsbok that O'Brien had brought
back with him, dried much of it and hung it in the larder at the back
of the cave.

O'Brien went off each morning and came back in the late afternoon with lizards he found in the far canyons. Grace and Grimmelmann went together and searched the nearby cliffs and the old haunts they knew so well.

Another dawn. Another breakfast at the cave's mouth after they had carried out the night fire and gathered their food before it. O'Brien had found nothing in the last two days. The meat was gone. They ate melons and honey and drank warm water. In the evening perhaps they would have lizards.

"I saw bees the other day," O'Brien said.

"Where?" Grace asked.

"In the far canyon," he said. "I'd like to find another big store of honey. It's probably keeping us alive, more than the lizard meat and the other stuff."

"I'll go with you," Grimmelmann said. "We'll bring some comb and see if we can't find the hive. When the sun is just right you can see them flying, follow them."

"Good," O'Brien said. "You coming, Grace?"

She looked at him. "No, it's too far to walk and climb. I'll stay here this time."

Grimmelmann waved his hand, nodded. "It is far. Even for me it is too far but I shall go. I am good with bees, I have a feeling for them."

"If this doesn't work I'll have to start going off into the desert," O'Brien said. "We need some more gemsbok. If only one of them would come around . . ."

"Maybe Bain will come back in a plane," Grace said.

O'Brien nodded. "I hope so. I feel guilty about him, and Smith too. When you get out there you get the feeling that there's a fence or road beyond the next hill, over the next rise. It's sort of a strange disease that grips you."

Grimmelmann got up. "Let us find the bees," he said.

They left.

Grace cleaned up around the rock, washed away the grease stains, covered them with clean sand to keep the flies away. She fed the fire scraps of wood and carried the melon rinds away and buried them.

She was hot, sweaty. She went into the cave and found the small laundry bag with her clean clothes, her brushes and combs, all that she had taken with her from the plane.

[158]

She walked to the pool and took off her clothes. She took one of the cans, dipped it into the cool water and poured it over her until she was completely wet. The few bars of soap were only memories now and so she walked a few yards to where there was a sandy spot and rubbed handfuls of it over her, scouring the bronzed skin. She went back to the pool and doused herself, washed the sand away. She felt wonderfully clean and new.

She sat on the wet slab of stone and combed her hair, let the sun warm her. Her comb found snarls in the heavy blond hair but after a time it was neat, orderly. She searched for her scissors and trimmed her hair until it fell just short of her brown shoulders.

The sun had dried her. She found clean clothes in the bag, underwear that was shrunken and threadbare, a rumpled blouse, a skirt that was too large for her now. Her feet were bare; her flimsy shoes and loafers had fallen apart long ago.

She wished O'Brien were with her now. She wanted him to see her fresh and clean and beautiful.

She was hungry. She drank all the water she could, picked up her bag and walked back to the cave. She ate some honey and part of a melon and then fell asleep in the cool sand waiting for the men to come back.

It took O'Brien and Grimmelmann two hours to get to the place that O'Brien had described; they had to cross the main canyon floor, climb the cliff and walk along it until they found a way down. Then they rested for a time in the shade and walked in the opposite direction down the third canyon until they were able to ascend the next ridge. At last they found themselves in the most distant canyon, the one they had started calling Lizard Canyon. It was half as broad as the main one and the least known. The two men rested again in the shade close to the spot where they had descended.

"It was foolish for me to come," Grimmelmann said. "An old man should have more sense." He fanned himself with his hand.

O'Brien said nothing. He sat upright, not quite relaxed, trying to make out something far away on the opposite ridge. It might be a gemsbok. A baboon. Grimmelmann knew that the big man hadn't heard a word he'd said. He stood up.

"Well, where are all these bees of yours?"

O'Brien was on his feet, moving away, ahead of him. "This way, only a few hundred feet." Grimmelmann followed, not hurrying.

There was no need to hurry and he knew that his slowness upset O'Brien. And he was irked now with the hunter for not listening to him.

O'Brien stopped and waited for him. Grimmelmann came and stopped. Close to the rock wall in the clean sand, in a spot that was always protected from the sun, was the bottom of one of the suitcases that they had brought with them from the plane. It had been made into a packboard and contained several ostrich eggs held in place by thin strips of leather and cord. The two leather straps had been fixed to slip over each shoulder. It was much like the other packs he had made for Smith and Bain, like the one O'Brien had fashioned for himself.

"It's for you," O'Brien said.

The old man looked at the pack for a long minute.

"I had a feeling about you," he said. "Did you force Bain to go, and Smith? I thought of that once. We only heard your version of what happened. But I will tell you this. I am not going."

"I made them go and I'm making you go," O'Brien said. "You will go in an entirely new direction; you are the fourth and you will make it. I have a map for you which will lead you to three more shells I planted out there on the hunting trips. After that you can start on these."

"Why did you make them go?" Grimmelmann said. "Why are there always those like you who force others to their will, to destruction?"

"We can't all stay here," the big man said. "You know that better than any of us."

"Then let us die," the old man said. "Let us eat the last melon and the last of the honey and the last lizard or whatever else and then die. There is no need for us to send each other to death in the desert. Sturdevant was a fool and went by himself but the others . . . you have killed them. Their blood is on your hands."

"They had to go," O'Brien said.

"You have no right to decide who shall go."

"All of you will go," said O'Brien.

"I am not going," Grimmelmann said. "I'm going back to the cave. If I die there I have done my best. I will not throw my life away because of a man with a gun. I am tired of your kind. You have already destroyed me. . . ."

"Go," O'Brien said softly. "Go or I'll kill you."

"I refuse," the old man told him.

"I'll shoot you," O'Brien said. He stepped closer.

"An execution?" Grimmelmann asked.

"Call it what you will," the hunter said. "It's all the same. Death."

The old man almost smiled. Threats, always threats. Always someone in front of him with a gun telling him to do what he didn't want to do. And always before he had shivered a little inside and then obeyed, telling himself he was not being bullied, telling himself all the lies he had always told himself. The blood that was on his hands now . . . Herero and Russian and the old SA members . . .

"I'll fight you first," he told O'Brien. He shifted his feet, fixed the brim of his hat. His right hand went into the pocket of his old windbreaker, found something there, something hard, the long flint, the spearhead he'd found among the ostrich shells.

"It's too late to fight," O'Brien said.

Grimmelmann nodded. Too late, too late. His fingers curled around the long flint; his fist felt heavy; he felt the sharp point protruding knifelike from his sweaty hand. He had a weapon.

"Pick up the shells," O'Brien said. He came another step closer, waved the rifle toward the pack.

Grimmelmann nodded. No. Never. He was conscious of being alone, as alone as a man ever could be: the Herero boy standing alone as the officer walked up and carefully leveled his pistol, the Russian *Kriegies* kneeling in the snow. . . .

He'd die fighting; he'd get O'Brien's gun, smash it; he'd hit the big man, scare him, hurt him. *He would not obey.*

His clenched fist came out of his pocket. He started forward.

"*Stop!*" O'Brien screamed. "*Stop it!*"

But the old man came on, his fist raised, the two inches of sharp stone protruding from his fist; he came like a man drugged, eyes fixed, his old face set in elation and hate.

"*Stop!*" O'Brien shouted and then the old man was upon him.

He waited until the last instant and then stepped aside, swinging the heavy rifle. The barrel hit the old man's right arm; Grimmelmann staggered, tried to catch his balance and went down heavily.

"You old fool," O'Brien said. "Can't you see that it's too late to fight?" He stood for a few moments and looked down at the old man. Then he turned and went off up the canyon.

Grimmelmann rested on the ground. His hand was bleeding. He had gripped the spearhead too hard. He sat up and let the flint fall in the sand. He was happy; not because he was alive but because of the great thing he had done. He had fought evil. He was a good man now. A good man.

A wave of dizziness came over him. He must get out of the sun, rest in the shade and then go back to the girl. O'Brien might be waiting somewhere to shoot him but it did not matter. He was old and had survived so much and now he was a good man . . . *good.* . . .

His hand felt numb. He brushed it against his leg, wiped away the bloody sand, studied the half-inch cut in the palm and knew that he was dying; that he would be dead in a matter of minutes.

The palm of his hand was blue black and there were streaks of blackness moving up toward the ends of his numbed fingers and up to his wrist. There was Bushman poison on the flint; he had squeezed it too hard, cut himself. He had beaten O'Brien but he would die now of old poisons.

He sat in the sun and he was not afraid. It was better to die in the sun than in the cold of Europe. The sun was warm; long ago he had been young here, a long time ago.

Long ago. A Bushman sitting cross-legged with his weapons and poisons, readying himself for the hunt or for war against the white man. He daubs poison of great virulence on the stone point of a new spear. Long ago . . .

He was suddenly blind and there was a ringing in his ears. He let himself down on the sand with his left arm, felt the earth begin to spin under him, faster, faster, faster.

The poison reached his heart; he shuddered and died.

A wasp, brightly barred, metallic, swift, flies low over the shimmering ground looking for spiders. It has a mud-daub nest somewhere in a lost cranny of the black cliff, a nest containing its own grub that it will fill with spiders and then seal.

A brown fly sees it and follows, a big fly, slow-moving, inoffensive. It follows the smaller insect, keeping high, in the sun. It waits. The wasp finds a web glinting in the light. It comes close, hovers in the air hardly moving.

Suddenly the brown fly has the wasp in its great long legs. They struggle as the fly lifts it higher into the air. The wasp tries to turn and reach the fly's body with its dreadful stinger, to stab it, paralyze it. The fly knows this, holds the wasp far away from its fat abdomen. The wasp, desperate now, tries to pull away, get free. It is no match for the powerful legs.

The long sharp proboscis of the fly comes down, stabs into the wasp's back. In a moment it is all over. The big brown fly moves away; the wasp's body falls to the sand and the breeze catches it and rolls it along. It is hollow. The fly has sucked it dry.

O'Brien came back to the cave as the sun was setting. Grace waited for him in the entrance with a few sticks of wood she had found. He was alone.

"Where's the old man?"

"He's dead," O'Brien said.

"I had a feeling when I saw you," she said. They were alone now, just the two of them. She wondered why Grimmelmann's death didn't shock her, and it came to her that she had somehow sensed it. And another thought came to her that she tried to shake away, that shamed her: there would be more food now for her and O'Brien and she would be totally alone with him.

"He cut himself on that Bushman flint of his," O'Brien said. "There was poison on it and it killed him. We were going along looking for bees and he fell behind. When I looked back he was staggering, reeling, as if he couldn't see where he was going. His hand was bleeding from a little cut. He sat down and his arm suddenly started to grow black. Five minutes later he was dead. There wasn't anything I could do. It was terrible, horrible. He found that flint with the ostrich eggs and carried it around in his pocket." He walked past her into the cave and put his rifle in the niche.

Grace carried the fire into the cave and dumped the glowing coals on the blackened embers of last night's fire. O'Brien's bag contained four lizards and a wizened narras cucumber. The lizards had already been cleaned and she cooked them quickly on the wire grill that Smith had invented. They ate the meat with plenty of honey and shared the cucumber.

Night came, bringing the cold. They piled more wood on the fire and hurried into the sleeping bag, shivering for a time, seeking the warmth of each other's body, relaxing.

"How did he happen to cut himself?" she asked. She dug her fingers into his heavy shoulders, felt the great power in them. There was something else about Grimmelmann's death that he hadn't told her, something vague and yet fearful that she could not voice.

"There's nothing more," he said. His fingers found her face and turned it, he kissed her mouth, her cheek, her neck. She thought of

[163]

her ex-husband and he seemed so far away . . . Andrew Monckton, a gentle lover, kind and considerate. And that's all he had been, kind and considerate.

"We can make it now," O'Brien was telling her. "You and I can beat this place. Live. The two of us."

But now she wasn't concerned. Her arms were around his neck and she didn't care about Grimmelmann or survival or anything else except *him*. There was nothing else in the black cold world except O'Brien's sweaty-hot body enveloping her, loving her, shielding her from the prehistoric night.

The two of them.

The sun rules. The naked rock shivers in the heat. The heat is intense.

A brown fly, old and thin, crawls over a pocket of powdered shale and wind-blown sand high on the narrow ridge. Its wings are frayed, shriveled, worn out, its sight is almost gone. It runs crazily across the hot stone now, wings whirring, leaving the ground briefly, falling back again.

The scorpion sees it, waits, follows. Its lobsterlike claws are readied, its segmented abdomen arched. In the last section of the long body is a sharp and deadly stinger; its enemies know this and are wary, for the potency of its poison is great. Men have died of it. The fly turns, sees the scorpion too late—a monster at eye level. It flees but the great claws take it, kill it, bring it to the cruel mouth.

The meal satisfies the big scorpion. It lingers in the sun, content, master of its narrow world. Brown flies are rare; ants and tiny red rock spiders are more common or bees overloaded with heavy nectar, resting on their flight to a secret hive.

Now the scorpion dies.

A young baboon reaches out over a rock, picks up the insect and holds it wiggling in the air. Some mystery of instinct teaches it that the stinger contains virulent poison; the humanoid fingers hold the segmented body gingerly. The scorpion struggles, tries to reach the hairy hand with its flicking tail. If it does the sudden pain alone might drive the young baboon mad and cause it to leap blindly off the sheer cliff. But the stinger is never used. With his free hand the baboon reaches behind the insect and snaps off the last of the seven segments from which the barbed stinger writhes in torment. The scorpion is helpless now. The baboon throws the stinger aside, examines his prize, pulls off the annoying claws and eats it in one quick, lip-smacking gulp.

Now the baboon turns and begins to wander back along the ridge to the great jagged base of the mountain. It has strayed from the troop but it has found food, a tasty tidbit; it has not been pushed aside by the stronger males, the violent females snatching everything for their babies. It moves along the top of the ridge on all fours, a loping, slow-motion run.

In the next instant it is dead.

O'Brien has stalked it for over an hour, a shadow, noiseless, crawling, inching from rock to rock even though a great distance separates him from his prey, hundreds of yards.

Then the single moment when existence narrows down to the black sharp lines in the telescopic sight. The hairlines converge on the baboon's back, the sweaty trigger finds release, the rifle convulses in his arms, there is the sharp smell of powder, the brassy *ping* of the ejected shell.

The young baboon catches the heavy bullet in the spine. It leaps high into the air, arch-backed, broken and dead as it comes down on a slanting rock and slides off into space.

The air is torn with the terror-filled barks of the baboon sentinels. The troop flees, shivering from the memory of the rifleshot. Death is among them; they do not understand it.

It becomes quiet again. Nothing moves. The heat sends shimmering waves over the stone and shale.

Grace Monckton sat in front of the cave warming herself in the morning sun. O'Brien had left while she was still asleep; when she had opened her eyes she'd been all alone in the cave, and it had frightened her. She quickly moved the fire outside, ate her meager breakfast.

Somewhere in a gorge was O'Brien, a big silent shadow moving from rock to rock, seeking things to kill, things to eat. . . .

She added a few gnarled sticks to the fire. She and O'Brien were alone now and they would never leave the black mountain. They would not be rescued. They would stay here and grow old and die.

It had been obvious from the start. If they had been close to the outside world, close to water, there would be sheep in the canyon or a few head of cattle. The precious water and the grass would be used by someone; there would be signs of white men or black, old campsites, wagon tracks from the old days of the *trekboers*, something to show that they were within the pale of civilization. But there were no traces of man, nothing to show that anyone had ever been in the canyon except the Bushmen, and that had been a long, long time ago.

They would not be saved. A plane might fly over and see them. A motorized expedition might cross the vast sand wastes and find them, but it might be in the next century.

She went into the cave and drank what was left in one of the water bottles. She picked up one of the empty ostrich shells and walked out into the sunlight again, headed for the pool. She would bathe and re-fill the water containers.

She made her way up the canyon to the pool, stood before it at last, started to undress.

Something moved in the rocks to her left. A man. Fear stabbed her heart . . . *a wild Bushman* . . . she turned wildly and began to run, heard herself screaming for O'Brien.

Mike Bain caught her and held her, cupped his hand over her mouth. She stopped struggling, terror fled from her eyes. He let go.

She stood before him, sobbing. But the tears welled up from happiness now. *Mike was back . . . he was not dead, he was not dead.*

"Where's O'Brien?" Bain asked. His voice was tense and hard.

She couldn't talk, she was wiping tears from her eyes, trying to button her open blouse.

"Where's O'Brien?"

"He's hunting," Grace said. "Where did you come from? O'Brien said you left him, tried to reach the outside. We thought you were dead."

Bain took her arm and led her into the shadow of a rock slab. They were out of sight here.

"O'Brien abandoned me out there, Grace. He told me to keep walking, not to come back. He had his rifle on me, said he'd kill me if I returned. And he did the same thing to Smith. He admitted it."

She didn't believe him. He was filthy and haggard and his voice cracked; he looked as if he might faint any moment. The sun had made him a little crazy.

"Sit down, Mike," she said. "We've got some food. You need rest, lots of rest . . ."

"He'll kill you next," Bain was saying. "And Grimmelmann and me. If he finds I'm back he'll shoot me. That's why I waited for you here, to tell you."

"Grimmelmann's dead," she said.

"Dead?"

"He's dead," Grace said. "He cut himself on that flint spearhead he found; it still had poison on it."

"Who was with him? You?"

"No. He went off with O'Brien to look for honey. In one of the other canyons."

"O'Brien's a murderer, Grace. He killed Grimmelmann. He tried to kill me. He made Smith go off in the desert at the point of a gun. Two days out from here he did the same with me. Don't you believe me?"

Grace Monckton slumped down in the sand. "It can't be true, Mike. You must be wrong. You've *got* to be."

"You believe me," Bain said.

She looked at him for a long time. "I don't know. There's a streak of ruthlessness in him. He might be capable of it." But she loved him. She belonged to him.

"Do you need water?" Bain asked. He nodded toward the bottle and the big shell.

"Yes."

"Let's get it then and get back to the cave," Bain said. "We've got to be there when he comes back. I've got to get the rifle away from him. He'll kill me if I don't get him first."

"*Kill* him?" Grace asked.

"If I have to," Bain said.

"What are you going to do?"

"I don't know. I should kill him, I suppose, but I'm not capable of executing a man, not even him."

"I can't believe it," Grace said.

"There's a good chance of O'Brien being the sole survivor," Bain said. "Some guy will fly over. O'Brien will be waiting. Alone. He'll tell them about the crash and how we all died one by one. Grimmelmann died of poison and I died of snakebite and you died of sunstroke. O'Brien will survive."

Grace shuddered. "Stop, Mike. It's too horrible." It was impossible. . . .

They hurried away from the pool.

She wondered if Grimmelmann's death was accidental. She'd felt something when she'd seen O'Brien coming back alone but it had all been swept away by her need for him. *She hadn't cared.*

[167]

They waited in the cave for O'Brien.

And he came. Grace stood in the entrance, hands on hips, and saw him in the distance. Her lover.

"Here he is," she said simply and in the darkness Bain grew suddenly frightened; his hand began to sweat on the wrench. If something went wrong he would be dead in a very short time and he did not want to die now that he had lived through so much: the crash, the first terrible week with the fever and the infection and the desire to die strong in him. He crouched in the darkness and began to pray that he'd beat O'Brien this time.

O'Brien came. Barefooted, hatless, without a shirt, hard, long-haired, beautifully muscled and burned cordovan brown by the African sun—a man who thrived on privation and hardship.

"Very soon now," Grace said. She stood and waited and wondered if she could go through with it. O'Brien was a hundred yards away now, fifty, twenty-five. He carried a lumpy bag in his left hand. Tsamma melons. He held them in the air.

"I found some nice ones," he said.

"Wonderful," Grace said.

He came on, stood before her, the rifle in one hand, the bag in the other. He bent down suddenly and kissed her, her lips, her neck.

He started into the cave.

"O'Brien?"

He turned, scowled.

"There's something I've got to tell you."

O'Brien waited. He wanted to go into the cave to drink and rest.

"I've got a feeling about Grimmelmann," she said. She took a deep breath. "I think you killed him." She had to know, she had to decide before she'd let him go into the cave where Bain waited in the darkness.

"I didn't kill him," O'Brien said.

She believed him. She had a choice to make between truth and hallucination, between the men.

He started into the cave again.

"Stop," she said. "Mike Bain's in there. Don't go in. He's waiting for you with his wrench."

O'Brien swung his rifle up and backed away. Grace moved away from him. "He's in there in the dark," she said. "He said you abandoned him in the desert. He's in a terrible state, imagining all sorts of things. We've got to help him. . . . He thinks you're going to shoot him."

But O'Brien didn't seem to hear her. He stopped, moved backwards. It grew very quiet. There was the hum of insects and the implacable heat beating down on the hot stone. A long minute passed. Two.

Mike Bain walked out of the cave. He stopped and looked at Grace and then O'Brien. He seemed to weave, to totter, a dirty, bearded man in tattered rags that had once been a white linen suit, squinting in the harsh sunlight. His left hand was knotted into a fist, his right hand held the big wrench.

"Tell her the truth," he said. He started to walk to the big man.

O'Brien backed away. "Don't come any closer," he said. "Stay away. I'm warning you."

But Bain didn't stop. "Tell her the truth!" He came on, the wrench held higher, the left fist reaching out.

O'Brien backed away. "Stay away from me, Bain, or I'll have to hurt you. You've been in the sun; you're sick. Put the wrench down."

Grace sobbed and ran toward Bain. She grabbed his arm and for a moment he was helpless. O'Brien was running toward him.

He swore and flung Grace away with a sudden desperate fury. The girl fell heavily in the sand. Bain leaped away and crouched with the big wrench ready, waited for O'Brien.

But the big man stopped. They were ten feet apart.

"I'll shoot you," O'Brien said. "Put the wrench down or I'll kill you." He was afraid of what the wrench might do to his rifle. If Bain rushed him and struck the barrel, it would be useless.

He stooped and placed the rifle on the sand. Then he rose.

Grace Monckton sat up in the sand. The cliff above was weaving; there were two suns; the ground swayed under her. Her elbow hurt. She rubbed it and saw that the skin had been scraped raw, that it bled.

She got up and walked toward O'Brien and Mike Bain, shouted at them. The ground spun and she lost her balance and slumped to the sand.

She saw Bain and O'Brien circling each other like boxers in a ring. Bain's wrench glinted in the sun. The big man was barehanded and feinting. Once he got his hands on Bain it would be over in an instant. He was big enough and strong enough to pick the smaller man up and hurl him ten feet.

And then he charged Bain, reaching for the big wrench. For one terrible instant Bain hesitated; then his left fist opened and he flung the fine cave sand into O'Brien's face. And in the same instant he swung on his left heel, the wrench held straight out from his body. He spun completely around, his back toward O'Brien who momentarily fought blindness and imbalance. The wrench hit the black-maned head. O'Brien took one step, then fell to the sand.

Grace blinked. Bain had won. O'Brien had underestimated him. And maybe she had. Maybe he was telling the truth. . . . O'Brien had been afraid of him, strangely afraid.

She got up and went to Bain.

"He was afraid of you," she said.

"*Believe me,* Grace, believe me for ten minutes. If I can't prove it, I'll let him go."

She nodded. They dragged O'Brien out of the sun into the cave. Bain tied his hands behind him with a piece of the long rope.

"Can I trust you to bring me the rifle?" he asked.

Grace left. She came back and handed the rifle to him. It was loaded. He found more shells in O'Brien's small bag.

They examined O'Brien's head, saw that the skull wasn't fractured. Bain poured some water on his bearded face and the big man groaned and started to regain consciousness. Bain motioned Grace away. She left him, retreated into the darkness deeper in the cave.

O'Brien opened his eyes, struggled up, cursed when he realized his hands were bound in back of him.

"Untie me, Bain."

"Not a chance," Mike said. He stood in the cave entrance with the rifle. O'Brien could be dangerous even with his hands tied. He was taking no chances.

O'Brien looked around. "Where's Grace?"

"She went to the pool for more water," Bain lied. "We poured a lot of it over you."

"Look," the big man said, "I'm sorry about what I did to you out there. But I had to do it, don't you understand? You and Smith would never have gone off by yourselves; you're not the type. You needed me to push you. And you came back anyway, so what's the kick?"

"What did you do to Grimmelmann?"

"Nothing," O'Brien said. "You think I killed him. You're wrong. He was a stubborn old fool. I wanted him to take a crack at crossing the desert but he refused to go. I had the whole thing set up: water points, a map, a pack of shells, everything. But he wouldn't go. Then he came

[170]

at me with that spear point. He fell and cut himself and died from the old poison on it."

"Then you did kill him," Bain said.

"I told you the truth," O'Brien said. "I didn't kill you, did I? I could have shot you. . . ."

"Why didn't you try to make it across the desert?" Bain asked. "Why old Grimmelmann?"

"His luck was as good as mine," the big man said. "He was old and his life was almost over anyway. If he'd failed he still would have helped us."

"One less mouth to feed?" Bain asked.

"Sure," O'Brien said. "What else?"

Grace Monckton came out of the blackness, walked into the sunlight and stood next to Mike Bain.

"You lied to me," she said to O'Brien. "If you'd told me the truth I might have gone along with you even if it was so terrible, so wrong. Now I can't trust you. I can't believe you. Ever."

"And I'm afraid of you," Bain said. "If I turn you loose, give the rifle back, I think you'd shoot the two of us. Then you'd have all the food."

O'Brien threw back his head and laughed long and loud. He looked at Grace. "Do you really believe that?"

"Yes," Grace said. "What you did to Smith is close to murder. It is murder."

"I thought he could find help for us," O'Brien said.

"Why didn't you try it?" Bain asked.

"I told you. I'm more valuable here. I can hunt. I got meat for you, didn't I? I knocked off a lot of baboons. What did Smith ever do for us? The old German was okay because he was smart and knew about the desert. And I came next in importance because I'm a hunter. I had no real right to make Smith go, or to make you go, but you have no right to tie me up either. You're wrong now. There are three of us left. We've got to stick together."

"We're going for a walk," Bain said. "Get up."

"Where?"

"Get up!" Bain turned to Grace. "Bring the coil of rope and the canteen filled with water. He's going in the pit."

"Don't be silly," O'Brien said. "Let me loose." He turned to Grace. "Don't let him do this to me, Grace. Can't you see what he's got in

[171]

mind? He wants to kill me. He wants you. The sun drove him crazy out there. . . ."

But Grace was gone. He got up slowly and shook the sand from his head. They moved out of the cave.

"I have no choice," Bain said. "It's me or you."

O'Brien stood and looked at Bain for a long while, studying his face. Then he walked off up the canyon toward the pool. Grace came out of the cave with the coil of rope and the canteen. She walked in back of Bain.

They came to the pool and went on and began climbing the cliff. Bain kept well behind O'Brien, certain that the big man would try something. Then they reached the top and stood high above the desert on the inky rock and felt the slight breeze. The sun beat down on them, glinted on O'Brien's sweaty muscles.

Bain motioned with the rifle and they went on and five minutes later they came to the strange round hole that they had discovered so long ago. It was fifteen feet deep and almost as wide, an unusual pit in the living rock with sides as smooth as glass, scoured by the wind-blown sands of thousands of years.

"Lie down," he told O'Brien.

"Help me, Grace," the big man said. "Don't let him put me down there. I can't help you from there. You'll be all alone with a crazy man."

"Lie down," Bain said. "Don't make me knock you out again. It might be fatal next time."

O'Brien got down to his knees and then rolled sideways until he was prostrate. Bain moved away and circled the pit, found a suitable place to tie the rope. He made it fast around an elevated slab and threw the other end into the hole. He went back to O'Brien and stood close to him, the rifle pointed at his head.

"Untie him, Grace," he said. "Loosen the knot and then back away." The girl bent down and began working on the tangle of rope around the big man's wrists. In a few minutes they were loose and she backed away behind Bain, out of O'Brien's reach.

"Don't get up now," Bain said. "Do just as I tell you. If you get to your feet I'll shoot."

"I believe you," O'Brien said.

"Crawl to the rope," Bain said.

"You're afraid of me, aren't you?"

"You're damned right I am," Bain said. "That's why you're going in the pit."

"I think I might stand up and take my rifle back," O'Brien said.

"Go ahead," Bain said. "It might be better for you that way."

But O'Brien didn't get up. He crawled to the rope and slid down it to the bottom of the pit. Bain pulled up the rope and threw down the canteen of water. "We'll be back later with some melons and honeycomb and whatever we can find for you," he told O'Brien.

"Thanks," the big man said. "I'll remember when I get out of here. I'll be nice to you for a while." He walked back and forth in the bottom of the hole like a caged animal.

"Can he get out?" Grace whispered. She was suddenly afraid, seeing him loose again.

Bain shook his head. "A lizard couldn't get up those walls."

"Bring some clothes too," O'Brien said. "It'll be cold here at night."

"You mean you plan to stay?" Bain asked.

"I'll be down some night to wake you up," O'Brien said.

"Make sure it's me," Bain told him.

O'Brien laughed. "Get me out of here, Grace, before it's too late. When you realize what he is, come back and get me out."

But Grace didn't answer. She backed away from the hole and walked off in the direction they had come. Bain coiled the rope and followed her.

O'Brien heard them leave, listened as they walked away. He was beaten; they had tricked him but his day would come.

He walked around the walls. Impossible. Rock as hard as steel and slippery; overhang; a centipede couldn't escape. There wasn't any point now in thinking of escape. Bain wouldn't leave him without food and water. He would wait. His weapon was time.

Solitary confinement. The nights would be cold. He'd have to beg Bain for an old coat, a jacket. He could be here forever . . . for years. He shook the thought from his head. He was here for one day. One day at a time. And a day was coming when he would be up and out of the pit and then he would never again be imprisoned.

Before night came Bain and Grace returned to the pit. They threw down two blankets, Sturdevant's sleeping bag, a sweater. The nights were cold on top of the escarpment but it would be impossible to bring enough wood for a fire. And it would be dangerous. Bain wasn't fully convinced that O'Brien was helpless in the big hole; he did not relish the idea of throwing wood down for the big man. O'Brien was too inventive, too clever.

They tossed six melons down to him and some honeycombs and two pieces of the dried meat.

"Get me out of here," O'Brien said.

"I'm afraid of you," Bain said. "And so is Grace."

"That can't be true."

"It is," Grace said. "Something happened to you, something I feel, something I don't even understand."

O'Brien put his head back and laughed; his white teeth flashed and the long black hair hung down, touching his muscled shoulders. He shook his head as if it were all some enormous joke. Grace glanced sideways at Bain and for a moment they both felt sorry for the big man in the hole. Maybe it was all a mistake.

"You better let me come up, Bain," O'Brien said. "I'll go along with this for a while because you're upset and you're blaming me for everything. In a couple of days I'm going to get mad and get out of here and then I might put you down here. Both of you. Better let me out while I'm in a good mood."

"You can't get out," Bain said.

"We'll see," O'Brien said. "Sometime you'll come here and see that I'm gone and you'll look in back of you and hurry back to the cave. And maybe I'll be there waiting for you. Or I might be watching you from the cliffs, waiting for the night to come, waiting for you to fall asleep over my rifle."

"You can't get out," Bain said. "You look like a bug in a drinking glass. You need wings to get out."

"I'm warning you, Bain, for the last time. Let me out."

"I'm sorry," Grace said. "We can't do it. You turned Smith and Mike loose in the desert and you tried it with the old man. We'll keep you here until help comes." She turned to Bain. "Let's go now, Mike."

They left and O'Brien was alone again. Night came and it grew cold and he lay in the sleeping bag, his brain turning slowly on the possibilities of escape.

And he would escape; there was no doubt in his mind. He would escape because he would direct his entire energy and will to it. Escape from the pit was survival and the secret of survival was adaptation. It was as simple as that. You adapted to a situation or a time or a place or you died. The survival of the fittest was the survival of the most adaptable; that was why man had come the long way from forager to

[174]

master of all. The human body was a weak and pathetic thing. But it could adapt; it could do nothing well but many things half well; it had the miracle of change within it and through the great gulfs of time it did change and adjust and survive while thousands of other forms vanished.

For modern man, survival meant mental change. The stubborn died as martyrs; the fanatic and the philosopher perished in the face of sudden change. To survive now one had to be pliable; one had to adjust to new codes and ideals and morals. The mind had to change.

O'Brien grunted. He'd survive because he was the most pliable of all of them. He had no beliefs to discard, no codes, no rules; for him it was easy.

CHAPTER VIII

BAIN visited the pit twice each day and saw that O'Brien had water and food.

"Bring me some more dried meat, will you?"

"No."

"When I get out of here, you'll be sorry."

"When you come out of there," Bain said, "you're going to prison, maybe worse."

"Don't be silly, Bain. I'm going to escape from here very soon now. And when I do, be careful. I'm going to hunt you down. In the dark . . ."

Bain left and went back to the cave. It had grown cooler and by the time they had carried the embers inside and built the night fire, the wind had picked up and there were distant rumbles far away. They heated some of the biltong and ate it with tsamma melon and honey and before they were finished a strange phenomenon occurred.

It began to rain.

The rain did not fall on soft land, heavy land, land that would absorb it, store it, hold it.

It fell on parched, bricklike slopes; on land that had never known roots; on land long ago gullied and scoured and creased with a billion hard wrinkles. It fell in the desolate gorges, and on the high ridges of the black mountains.

It gathered in pockets and broke through the tiny shale dams that held it back. It ran downhill, joined other rivulets, cascaded into older gullies.

Powerful now, running on, joining other tiny tributaries. The land takes its toll, sucks some of it away; but there is too much, it has fallen too fast. It traps desert creatures in holes and nests and burrows: mice and lizards and spiders and snakes. It drowns them, carries their bodies along. Now a waterfall, a turbulent stream running downhill, finding new power, roaring on. A heavy rock is undermined and rolled along; it gathers speed, smashes at the soft sides of the watercourse. It rolls on, smashing other stones, grinding heavily on a granite bottom, becomes lighter. It is swept over another waterfall, splits in half. Soon it will become gravel.

A million streams reach the canyon floor, spilling down the grooves cut by old rains, eon-old, time-worn.

Mike Bain and Grace left the fire and walked slowly out of the cave and stood in the rain, lifted their faces upward, let the water pelt them. It was cold and wonderful; they began to laugh and cavort. Bain grabbed Grace and kissed her and shouted something to the sky. She ran away and splashed through a shallow pool that was growing in one of the saucerlike depressions a hundred yards from the mouth of the cave. Bain followed and she turned suddenly and kicked water into his face. He caught her and they stumbled and fell into the water. He kissed her again and she grew quiet; they sat in the great pool of water which grew around them, almost unaware of it.

"I loved O'Brien," Grace said. "I've got to tell you that. I might still love him."

"I'm sorry," Bain said. "I understand."

"I thought he killed Grimmelmann but somehow it didn't seem important when we were both alone here. Nothing mattered. We were two people. And I wanted him, Mike. He was all I wanted and then you came back with your damned rules . . ."

"I know," Bain said. "I liked him too, in a way. I'm sorry."

"I knew he killed Grimmelmann," Grace said.

"Forget it," Bain said. The water fell about them; they watched it striking the surface—a billion skipping drops that made a wild music.

"I didn't *care*," Grace said. "That's what bothers me. It was wrong, so terribly wrong."

"Wrong ended when the plane crashed," Bain said. "I wanted to kill myself rather than starve to death. You wanted to live and you wanted him. Don't brood about it. It's past."

"But it was wrong."

[177]

"I wanted to die and you wanted to live," Bain said. "We both did the wrong thing. We closed our eyes for a little time."

"We all followed our natures," Grace said. "I wanted a certain man and you wanted to quit and O'Brien wanted to survive. We might be as bad as he is. . . . Maybe Grimmelmann's death wasn't murder, maybe Smith and Sturdevant are alive. How can we judge him?"

"I'm not judging him as much as protecting myself from him," Bain said. "I want to live too; and I want you to live. We're all guilty, but you and I worry about it, we're sorry. That's what makes us different from O'Brien."

Grace nodded. The rain was building up to the point where it was difficult to talk, to see more than a few yards.

They stood up and ran back to the cave, to the shelter, to their fire. They dried themselves on rags and bits of old clothing, threw extra wood on the fire.

"Don't kiss me again, Mike," Grace said.

"I'm sorry."

"If we weren't here alone it would be different. I wouldn't care. It's too easy this way. I like you too much."

"Is that why you helped me take O'Brien?"

She shook her head. "I helped you because I didn't feel safe with him any more. I was afraid of him."

"And that outweighed everything else?" Bain asked.

"Yes," she said. "I wasn't secure with him after he told me about Grimmelmann. I thought that maybe someday he'd send me off in the desert too. You wouldn't do that. You'd starve to death along with me."

"Would I?" Bain asked. He'd never thought about it.

"Yes," she said. "Or you'd go yourself. You're not like him."

"We don't know what we'd do."

"O'Brien does," she said.

"Okay, so he's evil, he's no good," Bain said. "That I know."

"He's not evil, Mike. He just has a different set of laws than we have. If right and wrong ended when the plane crashed, then something else took over. Maybe it was O'Brien's way, I don't know. The situation here is bad, not O'Brien; he just tried to cope with it in his own way."

"Survival of the fittest," Bain said.

"Something like that."

There was a long silence.

"When we get out of here I'm going to start courting you," Mike said suddenly. "If you're available, I mean."

"Try me," she said.

"You mean it? Me?"

"We've got a lot in common, Mike," she said. "I don't know how I'd get along with anyone else; we've been *here*, Mike, other people haven't. They'll never really understand us after this."

They were warm now. The fire felt good. Outside the rain continued to fall.

"You better be sure with me," Mike said. "You have a knack for picking the wrong guys."

"The story of my life," Grace said. "I hardly remember my ex-husband now. I suppose I married him because he was the first one who asked me and he was going to London. I was lonely and I loved him very much but I don't think he was capable of returning it. It was a second-class relationship."

"I'm sorry," Bain said.

"And then O'Brien," Grace said. "Maybe it was all physical or clinging to something strong but I was his all the way, Mike. I want you to know that. Whatever else he is, he is male. So much different from my Mr. Andrew Monckton. For a while it was enough for me."

"I know," Bain said. "I've had women like that too. I know what it's like." He thought of a girl in Rangoon, of another in Casablanca.

Night came. They ate again and went to bed.

The rain fell on O'Brien.

He opened his eyes and got up slowly like a tiger uncurling after a long day's sleep. He lifted his face to it and smiled; it spattered on his face, his lips. He turned his palms upward in a gesture as old as man, assessed its power, welcomed it. He walked around the sheer walls, wet now and glistening. Tiny rivulets spilled down from above and he stood under one of them and let the water shower over him. The rain built up. He was standing in an inch of it now, two inches, three; the tiny waterfalls pouring into the great hole were thicker, more violent, arching farther outward from the edge of rock above.

O'Brien stood in a foot of water. Fear struck him. *He was going to drown.*

He began to yell, to scream; he cupped his hands and shouted upward through the heavy rain.

Bain! Help . . . help . . .

And he knew that it was useless and stopped. He would die now and there was nothing he could do unless Bain came and Bain would not come until the rain was over and it would be too late. The pit would be half full of water and he would be floating in it like a dead fly in a tumbler of drinking water.

He found the center of the pit and stood and the rain became so intense that he closed his eyes. A yard of water covered the bottom of the hole; the little waterfalls joined now—sheets of water pouring down from the long inclines above, running off the smooth rock into a great cistern.

To drown after all the escapes from the desert, to drown in a world where water was almost never seen, to drown after he had sent the others off to die of the sun and thirst.

The water rose about him, inch by inch.

Bain sat up slowly, unzipping the bag. The cold air poured in on him. The fire had burned low and the rain outside had not slackened. He got up, shook Grace.

"O'Brien," he said. "We forgot about him. He's up there in the pit and it's probably half filled with water." He saw the big man struggling in the water, trying to hold onto the polished rock. It was something neither of them had thought of—the water, the sudden rain. Grimmelmann had told them about it but somehow it never seemed possible in such a pitiless desert world. Unless there was some unseen and unknown cleft in the bottom of the pit it would fill with water and drown whatever was in it. There was a good chance that O'Brien was already dead. . . .

Grace stepped out of the sleeping bag and hovered near the fire; it glinted on her golden hair.

"What are you going to do?" she asked.

"Go up," Bain said. "He might be hanging on, waiting for us. Maybe."

"He's not dead," she said. "Not him."

"We've got to see," Bain said. "We can't let a man die like that."

"No, we can't. That's the trouble with people like us. We can't do things like O'Brien."

"He may be up to his neck in water right now," Bain said. "That rain's been coming down all night."

"If you pull him out of the pit what do you plan to do with him?"

Grace asked. "It's pitch dark. He'll kill us. I don't see what we can do."

"We've got to see what the situation is," Bain said. "If he can stand up until dawn we'll wait. If he's swimming around hanging on, we'll have to figure out something. Throw the rope down and let him tie himself to it until daybreak. I know he's dangerous, but I can't leave him there, Grace. I can't kill a man that way."

"I know," Grace said, "but we'll have to be careful; the way up the cliff is going to be almost impossible."

"Let's go," Bain said. "Every minute counts."

Somehow they reached the pit, fighting the night and the rain and the slippery path. Bain carried the rifle and helped Grace with his free hand and they worked up the storm-lashed cliff and rested for a few moments when they were safe on the top of the ridge. The rain had diminished but the darkness was almost complete and they felt their way along the familiar path. An inch of water washed their bare feet and gusts of wind whipped at them. They slipped and fell and pulled each other along and after a long while they stood and looked at the pit.

In the darkness they could see only a part of it but they saw that it was completely filled and overflowing with water. It had not seemed possible in the cave but now, standing in the swirl of water that ran down the incline into the pit, they realized that the crevice had been filled in the first few hours of the downpour.

They circled the pit carefully, stooping low, peering into the water, calling out for O'Brien, but there was no sign of him and no answer.

"He's down there in the bottom," Grace said. "It wasn't our fault. We didn't think about the rain." She felt sick.

"He might be alive," Bain said.

"I know," Grace admitted. "I have the same feeling."

They were frightened now and shaken from the climb and the cold rain. Grace found herself praying that O'Brien was really dead. Bain no longer trusted the darkness.

They hurried away, back down the cliff, to their cave. The black night was O'Brien's province. They felt fear pressing on them from all sides.

O'Brien staggered away from the pit fighting the terrible nausea that had seized him once he was freed from the water and the glassy rock. He began to vomit and fell down again; his legs and arms shook from the fatigue and strain. He got up and went on in a stupor, almost unaware of the darkness and the driving rain and the slippery dangerous path he followed.

Some instinct pushed him along a way that he had traveled long ago and almost forgotten. The baboon's den, the cave where the troop had originally lived, the place where he had ambushed them the first time. He staggered along in the darkness toward the high peak and then turned and made his way down the great outside escarpment, where the wind pressed him against the side of the black stone, where the drop was straight down, hundreds of feet.

He came to the crevice where he had waited in the night for dawn to come, for the baboons to emerge. He went on and found the den and crawled into it, smelled the musky scent of the animals and then collapsed on the dry floor.

He awoke several hours later, his body stiff and painful. He crawled deeper into the den and massaged his limbs until the circulation improved, until his body tingled with the pain. He closed his eyes and waited for dawn. The rain would have killed many creatures as it had almost killed him; there would be dead things to feed on before the sun came and destroyed them: fat lizards drowned in their holes, luckless birds smashed against the cliff walls, rock pythons driven from their familiar lairs, easy prey in surroundings they did not know.

He fell asleep with the nightmare of the pit in his mind.

He relived it all again. The water reached his hips, his chest. He could see nothing now from the torrents of water cascading down on him. It grew dark. The water was cold and his legs were almost numb. He began moving them and lost his balance, fell sideways, found himself swimming, fighting the water to stay up.

Swimming!

He found the slippery sides of his prison, held onto a slight bulge in the rock. There was only the pitch-blackness of the night now and the water under him and the roar of water as it cascaded into the pit. He was going to live now, escape. He would endure the long hours until the water level permitted him to reach up and pull himself out of the hole. He was going to live, live, live. . . .

An hour later his raw fingers found a thin lip of granite and he lifted himself until his left hand grasped the edge of the pit. His whole body shook from the terrible strain but he swung sideways and his toes found purchase and he was up and out in a tremendous heave of his body, lying on the slippery rock like an exhausted fish, the water swirling past him.

Grace Monckton sat with the rifle in her hands, her eyes searching. She sat in the mouth of the cave and a few yards behind her, out of the sun, was Mike Bain. He was sound asleep.

A week had passed since the great rain. The valley was green; grass grew in the stony soil and trees came to life and bushes turned thick and leafy; the dry winter was over and summer was coming and everywhere there was life. Flocks of strange birds came and made nests in the inaccessible crannies of the black cliffs. Bees filled the air with their droning and swarms of them came from nowhere and colonized secret clefts that their scouts had discovered.

Two days after the rain Mike Bain shot a gemsbok within sight of the cave mouth. It had come like the first one, across the sands, unaware that a new force had come to the gorge to create a new balance of life and death. They skinned the big animal with care and butchered it as Grimmelmann had. The bulk of the meat was flayed thin and made into biltong. What they did not cure they boiled to make extract. Mike smashed the bones with his big wrench and made a soup from the marrow and bits of stray flesh. Nothing went to waste. They cleaned the hide and stretched it in the shade to dry; they had no immediate use for it but they were vaguely aware that it would be of value, that they should keep it.

They watched the miracle of life with an interest they had never known; they saw a dead land come to life, saw strange things push up from hard earth, from bulbous seeds once dormant and sterile; they almost sensed a change in the soil with their bare feet, saw insects multiply and listened to new sounds in the dusk. And they were part of it, tied to the great cycle of life and growth and death.

They had plenty of food and the nights were milder. They caught many migrating birds near the pool in nets and bizarre traps that Bain devised. In one week they had progressed from the brink of starvation and despair to a time of plenty.

But they did not enjoy it.

They felt that O'Brien was alive and waiting for them. They felt that his eyes were upon them, that he was high up among the crags and gloomy ridges following their movements, studying them while he bided his time and grew strong again. They knew that if he were alive he would strike soon, suddenly, without pity.

[183]

They went back to the pit and searched the whole area. The hole was filled with water but each day the level dropped. They knew that his body might be on the bottom but it would be a long time before they were positive, for there was ten or twelve feet of water in the big pool.

There was another possibility: he had been drowned and his body had floated out of the hole and lodged in some cranny or cleft on the downward slope of the cliff top. They spent hours searching and became convinced that this hadn't happened.

The third possibility was that he had been strong enough to stay afloat in the rising water until he could reach the top and crawl out, that he was hiding now in one of the gorges or high on the cliffs waiting for an opportunity to surprise them, kill them.

They saw no sign of him. They looked upward toward the black peak and scanned the fissured cliffs a hundred times each day, expecting to see him again, naked and black-maned, standing as he did, relaxed and graceful. They looked and saw nothing but as the days went by they sensed his presence, felt his eyes upon them.

They waited for him to come.

The cave, Bain knew, was a death trap for them if they wandered too far from it and allowed O'Brien to enter it. He could wait in the dark or hide in the tunnel they had found and creep upon them at night. They had been lucky and shot the gemsbok and had a great supply of food, but eventually they would have to move away from the cave to forage. It could trap O'Brien, of course. If they went off for the day and let him sneak into it they could wall it up and have him again—but it was too tricky; too many things could go wrong.

They stayed in the cave and took turns sleeping; they banked the outside fire and found that it lasted until dawn. They strung wire and cord across the cave's mouth and hung tins and utensils and other noisemaking things to give alarm if anything broke the string or pushed the wire. And then Bain dug an arc-shaped ditch six feet behind the wire, a ditch filled with pointed stakes to impale any intruder who might charge through the web of wire and string in hopes of taking them by sudden assault. They felt safe at night now, one of them always awake, waiting for O'Brien to come through the cave mouth.

And they were cautious outside as well. They stayed in the open, away from certain parts of the cliff where he might be waiting to crush them with rocks. They stayed in the valley, close to the cave, and hoped that another gemsbok would wander past.

"Maybe it's all in our mind," Mike said one day as they sat in the cave entrance.

"He's alive," Grace said. "I can feel him watching us from the high places. And sometimes in the night I feel that he's out here in the dark, creeping close to the cave. I'm afraid."

"I'm afraid too," Mike said. "But sometimes I wonder why. It seems that he'd have shown himself by now."

"We've got to act as if he were alive," Grace said.

"You're right. If he is alive then his only weapon is surprise."

They sat silently. Flies buzzed around them and from the cliffs came the bark of a baboon. Grace Monckton was deeply tanned, her blond hair blending with her bronze skin.

Bain scratched himself and yawned. He fingered his heavy beard and wondered if they would both die here. Living was easy now but the bad time was coming; the rains were over and it would be at least seven or eight months before they came again. They couldn't wait that long. He turned to Grace.

"Why the hell doesn't somebody *come!*"

"They will," Grace said. "We've got to believe that. Every day makes the chances better."

"I don't know," Bain said. "I get depressed once in a while. I know it's wrong but it happens. Smith and Sturdevant never made it. They couldn't have. It's so long."

"I'm afraid I agree with you," Grace said.

"I had an idea the other night," Bain said. "I was sitting on guard and I thought about the birds, the ones I managed to catch in those traps by the water. If there was only some way to use them. Band them. Tie notes on their legs and set them free. Use them as they use homing pigeons or bottles cast into the sea."

"It's an idea," Grace said.

"You really think so?"

"No."

They both laughed.

"Okay," Mike said, "we'll continue to eat them and save our dried gemsbok."

"A bird in the hand," Grace said.

The canyon was green and filled with millions of tiny yellow flowers. The trees were fat with leaves.

"What would you do if O'Brien came down from the pool right this minute?" Grace asked.

"I hope I'd have sense enough to shoot him."

"Would you?"

"I think so. He murdered Grimmelmann. He murdered Smith. And he swore to kill me."

Another night settled over the black mountain.

An airplane flew over the valley.

It came so fast, so suddenly, that it was gone before they had recovered from the surprise. It was midday and at the outside fire they were roasting a bird that had strangled itself in one of the nets around the pool.

Bain bounded into the cave and came out with two torches.

"Run," he shouted to Grace. "Hurry."

The torches caught fire and he ran after her, two burning torches in his left hand, the rifle in his right. They ran down the valley, away from the cliffs into the flatlands. The plane was far away but the noise was still in their ears, the sound of power, civilization, salvation.

They ran easily. They would be seen now if the plane turned and made another sweep over the gorges. The ground leveled off, the stones and sand replaced by the hard-baked red soil; tender grass grew in some spots and delicate white flowers. They came to the first big pile of trash: thornbush and dead camel's-thorn and wads of dead grass. Bain set it on fire and handed the torch to Grace. They ran across the valley toward the other pile.

The plane came back, slower this time it seemed. They stood waving the torches and the roar of the engines was deafening as it passed overhead. They found themselves shouting. The plane went on, then turned sharply to the right. They had been seen; the plane was heading out of the valley so that it could turn and come in for a landing.

It was a small plane with lettering on one side, a fragile object floating in the sky above the jagged black cliffs, the type of small plane that is usually privately owned. It reminded Bain of the crop dusters he'd seen in many parts of the world; he wondered if it would hold two more people.

They threw down the torches and stopped running.

"What about O'Brien?" Grace asked.

"He'll be here," Bain said. "Any minute now." They looked to the cliffs, shielding their eyes from the sun; they searched the black walls around them and saw nothing.

"I'm afraid," Grace said. "Even with you and the rifle and the plane. I'm still afraid."

"If he's here, he'll come," Bain said.

"What do you mean by that?"

"He might not be here, Grace. It could all be imagination. Something that grew out of the fear you had of him. And my fear. If he survived the pit he'll come down and get in the plane. What's he got to lose? His word is as good as ours. We can't prove he did anything."

"You think he's dead then?" Grace asked.

"I think he's alive," Bain said. "But if he doesn't show, then I'll close the book on him. I'll consider him dead, drowned in the pit."

The plane was a speck growing larger. But they did not watch it; they looked toward the cave and the ridges on both sides of them. They looked for O'Brien.

And then the plane was almost upon them, roaring and blowing red dust over them—a plane on the ground now, moving past them on rubber wheels, a fantastic sight, almost beyond their belief. They ran toward it, found that they were crying, holding each other, laughing, waving.

The plane stopped and a small door opened. The noise of the engine died as it idled. A long leg came out of the doorway and a big man stood before them, a middle-aged man with rimless glasses and a clean white shirt. The lettering on the side of the small craft was plain: TSUMSEBI MINING, LTD.

The man looked at them for a long minute.

"Well, we found you," he said.

Bain smiled. It was difficult to talk. The man had eaten a real breakfast in the outside world, he wore shoes, he had a haircut.

And Grace was suddenly aware that she was almost naked; she drew closer to Bain, saw that the pilot was leaning away from the controls, looking out the tiny door at her.

The man was talking to them. "We volunteered to join the search when the word came out about you. They picked up some guy along the coast in the diamond fields. Said he was a pilot, that his plane was down here. They locked him up, didn't believe it, but somebody checked the story and discovered that he was telling the truth after all. Funny."

"Sturdevant," Bain said. "We thought he was dead."

"Did he really walk to the sea from *here?*"

"Yes," Bain said. "He was our pilot. He must have." So Sturdevant was alive. He wanted to cry.

"We can't cut the motor," the man was saying. "We're low on gas now. Are there any others?"

"Others?"

"They're dead," Grace shouted above the motor noise.

Bain looked back along the cliffs. No one. No movement. O'Brien was dead. In their fear they'd convinced themselves that he was still alive.

"The others are dead," he said. "We're the only survivors."

And they got into the plane and flew away.

O'Brien watched the plane go.

He stood on a great slab of black stone and the sun glinted on his bronzed body. He scratched himself and rubbed the short pointed stick against his hard calf. He was alone now. Bain and the girl were gone; Grimmelmann was gone; they were all gone. The mountain was his.

He walked along the slab until it ended and began making his way down the face of the cliff; he had a sudden urge to see the pool again and the cave, the old surroundings.

There were birds by the pool. He moved toward them and they grew nervous. Then he sprinted forward. The birds flew away and the stick he threw at them clattered against the stone and rolled into the water.

He drank deeply and walked down the path to the cave. He saw the smoke first and caught the smell of the bird that Bain had been cooking. He smiled and hurried on, squatted over the fire and ate the bird.

He could survive; he was not worried. The mountain had only one human belly to fill, not six. A new crop of tsamma melons was already growing. Game would wander into the gorges now that man's noise and smell were gone. There would be honey and yellow lizards and more snakes and more of the roots and tubers that Grimmelmann had found for them. He would hunt and forage and he would survive.

He got up and walked into the cave. He saw the alarm net and the pit with the sharpened stakes. He had been right about Bain; the man had guessed he was alive and had taken the utmost precautions. They would have killed him if he'd shown himself.

He found one of the torches, went outside and stuck it in the fire. He walked back and saw the dried meat and the smoked meat which hung high in the darkness; saw the remaining melons, the piles of ragged clothes. He would live here for a time, eat the dried meat and let the living things in the valley grow and multiply.

Something cool under his bare foot. He stepped back, knelt and dug in the soft sand. It was the big wrench, the one Bain had always carried. He hefted it in his hand. It had a good feel to it, a weapon-feel. He swung it in front of him in a wide arc.

He took a strip of biltong and went outside, sat in the warm sunlight. Somewhere far away a baboon barked.

He did not sleep in the cave every night but in any place he found in the gorges and high on the cliffs, in the old baboon den, in narrow clefts, in low caves where sometimes in the sand he found flints and arrowheads and Bushman beads made from shell and bone.

He made fire easily: a hardwood, pencil-sized shaft held and spun between his callused hands, spun into a flat piece of soft wood in a tinder-filled cavity. Then a small fire warming him in the neolithic night over which he roasted partridge and fat geckos and other things he found in the sand and crevices of the black mountain.

There were new rains. He stood naked and let the water cool him, felt the ground grow slippery and soft under his feet. The great sand sea surrounding the black mountain took the water and gave nothing back, but in the canyons more grass came and pink flowers bloomed and the trees came to life and budded. A billion seeds awoke and sent forth fibers seeking moisture and the sun; living creatures came to feed upon the tender grasses and ripe tubers and sweet saps: noble gemsbok like fabled unicorns from the mysterious sand wastes, sleek zebra in harlequin camouflage, nimble gazelles and a few slope-backed hyenas. They found their way to the rock island from some ancient instinct and fed upon its sudden ripeness.

And he fed upon them. He dug a shallow pit and fixed a vicious stake in the bottom, covered it with a matting of sticks and grass and a thin layer of sand. On the third day a zebra fell into it and the stake ripped mortally into its belly. He followed it into the desert and butchered it while flies fought him and planted their eggs in the fresh meat. He carried a hundred pounds of it to the cave and buried it in the cool sand to keep until the night when he would slice it thin and make biltong. He raced back to the rest of the meat but it was gone. Hyenas fought over the crushed bone and evil vultures flapped away at his approach. He cursed them and crippled one of the hyenas with a heavy stone. He hated them. They were like baboons and others who stole his kill.

And he fought the baboons, but he was more cautious now that the rifle was gone. They came down from the cliffs for the succulent rain-made tubers and berries and he chased them back with firebrands. He gathered food and stored it in the main cave, deep in the sand and high up in the *kloof* where Smith had found the Bushman bones and ostrich eggshells. In the winter he would live here but it was summer and he filled it with food. It became his storehouse.

The melons he left alone. They grew fat and ripe and did not have to be picked. There would be more than enough for him in the main canyon, for the baboons no longer came here. Once the canyon had been dominated by the animals. Now it was his canyon. Its summer wealth belonged to him.

And then one day the baboons trapped him.

He was hunting lizards along the top of the outside ridge, the smallest one that resembled a thumb from the top of the high peak. It was the shortest spur but there was no way down from it. It fell down in steps that were fissured and split, where rain water hid in shallow pools from the prying sun, where quick lizards waited for heavy flies, where bees found the saxifrage growing and blooming in impossible pockets of black soil.

He was halfway out on it when he heard them barking. He looked back and then climbed to a high slab and let them see him, let the wrench glint in the sun, shouted at them, grimaced. But for the first time they did not retreat; their leader urged them on, bristling at the enemy who was alone now in the sun.

Some of the animals hung back: the old ones who had known the ambush, known the terrible rifle; the females concerned with their young; the half-grown males afraid. But the others advanced down the narrowing spine, barking and chattering and boasting of their strength.

He shouted and advanced, threw stones at them. They backed away but came forward again. There was no time to build a fire, make a firebrand; there was no way down the dizzy cliffs that surrounded him. He began to back away, his mind seizing on a dozen ways of fighting them or escaping and rejecting them all. They had him. They'd trapped him. He would die.

Now they were drifting around him, closing in, forcing him to the edge of the cliff. And there was excitement in them, different from before: the young males boastful, edging closer; the few older males objecting, keeping to the higher places, the safe places, excited too, but cautious. They were going to kill him.

He edged away but the semicircle followed, closing in. A young male was in front of him, shifting and grimacing, gleeful, skipping from rock to rock, boasting to the troop. They'd rush him and it would be over. But he'd kill too; he'd kill one of them, maybe two. There was a cold cramp in his stomach but it wasn't fear, it was excitement. Not the frenzied excitement of the baboons but something he was above, something he controlled—excitement that was cold and logical and human.

He found his spot, the sun behind him. He waited.

The troop stopped moving. They found places and squatted on the ledges, on the flat black rock, watching him. Then one of them broke away and bounded toward him, sullen and cautious: the new leader. He was the first; the others would break away any moment now and swarm over him.

But the other big males did not move. They sat tense and motionless until the tension became too great; then they exploded in a fit of jabbering. The leader moved back and forth in front of him, twenty feet away, a mastiff with an ape's body. He charged, but in the last instant, before the spear jabbed him, he recoiled and rolled away. The troop screamed approval. Now he was up circling and O'Brien moved, knowing somehow that the others would not attack from behind. This was a duel, a trial by combat.

He stabbed with the short spear, keeping the weaving animal away, working him around, trying to keep the sun in his eyes. The leader rushed again; he jabbed viciously, hit the baboon's chest. The leader grabbed and the spear was gone, torn from his grasp almost without effort. Now there was only the wrench. He crouched lower, his hands sweaty on the hot steel. The leader backed away from him fingering his bloody chest. In the rocks around them the silence was total, no muscle moved. The animal looked at his bloody fingers, then seemed to forget the wound as he came closer and circled. There would be no feinting now; there would be a final rush and one of them would die.

They circled like boxers, waiting. The wrench glittered, swayed like a cobra's head. The leader's long arms searched the space between them, measuring it. Then the baboon lunged forward, mouth open, yellow fangs ready for the final, terrible bite.

[191]

But the wrench was quicker, guided by an instinct that was primitive, brutal, animal-fast. It flashed through the air, blurred, silvery. It smashed against the big head. The baboon stumbled away, forgetting him, reaching weakly for his head. Then he died and sprawled on the black rock.

O'Brien stood, fighting for breath. There was a low moan from the troop. All of them stirred, the hair rising from their necks, fangs bared. Now anything could happen. It was up to him. He stood glaring at them. He picked up the spear and walked toward the baboons as if they didn't exist, striding toward them with determination and force. A big male moved toward him, fangs bared; the troop waited.

O'Brien didn't stop. He leaped forward to a raised slab, filled his great lungs with air. Then he screamed: a wild, terrible scream that had never been heard before on the black mountain, a cry of such power and ferocity that it caused the young to whimper and cringe, back away, run. And then the females fled with their babies clinging to them in blind terror. There was a split second when the remaining males stood trembling, uncertain. Then O'Brien charged, waving the glittering wrench and the two-pronged spear. He ran straight at the big warrior in his path and another scream started and the air trembled and shook with it.

The animals fled, terrorized, beaten. O'Brien stood in the sun, chest heaving, muscles rippling beneath taut copper skin bathed in sweat.

He began laughing, and as he walked along, the narrow canyon below caught the sound and brought it back to him, deep and genuine and elemental.